W9-AOK-937

MY LORD LION

"I doubt if all books are worth your enthusiasm," the earl said. He picked up a book from the box at his feet, opened it at random, and handed it to her. "This one, for instance. What does this book say to you?"

Diana took the slender book and saw that it was a collection of poems by sixteenth-century poets.

"Read a passage aloud and weave your magic, Miss Gardiner," the earl requested.

His finger pointed to a passage by Ben Johnson. Diana felt her cheeks grow warm as she read, " '*Drink to me only with thine eyes / And I will pledge with mine / Or leave a kiss within the cup / And I'll not ask for wine.*' "

"This poet's producing a veritable thirst in me," the earl said, admiring her spirit. He could drink her in with his eyes; indeed, with more than just his eyes.

Other **Regency Romances**
from Avon Books

THE IMPOSTOR *by June Drummond*
AN IMPROPER WIDOW *by Kate Moore*
LACY'S DILEMMA *by Barbara Reeves*
MIDWINTER'S BLISS *by Cathleen Clare*
A MISBEGOTTEN MATCH *by Rita Boucher*

Coming Soon

THE BLACK DUKE'S PRIZE *by Suzanne Enoch*

Avon Books are available at special quantity discounts for bulk purchases for sales promotions, premiums, fund raising or educational use. Special books, or book excerpts, can also be created to fit specific needs.

For details write or telephone the office of the Director of Special Markets, Avon Books, Dept. FP, 1350 Avenue of the Americas, New York, New York 10019, 1-800-238-0658.

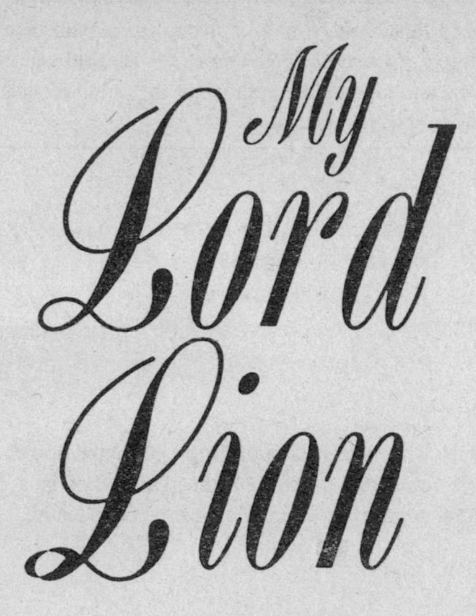

REBECCA WARD

If you purchased this book without a cover, you should be aware that this book is stolen property. It was reported as "unsold and destroyed" to the publisher, and neither the author nor the publisher has received any payment for this "stripped book."

MY LORD LION is an original publication of Avon Books. This work has never before appeared in book form. This work is a novel. Any similarity to actual persons or events is purely coincidental.

AVON BOOKS
A division of
The Hearst Corporation
1350 Avenue of the Americas
New York, New York 10019

Copyright © 1995 by Maureen Wartski
Published by arrangement with the author
Library of Congress Catalog Card Number: 94-96362
ISBN: 0-380-77804-1

All rights reserved, which includes the right to reproduce this book or portions thereof in any form whatsoever except as provided by the U.S. Copyright Law. For information address Howard Morhaim Literary Agency, 175 Fifth Avenue, Room 709, New York, New York 10010.

First Avon Books Printing: April 1995

AVON TRADEMARK REG. U.S. PAT. OFF. AND IN OTHER COUNTRIES, MARCA REGISTRADA, HECHO EN U.S.A.

Printed in the U.S.A.

RA 10 9 8 7 6 5 4 3 2 1

For Annette Bain

1

"Hell and thunder! the devil take the lot!"

Lionel Cramer, earl of Blaize, glared about him. "And confusion take the old man too," he added explosively. "What did I ever to do him that he should play me such a plaguey trick?"

He flicked his riding crop, and a dozen books crashed to the ground. Dust motes spumed upward, dancing in the sunlight that spilled through the high oriel windows to reveal other books: boxes of books, stacks of books, a confusion of books, all banked haphazardly around the room.

The earl leaned up against a billiard table. Tall and broad shouldered, he was an ominous presence with dark brows that scowled over eyes as hard as jade. His mane of tawny hair, disordered from his morning ride, gave him the look of an angry lion.

"Books," he exclaimed in accents of loathing. "Molhouse, what maggot did Cousin Percival take in his brain that he should die and leave his library to *me*?"

This last was addressed to the slight, scanty-haired individual who was standing just inside the door. This personage was dressed impeccably in sober valet's garb, which was in direct contrast to the jaunty twist of his mustache and the worldly twinkle in his small gray eyes.

"Lord Duchemps did not know your lordship very well," he

suggested. "Per'aps 'e thought that your lordship would henjoy the books."

The earl snorted.

"Lord Duchemps was a bachelor, sir. 'Is library is reported to 'ave been the love of the old gentleman's life."

"It damned well isn't mine. Pack up the books and get rid of them."

"Yes, me lord. Er—'ow would your lordship suggest I do that?"

"How should I know? Give them away or chuck them out of the window—it's all one to me."

When his lordship of Blaize roared, lesser mortals did well to walk softly. Molhouse made haste to move out of the way as his employer strode toward the door, and the two footmen stationed in the hallway sprang to attention.

Lord Duchemps's bequest had arrived this morning, and quivers of unease were still rippling through the spacious halls of Blaize Manor. Though the earl had received notice of his late cousin's will, he had apparently not expected the books themselves to be delivered so quickly.

Now his lordship was in a stamping bad temper. Molhouse pulled his hand from behind his back and doubtfully surveyed the letter with the ducal crest emblazoned on it. Perhaps he should wait until the earl's temper had cooled before delivering this, he thought.

"Molhouse! Where the devil are you?"

The earl's roar caused the little valet to drop the letter. Scooping it up, he called, "Coming, me lord," and fairly ran down the hall. As he passed the footmen, one of them spoke out of the corner of his mouth.

"Don't envy you 'aving to attend Lord Lion today, Molhouse."

The valet shopped short. His eyes narrowed, his head snapped back, and he turned on the footman like a mongoose on a snake. "*Mister* Mol'ouse to you, an' don't you forget it," he snapped. "And 'oo gave you the right to criticize your betters? Get back to your duties, you hoyster-brained twiddlepoop, or I'll 'ave you cashiered without a character."

The hapless footman quailed and muttered apologies as his colleague added hastily that Witton hadn't meant any harm—he was just young and new to the position.

"That isn't no excuse," Molhouse said fiercely. " 'Is honor the earl of Blaize don't take no impertinence. If 'e 'ears what you called 'im just now, young Witton, 'e'll throw you lot out of the window!"

With a final glare, Molhouse hurried down the corridor and out onto the second floor landing where the earl was waiting impatiently. The valet noted that his employer was carrying his gloves and riding quirt and felt more hopeful. Perhaps after a long, vigorous ride, his lordship's spirits might improve.

"You're exercising Sultan, are you, sir?" he panted. " 'At's good. Very good, me lord. The weather's turned warmer since this morning. A fine day for a ride."

"Stop nattering," the earl interrupted crisply, "and give me that letter from my father."

It was no use, Molhouse thought. There was no fooling the earl. His ability to see through subterfuge of any kind together with an almost uncanny memory had made Blaize a brilliant officer during the war with the Frogs.

It also made him a very difficult employer. With a heartfelt sigh the valet surrendered the cream-colored envelope with the ducal crest. " 'Ow did you know 'oo it was from, me lord?" he ventured to inquire.

"Why else would you have held the envelope so carefully behind your back?" Deliberately, Blaize unfolded a sheet of heavy vellum, scanned its contents, then handed it wordlessly to his valet. "So it was my estimable father who put the maggot in old Percival's brain."

Molhouse glanced down at the elegant copperplate handwriting and agreed in a subdued voice that it would seem to be so. "Naturally his grace has his reasons," the earl continued.

"Seems as though 'is grace wants to see you install a fine library at Blaize. 'E says 'e looks forward to seeing hit on 'is next visit 'ere."

Molhouse shot a nervous look at his employer, but the young earl said nothing. He neither frowned nor shouted nor evinced any other displeasure but simply stood tapping his riding crop against his hard thigh. A bad sign, Molhouse thought sadly.

When he spoke at last, Blaize's voice was almost silky. "My fond father forgets I'm no longer a chitty-faced brat. Blaize is mine, and I do what I like here. Burn the books, Molhouse."

"M-me lord?"

Looking more lionlike than ever, the earl said with a growl, "You dare to disagree with me?"

Molhouse drew a deep breath, mentally crossed his fingers for luck, and took the plunge. "Yes, me lord," he said. "With respect, sir," he added, his cockney accent growing broader as his agitation increased, "whatever you think of them books—and of 'is grace the duke, come to that—Lord Duchemps loved 'is library. 'E spent 'is life collecting rare books and old books and books 'e loved."

"Is there a point to this?" the earl asked.

Molhouse drew himself up and with obvious effort looked into the hard, angry, handsome young face.

"Yessir. The way I see hit, me lord, no man 'as the right to destroy so much love as your cousin put into 'is library. Love's not easy ter come by, sir."

Molhouse held his breath as Blaize's eyes narrowed almost to slits. Then, surprisingly, the earl smiled.

"Curse your impudence," he said, quietly. "Thunder and hell—what do you suggest I do with the damned things, then?"

Molhouse let out his pent-up breath. "Per'aps, me lord, you could 'ire someone to take charge of the books," he suggested. "A librarian or some such person. 'E could do 'is job, see, and never bother you about anything. Per'aps you know someone 'oo can be trusted, some nice gentleman 'oo might suit."

"I know no such." Abruptly the earl turned on his bootheel and started down the steps, then halted just as suddenly. "Dracot Gardiner," he exclaimed.

His deep voice softened as he remembered, "I met him at Harrow—that was before your time, Molhouse. Dracot was a year behind me. He lived in Somerset, near the town of Landover."

"Mr. D. Gardiner," Molhouse repeated. "Town of Landover, Somerset. Shouldn't be 'ard to find 'im, me lord. You think Mr. Gardiner might be interested in the position, then?"

"Dracot was a good fellow, and we became friends," Blaize mused. "He wasn't rich, and he was a bit of a bookworm, so the others made his life unbearable until I cracked a few of their skulls together. Jackals, all of them, always happy to torment and bully."

"What became of 'im, sir?," Molhouse asked.

"I heard he was in the war, but our paths never crossed after Harrow." The earl began to walk down the stairs again. "Writing to Dracot Gardiner will probably be a waste of time, Molhouse. For all I know the man's married and has a nursery full of brats. I doubt if he'll give a tinker's curse for Percival's books."

"Diana, *why* are you rainbow-chasing? I requested you to come to the morning room *at once*."

Miss Diana Gardiner looked up from the letter she had been reading, her brows thoughtfully puckered. Puzzled eyes, so dark as to be almost black, returned Lady Radley's agitated gaze. "I'm sorry, Aunt Hortensia. What was that you said?"

Lady Radley rolled her blue eyes upward, clasped her narrow white hands, and looked to be on the point of bursting into tears. "Your uncle will be in such a *taking*," she twittered. "You know how he is about punctuality. And Mr. Chadwick has been *waiting* for fifteen minutes."

"Do I know Mr. Chadwick?"

Lady Radley looked stunned. "Diana, you *cannot* have forgotten what I told you yesterday. The Honorable Mr. Hereward Chadwick, who is connected by marriage to the Viscount Blount, is doing you the honor of calling upon you."

"Another possible suitor." Diana sighed and tucked her letter into the pocket of her dark gray muslin day dress. "I have told you before, Aunt, that I do not intend to marry. I would rather find myself a position as a governess or lady's companion."

"Oh, Diana, do not *think* such dreadful thoughts," Lady Radley said. "Collect that you have *tried* to find such work before you came to Radley Place. It is not *easy* for a lady in reduced circumstances, especially if she has a brother like Archie."

Not easy indeed. Diana held her peace as Lady Radley continued earnestly, "You must *not* give up hope, my dear. Even though you are a *bit* past your prime, some gentlemen wish to marry sensible and mature females and not simpering misses out of the schoolroom." She paused to regard her niece critically as she added, "I will not wrap plain facts in clean linen. Your lack of a fortune is a problem but some gentlemen would overlook even that."

"How noble of them," Diana murmured.

As though she hadn't heard this last, her aunt continued, "Mr. Chadwick is a fine man. You must never credit the, er, *things* that have been said about him. After all, gentlemen have different—well, they are the lords of creation after all. They are made differently from us. They have different *needs*."

No doubt, Mr. Chadwick was a rake. Mentally, Diana catalogued the other candidates produced by her aunt and uncle during the three months she and Archie had lived at Radley Place. There had been a hard-eyed widower who had just buried his second wife and had six children at home; an old gentleman who was deaf as a post and had the gout; the simpering son of a neighbor who (it was rumored) enjoyed the company of young boys too well. The boy was being driven into matrimony by his worried mama—just as she, Diana, was being driven. Lord Radley had made it clear that he did not intend to support his wife's impoverished kin forever.

"Once you are married and have your own household—"

Lady Radley's speech was interrupted by a screech in the hallway followed by a thud and the sound of swiftly running footsteps.

"What on earth—" Diana stepped swiftly across to the door and, looking into the hall, found the second housemaid sitting on the floor surrounded by scattered clothing.

" 'Twas that Master Edward, miss," the girl wailed as soon as she saw Diana. "T'little devil jumped out o' the closet and scared me out o' me wits an' made me drop the clean wash."

She broke off as Lady Radley appeared beside Diana in the doorway. "I am persuaded that Edward would not do such a thing," Lady Radley cried indignantly. "It must have been Archie."

Diana exclaimed in protest, and the girl shook her head. "Master Archie is outside," she said, " 'elping in the stables. No, t'was Master Edward."

As Diana helped gather up the laundry, Lady Radley plucked at the costly Spanish lace that edged the sleeves of her dress.

"I had *hoped*," she sighed, "when your papa went to his

reward, Diana, and your poor mama fled this vale of tears, thus leaving us the duty of taking care of her defenseless children, I had prayed that Archie would be an older companion to dear Edward. But that, alas, was not to be. How is it that your brother wallows in stables and pigpens, Diana?"

"Archie is fond of animals," Diana protested. "And he does not wallow in pigpens."

"Master Archie was it 'oo 'elped Boorse nurse the master's 'unter when it took so sick," the housemaid put in eagerly. "Ever so clever Master Archie is, Boorse says—"

"Take those things downstairs, Etty," Lady Radley interrupted. "I am persuaded that a gentleman's son has no need of a *groom's* recommendation. Diana, they are waiting for us in the morning room."

Without waiting for a reply, she scurried down the hall toward the stairs. As Diana followed, she caught sight of her cousin peering out from behind a statue.

"There is Edward now," she said.

Seeing that he was discovered, Master Edward showed himself. He was tall for his eight years and had his mother's fair hair and eyes that were as blue and as innocent as a baby's.

"Ah, Edward," Lady Radley exclaimed in melting tones, "I must speak to you, my dearest. It is very vexing of you to frighten the maids."

"I didn't want to, Mama—it was Archie who suggested it. He wanted to see Etty cry." The boy turned those guileless eyes up to his mother. "He said he'd beat me if I didn't scare her."

"That is utter nonsense," Diana exclaimed.

Edward looked mournful. "Of course *you* wouldn't believe me," he sighed. "Nobody believes how beastly Archie can be."

Not for the first time, Diana's fingers itched to box her young cousin's ears. "Another lie," she snapped. "Aunt Hortensia, Archie is the gentlest soul. He could never terrorize anyone."

But of course, Edward's fond mama would never believe that. Diana felt a wave of outrage mixed with despair as she reminded herself how easily her aunt swallowed Edward's lies.

Only last week Aunt Hortensia had believed Edward's fib

that the chambermaid had filched some money. Diana suspected that the boy himself had pocketed the cash, but it had been the wretched servant who had been dismissed without a character. And lies and stealing were not the only arrows in Edward's quiver.

The boy had a vicious streak. The tricks he played on the servants were cruel, and Diana had often seen Edward torment a small, stray dog that Archie had befriended. Yet Aunt Hortensia was convinced that Archie was a bad influence on her precious son.

Lady Radley was still speaking to Edward. "I will talk to your cousin later. Meanwhile, *avoid* him, dearest. You must not be corrupted by bad influences." She patted Edward's cheek, then hurried down the stairs and into the morning room.

Ignoring the face that Edward pulled at her before darting off downstairs, Diana followed her aunt.

Two gentlemen rose to their feet as the ladies entered. One of them was a small, round man with a round, pink face set with small, pink features which might have appeared benevolent in any other face. In the case of Simon, Lord Radley, the small eyes were sly, the buttonhole mouth intolerant, the chin weak. A habitual scowl had formed a permanent crease between his brows.

He snapped open a watch and glared at it as they walked into the room. "Late, by my head, madam," he said with a growl. "Don't I always say that punctuality is the pride of princes? Hey? And here Chadwick and I have been waiting here for twenty minutes. Cooling our heels, madam!"

"I am sorry, Simon," Lady Radley said meekly. "Diana was not ready."

Lord Radley glowered at his niece and demanded, "What was you up to that you couldn't tear yourself away?"

"I beg your pardon, Uncle," Diana replied quietly. "I had received a letter and was reading it."

"No doubt a letter from an admirer," said the second gentleman gallantly. He was of medium height and as bony as a fish, and under his rouge and paint his features had a decidedly dissipated look.

"Chadwick, this is my niece," Lord Radley said. "My wife's

late brother's daughter. Don't resemble Lady R., neither. Bartholomew Gardiner was gypsy-dark like his chit here."

Diana curtsied meanwhile thinking that her aunt and uncle Radley were indeed scraping the bottom of the barrel. On closer inspection, Mr. Chadwick had the wrinkled skin of an ancient turtle, a red nose, and hands that shook when he raised his quizzing-glass to his eye.

His stays creaked as he bowed. "Miss Diana Gardiner, y'r most obedient servant. Sorry I wasn't acquainted with y'r late father, ma'am."

"You might've sat down to cards with her uncle Thomas Gardiner," Lord Radley said. "Fellow was a gamester—unlucky on the exchange, too. In the end, this chit's father had to use most of his own fortune to frank his brother. Shatterbrained move, by my head. Result was that when he and his wife died, he left his own brats in dun territory."

Lady Radley looked alarmed at this public washing of the family linen and twittered hastily that one must look after one's own and, at any rate, *dear* Diana was very well connected. "Her late father was the second son of Sir Reginald Gardiner, and her late mama was the Honorable Caroline Devereaux, whose grandfather was a marquess."

They might as well have been discussing the bloodlines of a horse. The first time this had happened to her, Diana had been so mortified, so degraded, that she had cried herself to sleep. Now, she had learned to blank her mind to what was going on.

Ignoring her relatives and Mr. Chadwick, she returned to the problem which had been gnawing at her heart ever since she and Archie were orphaned. *How am I going to provide a home for Archie*? Diana asked herself.

It was bitter truth that an unmarried female without money had little chance of making a life for herself and her thirteen-year-old brother. All of Diana's inquiries regarding employment had come to nothing because no one was willing to take in Archie. The Gardiners had been in dire straits when Lord Radley had at last extended his grudging charity.

But Radley Place had hardly proved to be a haven. Almost as soon as they had arrived in early December, Edward had begun to torment Archie. Sensing in the big, gentle youth a perfect victim, he had tried to goad Archie into losing his temper. When he found that he could not do so, Edward had begun to poison his mother's mind against his cousin. He had also convinced his father that Archie was feeble-minded.

A surge of love, hot and protective, filled Diana. Archie wasn't feeble-minded. Trusting, childlike, but with his own strength and wisdom, Archie was just . . . Archie. And anyone who would hurt him must first deal with her—

"Diana, are you rainbow-chasing *again*?" her aunt asked anxiously. "Mr. Chadwick has asked you a question."

As Diana glanced at the man, he winked at her. The old rake doubtless thought he was doing her a favor by courting her.

"What was it you asked me, sir?" she asked coldly.

"About the letter." Mr. Chadwick grinned. "Sounds intriguing—a lovely lady, a mysterious letter."

"Who was it sent the letter?" Lord Radley demanded.

Reluctantly, Diana replied, "The letter is from Cumbria. From the earl of Blaize."

Her uncle stared, then gave a bark of amusement. "By my head, you're saying that an earl—the duke of Naunce's son—wrote to *you*? Give it here, girl."

Diana barely removed the letter from her pocket before her uncle snatched it from her hands and scowled at it. "Can hardly make out the address," he said. "*Looks* to be addressed to Miss D. Gardiner, Landover Town, Somerset." He looked up to explain, "Chit used to live in Somerset, Chadwick—before I took her and her brother in."

He broke off and gasped, "By my head, the chit wasn't lying. This *is* from Blaize."

Lady Radley looked shocked. "What—*what* does his lordship require of Diana?"

Lord Radley raised a pudgy hand for silence and read aloud, " 'You are offered the post of librarian at Blaize. Communicate at once if interested.' That's all there is to the letter. Now, by my head, what's to be made of that?"

Lady Radley gave a horrified gasp and sank down into a chair. "Librarian—but you must be joking me," she exclaimed. "What *sort* of proposition is that to make an unmarried female? To whisk her away from her family to Cumbria—to the ends of the earth. It is *highly* improper. The earl cannot be in his right mind."

"He's as rich as Croesus, though," mused the lord and master. "Men of his rank have their whims. Perhaps he saw the chit somewhere and fancied her."

Everyone looked at Diana. Mortified, she said, "I never even met the earl. I received the letter this morning, but I am persuaded that it was meant for—for Dracot."

"Who is Dracot?" Mr. Chadwick asked.

"My late cousin, sir. He was killed at Waterloo."

The silence that followed Diana's low voice was broken by a sob from Lady Radley. "Poor boy," she said mournfully while dabbing at her eyes. "So full of promise! Killed along with his father, my youngest brother, Thomas."

"But why should Blaize write to Dracot?" Lord Radley was rumbling. "He didn't have a title—nor warm pockets, neither. Not the sort that a duke's son would even notice."

"Dracot came to know the earl while they were both at school. He told me they had become friends." Talking about her lost cousin brought a pain that time had not softened, and in an unsteady voice Diana went on, "Dracot enjoyed books as much as I do. He would have been happy in the earl's library."

As I would. The thought that had teased her all morning returned, unbidden. Of course it was Dracot that his lordship of Blaize wished to employ. But supposing she dared answer this letter, what then?

"Of course you will refuse this summons," Lady Radley said indignantly. "You must write at *once*, Diana. No doubt the earl does not know that poor Dracot is deceased."

"Yes, by my head." Lord Radley held the letter out to Diana. "Take this and answer by return post. Accept the position."

"Simon!" wailed his lady. "That *cannot* be. No respectable female would be so bold!"

"Spare me your spasms, madam. Girl's a D. Gardiner, too, ain't she? Letter was delivered to her. Hey? Could very well have been meant for her."

Lord Radley hooked his thumbs into his waistcoat, leaned back on his heels, and surveyed his niece with uncharacteristic approval. "Think of what it'll mean to us if the chit worms her way into Blaize. An earl who's connected with one of the noblest ducal houses in England—by my head, that's *something*!"

Wordlessly, Diana collected her letter. If she dared to respond to the earl's offer, she told herself, she would have a way of escaping the Radleys. She could take Archie to a place of safety. Diana held the letter tightly. *Did she dare*?

"But the earl will be expecting *Mr*. Dracot Gardiner," Lady Radley protested.

"Rubbish." Lord Radley's eyes held an almost reverent glow. "His grace of Naunce—now that's a man to be reckoned with. Brilliant gentleman! Followed his career in the house but never thought I'd ever have an entrée into his set. And now—"

"Y'won't have an entrée through Blaize," Mr. Chadwick interposed somewhat sourly. "Blaize is considered the black sheep of his family. That's why he's buried himself in Cumbria. Naunce ain't had anything to do with Lord Lion for years."

Seeing that he had everyone's attention, he assumed a superior expression. "M'brother-in-law told me all about Blaize. Lord Lion's his nickname because of his black moods. Nearly got tossed out of Harrow for fighting and laziness. Y'can imagine how Naunce took *that*—"

Mr. Chadwick was interrupted by a shout and a yelp of pain from the courtyard below. Diana, who was closest to the window, looked out and saw her cousin Edward beating a small, black-and-white mongrel.

She wrenched open the window, leaned out and shouted, "Edward, you beast—stop that at once."

Grinning, Edward raised his crop again, but before the blow could fall a towheaded youth came running out of the stables, grasped Edward's hand, and wrenched away the crop. The smaller boy bellowed as he was lifted up by the scruff of the neck and shaken.

"Don't you *ever* hit Claude again," Diana heard her brother cry. "I warned you the last time that I wouldn't stand for it."

"Oh, that is *Edward* calling for help!" Lady Radley pushed Diana from the window and leaned outside shrieking, "Someone stop that *monster* before he murders my son!"

There were several grooms, footmen, and servants within hearing distance, but no one answered their lady's cry. Master Edward had tormented the staff too long for anyone to care what happened to him.

Screeching like a banshee, Lady Radley ran out of the room. She was followed by Lord Radley, who was cursing at the top of his lungs. "If that want-wit has hurt my boy," he vowed, "I'll make him sorry he was ever born."

Picking up her skirts, Diana ran down the stairs after her aunt and uncle. She could hear Mr. Chadwick creaking behind her as she burst out of the house in time to see Lord Radley strike Archie with the riding crop that Edward had dropped.

"You vicious rat," he said with a roar.

Archie let go of his cousin and turned a flushed face toward his uncle. "But he was hurting Claude," he protested. "Edward was beating my dog for no reason, Uncle Simon."

Blubbering, Edward ran to Lady Radley, who clasped him to her bosom. "Mama," he wailed, "that horrid little dog bit me."

"You are lying, Edward." Diana cried. "I've seen you strike that poor animal for no reason."

She turned to reason with her uncle, who was glaring malevolently at his nephew.

"Won't have idiots and rabid dogs around me," Lord Radley sputtered. "I'll have that mongrel cur drowned."

"No!" Archie shouted. He knelt down to put protective arms about the shivering dog. "Claude didn't bite Edward—I swear it. You can punish *me*, Uncle. I'm the one that hit Edward."

"So you did—and for that you're going to the madhouse," Lord Radley vowed. "Took you in out of the goodness of my heart, by my head, and this is the thanks you give me."

"But Edward was hurting my dog." Archie was almost in tears. "Claude was asking me to help it."

"The *dog* asked for y'help?" The pop-eyed Mr. Chadwick had begun to edge away. "Not m' affair. Family matter, as I see it. Beg to take m' leave." But no one paid any attention to him as he turned and walked away.

"Lying little gutter rat," Lord Radley said with a snarl. He raised his riding crop once more—and found himself facing Diana.

"Don't you dare touch my brother," she told him.

Her voice was calm, but her eyes blazed. Lord Radley wanted to strike his niece down, but the look in Diana's coal black eyes checked him.

With a disgusted snort, Lord Radley turned away. "That's the outside of enough," he said over his shoulder. "You and your idiot brother get off my property."

"Gladly!"

Cursing and fuming, Lord Radley, followed by his wife and son, stormed back to the house, then stopped halfway to deliver his final insult. "You brazen slut! When you and your precious brother are in the gutter, don't think of coming to me. Hey? By my head, I'm done with you!"

Diana watched as the Radleys disappeared into the house and then looked down to see Archie eyeing her anxiously. "Are we really going away, Di?"

When she nodded slowly, he heaved a deep sigh of relief. "I'm glad. This is a bad place, and I've hated being here. Claude hates it, too."

He rested his cheek against the top of the dog's scruffy, black-and-white head. "Don't worry, Claude, you're coming with us," he said softly. "But—where *are* we going, Di?"

In answer to her brother's hopeful question, Diana took the rumpled letter from her pocket.

There was no point in hesitating any longer, Diana thought. Blaize may have wanted Dracot, but he had sent his almost illegible offer to *her*. She was as well read as Dracot had ever been, and she could work at least as hard as he. Given a chance, she could prove that she could earn her keep.

But what if the bad-tempered earl sent her away? A sliver of fear slid through Diana's blood, and for a second she felt paralyzed. Then she rallied.

After all, what else was there to do? Even if the earl were a man-eating ogre, she and Archie had no choice but to leave Radley House. And Blaize was the only place left to go.

She willed herself to smile into her brother's trusting face. "Archie, we are off to 'the ends of the earth' as Aunt Hortensia puts it. We are going to meet Lord Lion."

2

This truly had to be the ends of the earth, Diana thought as she gazed up at the mountains with their summits hidden by lowering clouds, and instinctively retreated deeper into her inadequate cloak.

A fine drizzle was falling, and the air was raw. Mist clung like cobwebs to the craggy mountainsides and to the town which huddled dispiritedly around a rain-swollen, leaden gray stream. Even the Gable Arms, the inn near which the driver had stopped, looked so unwelcoming that Diana had a hen-hearted impulse to run back into the coach that had brought them on the last leg of their journey.

They had traveled by mail coach through Lancashire and into Cumbria, and it had been a long, cramped, bone-rattling journey lasting several days and nights. At Grasmere they had changed to another and smaller conveyance, which in turn had jolted and jounced for miles on end until they reached the town of Kernston-on-Stream.

"If this is the end of the world, won't we fall off the edge?"

Diana turned to look at Archie, who had emerged from the stage and was looking around him with awed eyes. He looked rumpled and dusty and smelled of the camphor in which his seat companion's clothing had apparently been stored. In his arms he clutched a large, covered basket.

The portly matron who had been squeezed in on one side of Diana clicked her tongue. The red-nosed gentleman who had crowded her from the other side tapped the side of his head significantly. They both looked at Archie with such pity and scorn that Diana felt her throat close up.

Ignoring them she asked, "How is Claude?"

Archie set the basket down and opened the lid, whereupon a small, black-and-white head poked out to sniff the air. "I told you he'd be good and not make a fuss," Archie said proudly. "Claude is very, very clever."

"Which is more'n can be said for his master, us'd say," muttered the red-nosed gentleman. Diana glared at him and suggested to Archie that it was time to collect their luggage.

Afterward, Archie surveyed the two small bags and the box they had brought with them and asked, "Is someone going to meet us, Di?"

Diana shook her head. "We didn't have time to write the earl, so he will not know we have arrived. We will have to ask directions at the inn and find our way to Blaize Manor on our own."

She spoke stoutly, but brave speech did not allay the sinking feeling in her heart as they approached the Gable Arms. That sensation worsened when the shriveled landlord met her inquiries with an astonishment bordering on shock. "You want t'go *where*, mum?" he said, wheezing. "But 't earl's manor is miles and miles to the west o'us."

"Oh, distance doesn't matter—my sister is going to work for Lord Lion," Archie announced cheerfully, whereupon the landlord's wife threw up her arms and called upon St. George to preserve them in the day of disaster.

" 'Tis better you should stay and sup here," the woman declared. "There's stew on t'fire and a draught o'ale t'go with it." She added significantly, "Precious little cheer you'll get at t'manor, I'm thinking."

Diana had been thinking so, too. The warmth of the inn was inviting and so were the fragrant scents of stew which emanated from a cauldron on the stove. Archie looked hopeful, and Claude wagged his stump of a tail and licked his lips.

Diana desperately wanted to stay, but she knew that if she did not make a push now, she might never again have the courage to face the earl. Besides, she had no money to finance a night at the inn. The mail coach fare had taken almost all of the money she had gleaned from selling her last link with the past—a golden chain that Dracot had given her before he went to war.

"Is there some way we can go to the manor?" she asked. Both the landlord and his wife exchanged doubtful glances. "Perhaps there is someone with a trap that I could hire?"

After some discussion, the landlord's wife recalled that her sister's cousin's husband had a market cart. "But happen it won't be what you're used to," she cautioned.

Beggars could not be choosers. Grudging every one of her dwindling coins, Diana hired the cart, which rolled and jolted and squealed so abominably that she half wished she had not taken the offer. It made her think of the tumbrils that had taken the French aristocrats to the guillotine.

In spite of the incessant jolting, Archie fell asleep with Claude in his arms. Diana remained watchful as the cart turned inland, and she was still wide-awake an hour later when the sun unexpectedly burst out of the clouds and flooded the countryside with light.

"How splendid!" Archie exclaimed, waking up. As they rounded a curve in the road, he added, "That must be Lord Lion's house."

Diana had to admit that Blaize Manor was a pleasant surprise. After hearing so much about the earl, she had half expected a dark and brooding castle, not a handsome home built near a lake. The earl's manor commanded a splendid view of the mountains, and his acres were broad and gleamed like emerald velvet in the sun. As the cart rattled nearer, they could see horses grazing in a large paddock at the back of the house.

"Look, Claude—horses!" Archie breathed, and the dog barked excitedly. "We are going to be happy here, Di. I know it."

The countryman driving the cart muttered something under his breath and added aloud that he could drive them no farther than the gate. "T'earl don't like t'have visitors unexpected like," he explained.

Diana's stock of courage dipped lower. From the formidable iron gate and stone walls that formed a circumference around the manor house, it was evident that Lord Lion was jealous of his privacy.

Mindless of her anxiety, Archie jumped off the cart, touched his cap to the driver, then went around to the horse that had pulled the cart. "Thank you," he said politely. "It was kind of you to bring us all this way."

He then whistled for Claude, hefted the box, and followed Diana, who had picked up the bags and was walking steadfastly toward the gate.

The spurt of sun had disappeared as quickly as it had come, and gray mist gathered close again. Forcing herself to sound calm and confident, Diana gave her name to the gateman. That worthy looked at her askance, scratched his head, and requested to see the letter of invitation.

Diana withdrew Blaize's letter. The gateman seemed unable to read, but he recognized the coat of arms on the envelope. He touched his hat and said, "That's all right then, mum." He then added apologetically, " 'Twould have meant my place here, see, to let you in without the earl's orders."

The iron gate creaked open, and Diana and Archie stepped through onto a carefully maintained road that led toward the manor house. As she passed, Diana saw gardeners at work in a fine rose garden and others busily clipping the hedges that lined the lawn. They looked up curiously and touched their forelocks as the Gardiners passed.

"Lord Lion must live in a palace," Archie said, his voice soft with awe. "And look, Di, look at those beautiful horses! Do you think he owns them all?"

He started toward the paddocks, but Diana held him back. "We must first meet the earl of Blaize." *And see if he will let us stay*. "Don't call him 'Lord Lion,' Archie. He may not like it."

As she spoke she reached the lowest of several marble steps that led up to the house, and a surprised-looking young footman in gray livery appeared at the door. Once more, Diana produced her letter. Glancing at Claude, the footman then informed her that the earl was not in. Would madam care to wait?

Madam had no other choice. "Yes," Diana said, "yes, we will wait."

"And don't worry about Claude," Archie added reassuringly. "I've told him to mind his manners, and he won't make a mess."

The footman ushered them to a small sitting room on the ground floor and left them there. "I wish," Archie sighed, "there was a dish of water for Claude. He doesn't like to make a fuss, you know, but he *is* thirsty."

"I am sorry," Diana said, gently. "I collect that you are thirsty, too—and hungry as well. But until I see the earl, I don't dare ask for anything."

She looked around the room as she spoke and was not reassured by what she saw. Furnished with massive dark wooden chairs and hung with dark green drapes roped with gold, the chamber had been scrubbed and polished and waxed to within an inch of its life. Everything was precise, orderly and uncompromising in its perfection.

On one wall hung a life-size portrait of a tall man in court robes. Still holding Claude, Archie got up and walked across to look up into the proud, painted face. "Is this Lord Lion?" he wondered, and then corrected, "I meant to say, the earl."

"Oh, no, that is not my cousin Lionel. It is a likeness of his grace the duke of Naunce."

The new voice was breathless, as twittery as old paper rustling together. Diana rose quickly as she saw a tiny, bespectacled lady hovering in the doorway. She was dressed in a costly but too-large brown cambric gown, and at first glance she looked little more than a child. Then she turned her head, and Diana saw that her hair under the neat little cap was white.

"Oh, pray, do not get up on my account," the lady exclaimed. "I heard Witton at the door and wondered if it could be true that there were visitors."

She spoke as if visitors were a rarity, and Diana recalled the gateman's warning. She introduced herself and Archie, who added, "And this is Claude, ma'am."

Claude sat up on his haunches, raised both paws in the air, and barked once. "How charming. I am Miss Flor," said the little lady. "What a clever dog you are, Claude."

She held out her hand to the dog, who pattered over, sniffed, then licked the extended fingers. "He likes you," Archie declared. "He says you're a kind person who likes animals."

He smiled ingenuously at the small lady who meanwhile was engaged in scratching Claude's ears. "Oh, yes, I do indeed," she replied. "I once had a dog of my own, whose name was Bruno. He was a mastiff, and he enjoyed eating mama's flowers. That was when we lived in Kent, before I went to live at Naunce. Alas, he is dead now."

She looked sadly at the Gardiners. Diana did not know what to say, but Archie said sympathetically, "I'm sorry to hear that, ma'am, and so is Claude. He thanks you for scratching his ears. You have just the right touch, he says."

Miss Flor blushed. But her look of pleasure changed sharply to dismay when Archie added, "I hope Lord—I mean, the earl, likes dogs, too."

"Did you truly come to see Lionel?" she asked Diana in such a disconcerted voice that Diana's courage sank still further. If the terrible earl's own cousin feared him, what could strangers expect?

Not so Archie, who announced, "Di has come to be the earl's librarian."

Miss Flor gave a little moan. "Oh, dear, *dear* me. Those dreadful books. How extremely unfortunate."

"How so?" Diana asked, but Miss Flor only shook her head.

"I think it is better if you speak with Lionel himself. If you will follow me, I will conduct you to the library."

Her heart hammering, Diana followed silently as the little lady led her up a curve of circular stairs to the first floor. They traversed a staircase landing and a hallway unadorned save for a rather depressing mural of Boadicea defending Britain against the Romans, and finally stopped in front of a closed door.

"This is the library," Miss Flor explained.

By now used to the almost military neatness of the rest of the house, Diana was unprepared for chaos. There were bookshelves in the room, but these were stacked with whips, quirts, and tankards and pipes. On the floor were the books—books in crates or spilling out of boxes, books mashed underfoot or stacked pell-mell on what looked to be a billiard table.

"Good heavens," she exclaimed faintly.

"The room, as you see, is somewhat confused," Miss Flor murmured apologetically. She then looked down at Claude adding, "While you look about, Miss Gardiner, I will take the little dog to get something to eat. Will you come too, Master Gardiner?"

She smiled shyly at Archie and, calling to Claude, left the room. Claude followed at once, but loyalty held Archie back until Diana nodded and smiled a reassurance she was far from feeling and said that she would do very well.

Left alone, Diana took a few steps into the room and gazed at the confusion around her. Dismay was too easy a word for what she felt. She had expected to find a library such as the one her father had loved so dearly, or the one Uncle Thomas had maintained. She had suspected that the earl's library might have been neglected, gone to dust and spiderwebs, perhaps even become disordered or untidy. But *this*!

This was impossible. Bringing this mare's nest to order would take her weeks, *months*. And would the fearsome Lord Lion brook such delay? "Not likely," Diana muttered.

The earl of Blaize was, no doubt, the sort of employer who would demand instant results. If she could not produce them—and who could—she would be dismissed.

And Archie and Claude and she would be beside the bridge. Despairing, Diana took a step backward and realized to her horror that she was actually standing on a book which had been lying open and facedown on the floor. Automatically, she rescued the volume.

"This is a first edition," she mumbled in disbelief.

She bent down and began to lift other books from the floor. Here was a valuable Homer, and here an illustrated Chaucer. "This is—this is beyond everything," Diana gasped. "No one should treat treasures in such a way. It is—it is criminal!"

Forgetting her earlier despair, forgetting even Lord Lion, Diana knelt down amongst the books, exclaiming and commenting and wiping dust away with a corner of her skirt. She mourned over an ill-used Shakespeare, and almost wept over a book of poems which had been ripped nearly in two. There could be no question now of hen-hearted behavior. There was only one thing to be done.

Determinedly, Diana set to work reclaiming the earl's library.

* * *

"I told you," Archie said to Claude, "I *told* you we'd like it here."

Life was good. Claude was full to bursting with bread and scraps. Moreover, the earl's balding and fearsome cook, at Miss Flor's request, had given Archie a thick slice of meat pie, and damson tart drowned with custard sauce.

Archie's appreciation of these treats had been so heartfelt that the cook had melted, called him a good lad, and had given Archie a large cake to take with him outdoors. Now, sharing the cake with Claude, who bounced happily at his heels, Archie was looking for the earl's horses.

Boy and dog passed a pleasant kitchen garden and followed a path of neatly trimmed bushes toward the paddock. They had almost reached their goal when a terrible din erupted.

"Now tha's gone and done it," a disgusted Yorkshire voice shouted. "Did I tell thee, or did I not tell thee that no one was t'ride Thunder? Mathews, tha great gowp, get down!"

There was the sound of a horse whinnying as if in rage or pain. Following the direction of this sound, Archie ran down the path until he came within sight of the paddocks. Here a rider was attempting to ride a furious black stallion.

It was an impossible task. The animal bucked, reared, and pawed the air. Now, as Archie watched, the horse gave a mighty heave and unseated its rider, who flew through the air and landed on the ground with a sickening thud. A thin, stoop-shouldered individual standing near the paddock flung his cap down on the ground and commenced waving his arms.

"Now, tha's done it, Mathews! Get him out of there, lads, afore his head's bashed in," he yelled.

A half dozen grooms surged toward the paddocks but fell back in fear before the horse's slashing hooves. Claude barked and pushed himself protectively against Archie's legs as the black horse reared again. But before it could crush its fallen rider with its hooves, a tall, broad-shouldered man in a buff coat and riding breeches vaulted the paddock fence, reached the enraged beast, and seized its bridle.

"My lord—oh, my God, my lord!" The stoop-shouldered individual was also scrambling into the paddock. "Sir, that was a terrible risk you took—think on, t'horse could have trampled thee."

"Get Mathews out of here." The buff-clad gentleman's voice was so deep that it seemed to vibrate against Archie's bones. "Be quick about it."

Archie watched as several grooms dragged the unconscious man away. Meanwhile, the man in the buff coat controlled the plunging horse. A remarkably strong man, and a very cool one— "That must be the earl," Archie breathed. "He really looks like a lion, doesn't he, Claude?" The dog whined, softly. "Yes, I can see he's very angry. I think his grooms didn't do as they were told."

As if he had overheard Archie's remark, the earl snapped, "Urse, I gave orders that this horse was not to be ridden by anyone but me. I want Mathews dismissed."

"Nay, my lord, I beg tha'll reconsider," the head groom pleaded. "Mathews's young and foolish, sithee, and meant no disrespect. T'horse is a wild 'un. Mathews thought that he could gentle Thunder summat for thee—"

"Gentle it for *me*?" Lord Lion interrupted. His deep tones dropped to an almost-silky drawl. "Are you saying that I can't control my own horse, Urse?"

"Nay, my lord, but—"

"You've been with me for years, so I'll forget that you acted against my orders," Lord Lion went on in that same silky voice. "But if you ever disobey me again, you'll be dismissed without a character. Do you hear me? As for this brute, get rid of it."

Urse's jaw dropped open. "Dosta want me t'sell Thunder, my lord? But—but t'whom, sir?"

The earl's eyes flashed with impatience. "Sell it as a cart horse or to the knackers for all I care. Just get it out of my sight." Then he added as an afterthought, "Colonel Pratt was with me when I bought the horse. He took a fancy to the brute and offered me twice what I'd paid for him. Send a man to Pratt House and see if the colonel's still interested."

"Aye, my lord. At once, sir."

The earl started to turn on his heel, then paused to command, "And one more thing. The colonel must know exactly what kind of animal he's buying. Tell him exactly what happened and why I'm selling this devil."

Blaize could hear his head groom breathe a sigh of relief as he turned his back on the struggling horse and grooms and strode toward the house. He was furious with himself for having been fool enough to buy the black stallion when Forthingam sold some of his cattle this September. Because the handsome animal had shown such spirit, he had not questioned why Forthingam was so eager to part with him.

But spirit was not the word for Thunder, who seemed almost possessed. Blaize had seen horses like this stallion before, animals with a vicious streak. Such a horse could never be trusted, could maim and kill—*had* almost killed a man in his employ. The thought of what could have happened to young Mathews if he had not been there made Blaize grit his teeth.

Still seething, he reached the house, where he tossed his whip to Witton and strode up the stairs to the first floor. He was on his way to his rooms on the second floor when he heard a noise in the billiard room.

Blaize crossed the staircase landing and glanced through the half-open door. Here someone, almost completely hidden between the boxes of books, was busily stacking and sorting.

Thinking that it was Molhouse, Blaize demanded, "What the devil are you doing?"

The figure jerked upright, and Blaize was astounded to find himself face-to-face with a slender young woman. She had dark hair and dark eyes that had gone wide with apprehension. The thought crossed his mind that they were gypsy eyes. "Who are you?" he asked in a much softer voice.

Diana stared up at a tall gentleman who was dressed in a muddied riding coat and breeches. She had been so intent on the books that she had not heard his entrance.

It was the earl, she realized immediately, and Diana's courage went to powder. She wished to rise and curtsy and introduce herself, but her legs would not obey her and she could not seem to find her voice.

"What are you doing on your hands and knees?" The hardness in the deep voice was gone and Diana noted that under his tawny mane of hair, the green eyes had lost their angry glow. "The floor is damnably dusty. No place for a lady."

He crossed the floor and held out a hand to help her rise. It would be rude to refuse the gesture, and Diana swallowed hard as her hand disappeared into the earl's large, hard clasp.

"I'm Lionel Cramer," he was saying, "at your service."

Blaize felt the small hand he was holding tremble and regretted that he had frightened her with his earlier temper. He was not in the habit of snapping at females. He thought ruefully that living in the country away from so-called civilized influences had caused him to forget how to deal with ladies.

He had no idea who this particular lady was, but he surmised that she was one of his cousin's friends—or, more likely, the daughter of a friend. Decidedly she was pretty to look upon, with the vivid color in her cheeks and those remarkable dark eyes. Standing so close to her, he could draw in her scent, as delicate as roses and sunshine.

Blaize felt the distasteful events of the morning slip away as he asked, "Did my cousin bring you to this depressing room?"

Emboldened my his smile, Diana found her voice at last. "Miss Flor was kind enough to show me the way. But I must explain—"

He interrupted, "She could have guided you to a more congenial spot. Have you seen Guenevere's garden?" When she shook her head, he said, "I'm surprised. My cousin is fond of her flowers, and they'd suit a lady far better than these dusty tomes."

She could not believe that this was the fierce Lord Lion. He seemed pleasant, even kind. Diana's heart rose in a rush of hope as she countered, "But these books are the reason I am here, my lord."

Some females, Blaize reasoned, were inordinately fond of reading, but this one looked nothing like a bluestocking. "I would still suggest the garden," he told her. "Perhaps you'll permit me to escort you."

Diana's brain had at last grasped the fact that the earl was speaking to her as an equal, not as an employer. *Widgeon*, she called herself. She had not introduced herself or given any explanation for her presence, so of course the earl had no idea who she was.

She spoke in haste to rectify the situation. "I am Diana Gardiner, my lord. I have come in answer to—"

Once more he interrupted. "Diana *Gardiner*? Can you be related to Dracot Gardiner?"

"He was my cousin, sir." Diana drew a deep breath and plunged ahead. "And I—I am here because I received your letter offering employment as your librarian—" She broke off as a frown began to gather on the earl's forehead.

"There must be some mistake. That post was offered to Dracot."

"Dracot was killed at Waterloo." Ignoring the familiar, stifling pain under her breastbone, Diana added, "We are both D. Gardiners, my lord. Your letter was delivered to me, and since I am in need of work, I decided to accept your offer. I arrived today and Miss Flor kindly showed me where the library was."

With dismay, Diana noted that the earl's frown had intensified and that the warmth in his eyes had been replaced with something like chagrin. "I see," he said.

And, Blaize thought, he saw too clearly for his own comfort. To enjoy the company of a pretty woman was one thing. To have her live under his roof, work for him, tend the hated books, and perhaps learn, as Dracot had, of his situation was more than he could handle.

"I'm afraid it's impossible," he said abruptly.

"But *why*?"

The genuine despair in her voice disturbed him, made him uncomfortable and anxious to end the interview. Blaize now deeply regretted his earlier interest in Miss Diana Gardiner, an interest which might have misled her into thinking that she would be an acceptable substitute for her cousin.

"I'm truly sorry to hear about Dracot," he told her. "We were friends at school. Now that I think of it, I remember hearing him tell of his younger cousin in Somerset."

Was he softening? Could she make him change his mind? Praying that this was so, Diana said warmly, "He often spoke of you, my lord. He said that you relied on each other at school."

It was the wrong thing to say. Any possible signs of sympathy vanished, leaving the earl's eyes hard and searching. "What do you mean by that?" he demanded. Then, before she could explain he added, "I am sorry that you have made a wasted trip, Miss Gardiner, but my decision is final."

Diana felt a sickening wave of nausea. In spite of all her fears and foreboding, she had hoped that her reception might be different, that *somehow* Lord Lion would agree to let her stay and work for him. She wanted to weep with frustration and despair, but the last dregs of her courage made her say, "But you have not asked for my credentials. You don't know whether or not I can do the work."

His shrug said, why bother? "I know that you would not suit. My valet will reimburse you for your time and trouble."

It was over. She was dismissed. Bile filled her throat and with this a memory of Lord Radley's bad-tempered voice exclaiming, *When you and your idiot brother are in the gutter, don't think of coming to me. I'm done with you!*

"You are unfair, my lord!"

He was halfway out of the door, but this last made him wheel about to stare at her. In the gloom of the afternoon, her hair appeared very black against her pale skin. Her clothes, he now saw, were white with dust, and there was a scratch on her arm.

Blaize's eyes narrowed at the expression on Diana's face. It made him remember the look of men going into battle—men who were ready to fight recklessly because they knew they had little hope of surviving the charge.

"What are you talking about?" he demanded.

"You do not give me a chance to prove my worth. I am every bit as qualified as Dracot." He made a dismissive gesture. "You do not think so? Then put me to the test! I have read as much as my cousin. We had our lessons together before he went to school, and even later, I would help him study for his examinations. My father was a scholar with a fine library of his own, and —and I can put this disorder to rights for you."

Something in her voice made him uneasy, touched dark places and memories which he did not wish to examine. There was nothing to remind him of Dracot in her face, but even so Blaize made an effort to soften his voice. "I'm certain that you are eminently qualified, but not for this post."

"Because I am a woman or because you think I cannot do the work?"

"My reasons are my own." Blaize cast a look of loathing around his disordered billiard room. He was infinitely weary of the books and of Lord Duchemps's idiocy, and the sooner he saw the last of Miss Diana Gardiner the better.

"A moment, sir." Diana swooped down to the floor and picked up a Bible. It was a Gutenberg, costly and beautiful, and someone had stepped across it with a careless foot. "Look at this," she cried. "You cannot wish to have precious books treated so badly."

"Obviously they aren't *precious* to me." Now there was an underlying growl in his voice. "I'm sorry you misread my letter. I am sorry you made the trip. Now—"

"You are a fool, my lord earl."

"*What*?"

At his lordship's veritable roar, Diana went white. She wanted nothing better than to run out of the door, but the fact that the earl was standing directly in front of that portal made escape impossible. In a trembling voice she cried, "Only a fool would treat his valuable possessions as you do."

Diana threw out her hands to indicate the books around her. "Here are rare books, precious books, first editions—the collection of a lifetime. Men have labored to write them, sometimes even given their lives in the attempt. And yet you treat them like the dirt under your feet. Any man who destroys true worth like this has got to be a fool—or worse."

"And in your estimation no doubt I am worse." The earl's voice turned suddenly soft, silky, definitely menacing. "Very well, madam. I have listened to what you have to say, and I'm not interested in your services. That is the end of the matter, and I must ask you to leave my house."

The earl turned on his heel, slamming the door as he strode out of the library. As that awful sound echoed through the house, Diana felt her anger drain away. With it dribbled away her hope. "I have done it now," she whispered.

Within the space of a few days she had been ordered away both from Radley Place and from the earl's domain. Where would she and Archie go now? She had burned all her bridges.

She would have to find Archie and tell him that they must leave. Heart heavy, Diana left the library. The young footman, Witton, was standing some distance away, and from his blank expression she was sure that he had overheard her exchange with Lord Lion. Too dispirited to care, she asked where Archie might be and was told that he had last been seen walking toward the paddock.

Witton led her to a side door. It opened onto a path which led through a kitchen garden fragrant with herbs and flowers. Diana caught a glimpse of the lake as she followed the path to the paddock at the back of the manor, where a group of men—grooms by their attire—were huddled together talking in hushed tones.

"Nay, I never saw t'master so angry," one thin, stooped personage sighed. "We'st best get shut of that Thunder before t'earl claps eyes on it again, and so I tell thee."

They all gazed gloomily toward the paddock, where a splendid black horse was pacing back and forth. It shook its wild ebony mane, whinnied and pawed the ground.

"It's a shame, Mr. Urse," one of the others sighed. "Thunder'd be a fine animal if he didn't have the devil's own temper. It'd a killed Mathews if me lord hadn't stopped him."

At this juncture Diana spotted Archie. He was standing half-hidden by some trees near the paddocks. Claude was curled up at his feet.

"Where have you been?" she exclaimed.

"I have been talking to the horse," Archie explained. "Di, it's too sad. He has had a hard life."

"This is no time to be talking of horses," Diana interrupted. "We must leave this place at once. The earl did not see fit to employ me."

"But we can't leave now." Archie nodded at the black horse which was pawing the ground and explained, "I've been talking to him, and he's just beginning to trust me."

There were times when Archie's eccentricities became truly irritating. "We must leave *now*, Archie," Diana repeated sternly. "It will be dark before we reach the town."

They would have to walk unless some countryman with a horse-drawn cart passed them on the way. There would be no way to leave Kernston-on-Stream tonight, so that would mean she would have to pay for a night's lodging at the Gable Arms. Now Diana almost wished she had taken the money Blaize had offered her.

"But it would have been demeaning," she muttered to herself. "He was so overbearing and *hateful*."

"Yes, that was it, he was hateful," Archie agreed, absently. "He was always beating poor Midnight and abusing him. It's no wonder that he doesn't trust anyone."

"Archie, *what* are you talking about?"

"About the horse, of course. Midnight is confused, and afraid, and that makes him angry. He didn't mean to hurt that groom, really, but Lord Lion didn't understand that."

There was a footstep close by, a familiar deep voice at Diana's shoulder. "And what is it that I don't understand?" Lord Lion demanded.

3

For the second time that day, Diana found herself face-to-face with the master of Blaize Manor. There was no improvement. If anything, the earl looked even angrier than he had before.

"What is the meaning of this?" he asked in a soft voice which was, if anything, even more frightening. "Am I to understand that you know more about my horse than I do?"

Diana tugged at Archie's sleeve, but her brother simply said, "I think so."

"Then enlighten me."

Diana bit her lip. She saw that all the grooms had retreated to a safer distance and that she and Archie stood alone confronting Lord Lion.

Archie was saying, "You mustn't sell the black stallion, my lord. It would be wrong of you."

Almost speechless at such effrontery, the lord of Blaize glared down at the dusty, towheaded lad. "Who in hell are you?" he asked, bluntly.

Diana put a protective hand on Archie's arm. "He is my brother, sir."

Before the earl could react to this, Archie continued, "You really need to understand this horse, my lord." He pushed back a long lock of almost-white hair that had fallen forward into his eyes as he added, "That man Mathews used a crop to Midnight, and that made him remember the brute who owned him before, and how he was constantly whipped and beaten. He has been badly, *badly* treated, my lord, and that's what makes him act so wicked."

Blaize stared hard at the lad, who simply gazed back. The dark, steady gaze reminded the earl of how Diana Gardiner had faced him in the library, and he felt a faint stab of guilt when he recalled how he had snapped at her.

Irritated by this unwanted emotion, he rapped out, "Slum! That black horse is vicious." He raised his voice to shout, "Urse! I told you I wanted this brute out of my paddock."

Hastily the head groom stepped forward. "Sir, I've sent Seamus t'Pratt House, my lord. He hasna come back yet."

Urse paused, seemingly struggling with himself. "My lord, t'young master has t'right of it. Mathews did take his crop to t'black horse afore he were thrown. I dunnot know how he knew that."

"Midnight told me," Archie explained.

"He *what*?"

"He is not lying to you." Diana quickly leapt to her brother's defense as Blaize fixed Archie with a narrow-eyed gaze. "Archie is—is sensitive to animals. He can tell how they are feeling. I cannot explain how he does it, but—"

She was interrupted by a shout from one of the grooms. "Saints o' heaven, preserve us," the man said with a gasp.

Following the direction of the man's pop-eyed gaze, Diana saw that her brother had slipped under the paddock fence.

"Archie!" Diana gasped.

"Get back here at once, you fool," Blaize ordered.

Paying no attention, Archie proceeded to walk slowly toward the black stallion. The animal raised its head and whinnied a challenge. When Archie did not retreat, it reared up on its haunches and punished the air with its hooves.

Fearing that Archie would be trampled, Diana darted toward the paddock fence in an attempt to rescue her brother, but an iron hand clamped down on her arm and hauled her back. She twisted around to stare up into Blaize's hard face. "Let go of me," she cried.

"So you can be trampled, too? Stay here." Blaize let go of Diana's arm and then vaulted the paddock fence. "No, Urse—

stay where you are and keep the others back," he commanded. "I don't want the brute agitated further."

Diana gnawed her lower lip as she watched the earl walk purposefully toward her brother. Meanwhile Archie was standing only a few feet from the maddened black horse. Its eyes were rolling and its nostrils were distended, but Archie looked quite calm. Over the animal's snorts and whinnies, they could all hear the boy's soft crooning.

Blaize stopped a few feet from Archie and spoke in a quiet, steady voice. "I'm only a few feet behind you. Walk backward toward me without hurry or panic, and he won't hurt you."

"But he wouldn't hurt me anyway," Archie protested.

Blaize winced as the stallion reared back on its haunches. Its punishing hooves missed Archie's head by inches.

An orderly retreat was impossible, so the only way out was to seize the boy and then race back to safety. Even with the added weight, Blaize judged he could accomplish the rescue. He was about to make his move when Archie spoke over his shoulder.

"Please, my lord," he said, "stay where you are. You see, he is calming down."

"He's doing no such thing—" But Blaize broke off when he saw that the black stallion had ceased its frantic movements. It had retreated several steps and stood there quivering with nerves.

"Please stay very still," Archie went on earnestly. "Midnight doesn't trust you."

As he spoke, he slowly extended his hand. To Blaize's utter amazement, the black stallion dropped his muzzle into Archie's hand.

"Thunder and hell," the earl whispered.

Watching, Diana felt as though she had been running for miles. Her knees felt weak, her heart hammered, and she could hardly catch her breath. Behind her, Urse was swearing that he had never seen the like in his forty years of service. The other grooms were speechless as they watched the stallion nuzzle Archie's neck.

"And *that*'s t'killer horse, think on," Urse said.

Archie was still communing with the black horse. "You can come closer now, my lord," he said, "but please move slowly so as not to frighten Midnight. If you do it gently, you can pat him to show you mean no harm to him."

Carefully, the earl obeyed. He felt the taut, ebony neck flinch as he touched it, but Archie crooned softly, and the animal remained still. Blaize was conscious of deep quivers running through the powerful beast as he stroked the sweat-soaked hide.

"He doesn't want to be ridden, yet, but he'll come with me to the stable," Archie went on. "Shall I take him?"

Blaize looked down into the clear dark eyes that were lifted to his. It seemed he started to say one thing, then checked himself and said instead, "Urse will show you where to go."

Archie started to walk away with the stallion following. Halfway to the paddock gate, the boy stopped and looked back uncertainly at the earl. "Midnight thinks you are going to keep him and treat him kindly, sir. I told him you would. You won't sell him, or—or hand him over to the knackers, will you?"

Blaize shook his head and, apparently satisfied, Archie led the horse through the paddock gate where Claude was waiting. Then all three progressed to the stable. The stallion tossed his head nervously when he sighted Urse standing by the stable door, but Archie stroked him, and boy, horse, and dog disappeared into the stables.

"I'd give a great deal to know how he did that," Blaize muttered.

"I told you that Archie had a way with animals." Diana had come up to stand beside him. She had gone so white that her black eyes looked enormous, and her lips were trembling. So were her hands, though she clasped them tight in an attempt to control herself.

"There's no need to be afraid," Blaize said, abruptly.

"There probably never was," she replied. "I forget that no animal alive would hurt Archie."

Blaize felt a surge of respect as he realized that she had shown no fear when she confronted him in the library, and she was being even more courageous now. "Has he always had that gift?" he asked.

"Archie has always been—different. There are some who think he is simple because he does not think or act as other people do, and many times he has been teased and ridiculed for it." In a subdued voice Diana added, "I do not know if it is really a gift."

A somber, bitter expression touched the earl's hard face. Abruptly he said, "It can't have been easy for him—or for you."

Diana glanced uncertainly at the earl, but his set expression belied the note of sympathy she thought she had detected in his voice.

"While our parents were alive, it was not difficult," she said. "They realized Archie's talents and—and his limitations. They did not insist he learn his letters but let him be free with the dogs and horses, and he was happy. But when they died, we—"

Diana stopped suddenly, remembering to whom she was speaking. Fifteen minutes ago, Blaize had curtly demanded she leave his estate. Yet now she had been on the point of telling him her family history.

"All this is neither here nor there," she amended. "My brother and I will leave as soon as he is finished in the stables."

"Is it possible—how can it be? You are not leaving at this hour?" a breathless little voice behind them asked.

Both Diana and Blaize turned to see Miss Flor standing not far away. A basket full of herbs and flowers hung over her arm, and her small face was screwed up in distress.

"I have been picking thyme and rosemary for the gravy," she explained. "The cook said he would make his special sauce since we were to have guests for dinner."

"I am afraid that we must leave at once," Diana said.

"But will you not be frightened? It will be dark long before you reach town and who knows if you will find accommodation at the Gable Arms." Miss Flor looked pleadingly at the earl. "Please do ask them to stay, Lionel."

To Diana's astonishment, the earl smiled quite kindly at Miss Flor and said that, unfortunately, the Gardiners had made up their minds to leave. "My carriage will convey them to Kernston-on-Stream," he added.

Before Miss Flor could speak again, Archie emerged from the stable. He was walking shoulder to shoulder with Urse, and they were both in some deep discussion. Seeing his sister,

Archie called, "Oh, Di, isn't it grand? Mr. Urse and Midnight are going to be friends."

He hurried toward her, Claude bouncing at his heels. "Midnight likes Mr. Urse," he bubbled. "He feels Mr. Urse is a kind man, *not* like that brute of a groom who beat him before. And he admires you very much, my lord," he said to the earl, "especially since your gelding, Sultan, thinks so well of you. Midnight will come to love you as much as Sultan does if you are kind to him."

He paused to draw breath and further explain, "I know that 'Midnight' is not the name you gave him, but he likes it better than Thunder."

To Diana's surprise the earl spoke courteously. "Since he trusts you, I'd be obliged if you'll give Urse some suggestions on how to make Midnight more comfortable."

A slow smile creased the Yorkshireman's face. "Aye, my lord. T'lad an' me, we have a lot to talk about."

"How fortunate," Miss Flor said with a smile. "Now you *must* stay for dinner. I will tell Mrs. Pruitt."

After she drifted away, Blaize turned to Diana and said somewhat stiffly, "It will give my cousin pleasure if you will stay at Blaize Manor tonight."

"Collect, my lord, that you ordered me off your property. My presence in your house can hardly bring *you* pleasure."

The earl winced. "I was wrong to lose my temper about that curst library." He hesitated and then added, "I beg your pardon for my bad manners, Miss Gardiner."

It could not be easy for such a proud man to admit that he was wrong. And turnabout was fair play. "I, too, said several things that should not have been said," Diana admitted.

"I'll grant that you had provocation." Almost reluctantly, Blaize smiled and the hard lines of his face softened. "Guenevere is right—it's getting too late to set out, and besides, your brother and Urse apparently have business together."

Diana noted that indeed it was turning darker and that shadows were already spreading over the landscape. A bird called shrilly as it flew past, a reminder that night was coming and that all feathered creatures should return to their nests. It was also a reminder that the Gardiners had no home to go to.

"It *is* getting late," Diana agreed.

They were tired and hungry and Archie was content. For one night, at least, they could count on full stomachs and pillows on which to rest their heads, even if those pillows were to be found in the Lion's den.

Anticipating the acceptance of her invitation, Miss Flor had ordered the Gardiners' luggage to be sent up to one of the chambers on the third floor. Guided up the circular staircase by a pert young maid, Diana was shown to a large room in the west wing. It was handsomely furnished with a bed covered with gold velvet, a costly Aubusson carpet, and a rosewood desk over which hung a large, ornately framed portrait.

Next to the bed stood Diana's dusty box. She was grateful that the servants had not unpacked it, for her small store of clothing would have looked shabby and shopworn in such an elegant setting. While she attended to this, there was a knock on the door and Miss Flor peeped in.

"I hope I do not intrude, Miss Gardiner?" She inquired in her diffident little voice. "I have come to see if there was anything else I could do to make you comfortable."

"Thank you, Miss Flor. You have been very kind and everything is wonderful. But it was not necessary to go to so much trouble, ma'am," Diana responded.

Looking more childlike than ever, Miss Flor toyed with the lace that edged her plum-colored damask dinner gown. The lace, Diana noted, was as costly and as unflattering as the gown itself.

"I am pleased you like the room," the lady continued. "Her grace the duchess stays in this room when she visits Cumbria. I am persuaded that it is because she is fond of the portrait of her children, which was painted by one of the best painters of the day."

Sensing Diana's interest Miss Flor pushed up her spectacles and resumed, "That tall boy on the left is Nicholas, who will be duke of Naunce when his papa dies—such a clever boy, though he has a habit of compressing his lips in so daunting a fashion that one is always afraid of saying the wrong thing. Next to him are dear Eugenia and Arabella."

With gathering enthusiasm, Miss Flor described the young ladies' successful marriages. "And next to the girls is

Theodore, who is the man of the hour in the House of Lords—Theodore has a charming smile, does he not, Miss Gardiner? And there is Lionel standing behind his brothers."

Diana noted that even as a child the earl had been taller and broader of shoulder than either of his brothers. Moreover, unlike the other children, Blaize was not smiling.

Had Lord Lion been the 'black sheep' of the family even then? Aloud Diana asked, "Do their graces of Naunce often visit Blaize Manor?"

Miss Flor sighed. "Alas."

Alas, yes, or alas, no? Diana waited for illumination but the little lady had lapsed into silence. Diana reminded herself that the earl or his family was no concern of hers, especially since she intended to leave in the morning.

"Lionel is the second son. I have known him since he was a little boy when I went to live with their graces of Naunce. They took me in twenty years ago when Mama and Papa died. I was twenty-five, you see, and decidedly on the shelf, so there was nothing else to do." Miss Flor played with her lace again. "Lionel was always a chivalrous boy."

Chivalry was the last quality she would have attributed to the earl. Astonished, Diana listened as Miss Flor spoke of her days at Naunce. Difficult days, for though the duchess was kind, she was also busy, the duke hardly knew she existed, and servants sneered behind the poor relation's back.

"I was the girls' governess. They were such good little girls, but the boys were high-spirited, as boys will be. Nicholas—he was barely ten, then—used to enjoy leaving spiders in my room and Theodore would hide and jump out at me—just to tease, of course."

"And the earl?" Diana asked.

"Lionel was always a dear," was the warm response. "He brought me little gifts and helped me in the garden. We became such good friends that I missed him terribly when he went away to school. And later, when he had his own household, he asked me to come to Blaize and oversee the servants."

She paused. "Of course, that was a kindly whisker to salvage my pride. Mrs. Pruitt, the housekeeper, does everything so well. I fear, Miss Gardiner, that I am as I always was—a poor mouse."

She looked so dejected that Diana said gently, "I fear that Archie and I are poor mice, too, ma'am. And I beg you will call me Diana."

"Then we must be brave mice together," Miss Flor declared. "I am glad you have come here, Diana. I am old enough to enjoy the quietness here, but Lionel is too *young* to bury himself here in Cumbria."

She leaned forward confidentially to add, "People may think it strange that he does so, but Lionel truly hates London and what he calls the false society there. He says too many of the ton are frivolent and self-seeking and prefers to rusticate here with only Colonel Pratt for company."

Miss Flor paused, and Diana noted that her cheeks pinkened as she elaborated, "The colonel lives at Pratt House, nearby. He is a retired military gentleman and a friend of their graces. He used to visit Naunce often and as he is a—a single gentleman, he looked on the children as his nevvy. Lionel was his favorite."

Just then there was a knock on the door and Archie ran into the room. His eyes were bright, his cheeks flushed with pleasure, and he fairly bubbled with excitement.

"Midnight is so much calmer, Di," he reported, "now that he knows that Mr. Urse will treat him gently. Claude said he'd stay in the stables, too, because it's more interesting there than it is in the house, and—oh, I beg your pardon, ma'am. I didn't see you."

He broke off to bow clumsily to Miss Flor, who murmured that she would leave Diana to dress and drifted away. Archie looked bewildered. "Did I say something wrong, Di?"

Diana shook her head. "No, but, Archie, you must not become too fond of Blaize Manor. We must leave in the morning."

Archie's smile lost some of its brilliance. "Must we?" he pleaded. "Claude likes it here, and so do I, and Midnight needs me."

"We must face the fact that I am not suitable as the earl's librarian." As Archie's face fell, Diana spoke in a rallying tone. "We've always managed, haven't we? Let's have a good dinner tonight and we will face tomorrow when it comes."

This seemed to satisfy Archie. He went off to his room at the end of the hall to wash and change for dinner, leaving his sister to do the like. It took some time to brush out the creases of her well-worn gray muslin, and by the time Diana had brushed her thick hair and braided it into a chignon high at the base of her neck, the dinner gong was sounding.

Archie met her in the hall and together they followed Witton, who carried a silver candelabrum aloft as they walked downstairs. Once there they were conducted to the drawing room where a fire was crackling in the hearth and the earl was standing with his foot on the hob, staring into the flames.

He had changed into evening clothes of black superfine, and a solitary diamond glittered in the folds of his white cravat. Sober garb, but even so, the lord of Blaize resembled a lion.

The moods of the king of beasts were unpredictable and not to be trusted, Diana thought. Archie had no such qualms. He went directly up to the earl saying, "Good evening, sir. Midnight is settled all right and tight, as Mathews says."

Blaize had been thinking since the incident in the paddock. His initial wonderment at the way Archie had handled the black stallion had given way to uncertainty. His better sense told him that it was unwise to have invited the Gardiners to dinner, and as he looked keenly into Archie's open, eager face, a frown began to form between his tawny brows. It would have been simpler to send them to the Gable Arms and have them housed there at his expense.

Diana watched the earl's expression and felt sure that his lordship was about to ask questions. People curious about Archie's abilities tended to treat him as a freak of nature instead of a thirteen-year-old lad with feelings and sensibilities.

In order to deflect his lordship's fire, Diana said, "Good evening, my lord. I hope we are not late."

Before Blaize could answer, Archie explained, "It's my fault. Mr. Urse said Midnight would settle down even if I left, but I stayed with him to make sure he would be all right. And I had to see if Claude really wanted to stay in the stables. It's hard to sleep in a strange place."

Blaize watched Diana reach out to touch her brother's shoulder. Though he could not know why, the protective gesture eased his doubts, and he spoke more warmly. "It's all right, lad. Come and sit by the fire, Miss Gardiner. The night's turned chilly."

He stepped forward to conduct her to the chair, his hand briefly cupping her elbow. Sure hands the earl had, and strong. Diana found herself remembering something that Dracot had said about his school friend years ago. *He's a hard fellow to bridge, Dina, but a right 'un. And a man who doesn't know the meaning of fear.*

She listened carefully as the earl turned to Archie, saying, "I went to see Midnight myself and was astonished at the change in him. How did you know how to handle him?"

The boy looked bewildered. "He told me how."

Miss Flor now entered the room and Diana noted how Blaize greeted her with genuine pleasure.

"I am so glad that your guests have stayed for dinner, Lionel," Miss Flor was saying shyly. "I have cut my best dark red roses for the table. They are so vivid and full of spirit that they remind me of you, Diana."

Just then dinner was announced. The earl suggested that Archie escort Miss Flor in and then offered his arm to Diana.

"Guenevere's very fond of her garden. Being compared to her roses is a rare compliment."

"Miss Flor has been most kind to Archie and me," Diana said.

"She's kind to everyone." The earl's voice softened as he added, "Perhaps she's good at growing things because she can 'see a world in a grain of sand and a heaven in a wild flower.' "

Diana was surprised. From what he had said about despising books, she had not expected the earl to quote Blake.

She was thoughtful as they entered the dining room where Archie was staring with awe at the gleaming table. Molhouse, standing at attention near the door, cocked a shrewd eye at Diana as she entered, and she thought there was a trace of approval in his shoe-button eyes.

The meal was simple but abundant. Witton served up a tureen of fragrant broth, which was followed by a dressed sole and chicken cutlets wonderfully sauced. Archie ate with silent appreciation, the earl seemed to be lost in a brown study, and there was silence until Miss Flor finally spoke. "I am so grateful that you have invited Diana to be your librarian, Lionel."

"Actually, I wanted her cousin, Dracot, to take the post," the earl replied. "Unfortunately, my old school friend was lost at Waterloo, and my letter was delivered to Miss Gardiner by mistake."

"Dracot and Di were to be married," Archie volunteered.

Miss Flor gave a little gasp of sympathy. The earl said nothing but looked hard at Diana who said, "It is true—we were engaged just before his regiment left for Waterloo."

"Why didn't you mention this before?" the earl asked.

Diana looked around the table, saw that everyone was looking at her, and felt her cheeks grow warm with embarrassment. "I did not think it made any difference."

"Oh, my *dear*." The enormity of Diana's tragedy seemed to have shaken Miss Flor terribly. "What a misfortune. To lose the man you love at such a young age. No doubt your heart is broken and you will mourn him forever."

She wiped her eyes with her napkin. In the ensuing silence, Diana felt the old, hard knot of pain beneath her breastbone. She was only two years younger than Dracot, and they had been best friends since early childhood. Together they had climbed trees and gone wading to catch frogs. Together they had conspired to filch tea cakes from the kitchen. When they were older they had shared books, gone for long rambling walks, and debated philosophy for hours.

Truly, truly, she mourned her cousin Dracot. Perhaps that was what was meant by a broken heart.

The earl frowned down at his plate. "I'm sorry," he said. "If I'd known—"

If he had known, he would not have roared at her as he had. Blaize looked at Diana Gardiner sitting across the small table from him. Her obviously twice-turned gown was worn to a subtle silver hue and emphasized her striking coloring. Guenevere's odd comparison was apt, he thought. The woman did resemble one of the vivid, dark red roses. Or she would have, were she not looking so worried and unhappy.

"But how *brave*," Miss Flor said. "You have lost your true love and now you are making your way in the world."

"Di *is* brave," Archie said earnestly. "You should have seen her when she stood up to Uncle Simon and told him he couldn't send me to the madhouse."

Blaize raised a quizzical eyebrow while Miss Flor looked alarmed. Embarrassed, Diana said hastily, "Uncle Radley did not mean it."

"He did, too! And he wanted to drown Claude," Archie protested. "Or he would have done if Di hadn't told him we were coming to work for Lord Li—I mean, for the earl."

"Of course you are not mad and—oh, only a brute would want to drown that dear little dog." Miss Flor reached out to pat Archie's hand. "Don't be afraid. Lionel will protect you and Claude, too."

Diana opened her mouth to say that they would not avail themselves of his protection and that they were leaving in the morning. But before she could speak, Miss Flor continued, "How fortunate, Lionel, that Diana came to us. Now when your mama and papa come to visit, they will be so pleased."

Diana saw Molhouse shoot a glance at his employer. There was uneasiness in the valet's swift glance, but the earl's face remained bland. "Quite so," was all he said.

The rest of the meal passed in desultory conversation. But when Miss Flor rose, announcing that it was time to leave the earl to his port, Blaize called Diana back.

"I need to speak to you," he said.

Determined to face what was inevitable and take her fences cleanly, Diana agreed. "I understand what you wish to tell me," she said when they were alone. "There is no need, my lord. Tomorrow, we will leave."

He ignored this. "When did you and Dracot decide to marry?"

"Our marriage had been arranged by Papa and Uncle Thomas Gardiner when we were in leading strings," Diana explained somewhat stiffly. "We announced our engagement on the eve of Waterloo because Dracot said—" She broke off and then added quietly, "because Dracot wanted it."

There was a small silence. Blaize walked to the tall French windows and stood staring into the darkness. "Will you take the post?" he demanded suddenly.

"I beg your pardon?"

"I need a librarian. You need a position. It seems to be a sensible solution."

Diana could not credit what she was hearing. "But this afternoon, you said—"

The earl interrupted. "Please understand. I loathe that library. It was foisted on me by a bluestocking cousin I hardly knew. Thunder and hell—I haven't the time or the inclination to worry about a roomful of curst books. I wanted Dracot to come to Blaize and take the damned things off my hands. He was my friend and would have understood exactly how I felt—"

Abruptly, he stopped talking and faced her. "Your brother seems happy at Blaize. And besides, Guenevere seems to have taken to you."

In the next room Diana could hear Archie's voice rise and fall as he talked to Miss Flor. Yes, Archie could be happy here. And safe.

"Well?" he asked her. "I thought you wanted this post."

There was a challenge in his jade-hard eyes. *Perhaps,* Diana thought, *not so safe after all.*

The earl was powerful and autocratic. He would be a difficult employer. Though, at the moment, he was well disposed to her, there was no guarantee that this feeling would last. Tomorrow she might anger him again and he might send her packing once more.

"Yes, or no?" Blaize demanded.

She would deal with tomorrow when tomorrow came, Diana decided. Lifting her chin, she met the earl's eyes squarely and saw within their depths something she could not quite analyze.

"Yes," she said—and was surprised to see him smile.

4

Wrestling, tugging and pushing, Diana attempted to move a heavy carton of books across the floor. It resisted. Diana gritted her teeth, wiped damp palms on her now dusty skirt, and put her back into it.

"Where do you want the box?"

Startled, Diana sprang up and almost collided with the earl of Blaize. "I am sorry," she stammered. "I didn't hear you come in, my lord."

He nudged the box with the toe of his boot and repeated, "Where were you taking this?"

"By the shelves over there. But—my lord, wait! there is no need for this."

Without paying her the slightest heed, the earl lifted the enormous box. Muscles rippled under the gray superfine of his riding coat as he carried it across the room.

"You are paying me to organize your library," Diana protested, "not to do the work yourself. Pray don't trouble yourself, my lord."

Thoughtfully, Blaize regarded his librarian. There was no doubt that she took her work seriously. Her face was flushed with effort, and there was a smudge on her nose. A strand of silky black hair had escaped from the tight chignon at her neck and curled damply across her forehead.

She was up before dawn and at work long before he returned from his morning ride. During the past week he had never seen her at breakfast, seldom at lunch, and at dinner—*if* she appeared for dinner—she had worn a sleepwalking look.

His cousin Guenevere was worried about the girl and he himself did not want any employee of his working herself to death—which was the reason he had stopped in today.

"You look haggard." His deep voice held a sympathetic note, and he actually smiled as he added, "There's no need to kill yourself, Miss Gardiner. These curst books will outlive us all."

So far killing herself had done little good. It had been a full week since she had begun her task, but Diana felt that she had hardly made a dent. A morass of books lay about her everywhere. Though the servants had removed the billiard table and carried out the mess that had till now cluttered up the library shelves, crates, barrels, and boxes of books remained unpacked.

Blaize was looking about him critically. "Why not simply line the books on the shelves and have done?"

"The problem is that they already have been tossed haphazardly into boxes," she protested. "Here is an old and valuable edition of Aesop's *Fables* packed in with essays by Voltaire and a book on culinary recipes." She selected another volume. "This book is a treatise on the diseases of the throat and this concerns sheep farming."

About to say that he had absolutely no interest in either philosophy or sheep, Blaize held his peace. Another black curl had just tumbled across Diana Gardiner's forehead, and he was battling an insane desire to reach out and push it back. The urge was so strong that he could actually feel the stroke of warm, dark silk against his fingers.

The earl locked his hands behind his back and stared hard at the wall behind Diana's head. "Foolishness," he muttered.

She misunderstood him. "I agree," she said gravely. "It is no way to treat priceless things."

Something in her way of speaking reminded him of Dracot, and Blaize recalled another time when he and his school friend sat together with a heavy volume of Aristotle's *Ethics* between them.

Perhaps it was because she was Dracot's cousin that she moved him. Blaize watched his librarian setting up her books as carefully as if they were gems and asked abruptly, "Why do you value them?" She looked up at him in surprise and he explained, "Books are just bits of paper bound together in leather. There's nothing in them that amounts to a tinker's curse."

"But that is not true. Books are wondrous things, each containing undreamed-of magic."

Her eyes were bright, her cheeks full of vivid color, and enthusiasm softened her mouth. With an effort, Blaize forced himself to look away from those inviting lips.

"How so?" he heard himself ask.

"There are books of travel that will transport you to another country more surely than ever a magic carpet could. And books to catch the heart, to dazzle, delight—" Diana stopped herself. Even in her eagerness, she had noted how fixedly the earl was regarding her.

"You are an excellent advocate, Miss Gardiner. You almost make me believe you."

Diana was relieved at his lighter tone. She was afraid that she had angered him. After all, she was there to see to his library, not to deliver lectures.

"But I doubt if all books are worth your enthusiasm," the earl continued. He picked up a book from the box at his feet, opened it at random, and handed it to her. "This one, for instance. What does this book say to you?"

Diana took the slender book and saw that it was a collection of poems by sixteenth-century poets.

"Read a passage aloud and weave your magic, Miss Gardiner," the earl requested.

There was a challenging glint in his eye. Diana cleared her throat and began reading a poem by Thomas Lodge.

" 'Love in my bosom like a bee/Doth suck his sweet—' " She broke off.

"Go on," Blaize directed. His deep voice was soft in the sudden hush.

" 'Now with his eyes he plays with me/Now with his feet,' " Diana read. " 'Within my eyes he makes his nest/His bed amidst my tender breast/My kisses are his daily feast—' "

"Read on, Miss Gardiner," he murmured.

Diana was aware that the earl had come to stand behind her.

He was so close that when she breathed, she drew in the scent of leather and the clean, vital essence of the man himself.

If she moved back a step, she would be in his arms. Hastily discarding this ridiculous thought, she ruffled the pages of the slender volume. "It is a foolish poem, my lord."

"Then read another," the earl said.

His finger pointed to a passage by Ben Johnson. Diana felt her cheeks grow warm as she read, " 'Drink to me only with thine eyes/And I will pledge with mine/Or leave a kiss within the cup/And I'll not ask for wine.' "

"This poet's more to my liking. He's producing a veritable thirst in me," the earl said.

At his suggestive tone, Diana's blush deepened. Though clearly embarrassed, she continued to read, and her voice did not falter. Once again Blaize admired her spirit. He admired, too, the way Diana's long lashes cast shadows on her cheeks, the slender whiteness of her neck and throat. He could drink her in with his eyes, indeed, with more than just his eyes.

He was standing so close to her that at any time he could take her into his embrace. As the thought crossed Blaize's suddenly befogged mind, Diana stepped forward and out of danger. She closed the book and placed it on another part of the shelf.

"It is an old and valuable edition," she told him. "And it should have been carefully packed, not jumbled about with all these other volumes of lesser importance."

He said nothing. Striving to calm her confused senses Diana added briskly, "Your cousin must have been a man of great learning, my lord, but his servants must have been illiterate to treat his books so badly."

There was a small pause. Then the earl said, "I won't keep you from your work."

Surprised at the change in his voice, Diana turned to look at him over her shoulder and saw that his expression, too, had altered dramatically. He was unsmiling, and there was a harsh cast to his mouth.

"In the future," he added coldly, "call one of the footman to help you if something needs to be lifted. That's what I pay them to do."

Bewildered, Diana watched the earl stalk out of the library.

Now what had she said to displease Lord Lion? For a moment he had seemed so friendly.

More than friendly, a voice in her brain whispered. Diana's cheeks felt warm again as she recalled the earl's deep voice at her shoulder, her reaction to his nearness.

"Splendid! Oh, Midnight, you are a go-er!"

The familiar voice outside the library window shattered these unseemly thoughts. Thankful for the distraction, Diana glanced through the high oriel window and saw Archie riding past on Midnight. His hair shone silver in the sun, and though she could not catch what he said, she could hear the lilt in his voice as he cantered out of sight.

Archie was happy for the first time since their parents' death. She *must* not risk Lord Lion's displeasure again, for she could not lose this post. With renewed determination Diana returned to her work.

She ignored Witton's announcement that lunch was served and thereafter lost all track of time. Perched on a ladder, she was arranging books on a high shelf when the library door swung open again.

This time it was Miss Flor who peered in. "My dear Diana," she protested, "you are working much too hard. I have not set eyes on you since breakfast and here it is three o'clock in the afternoon."

"Is it really?" Diana asked, amazed.

"You should at least stop for a cup of tea." When Diana explained that she had just started to make progress, Miss Flor looked even more concerned. "Indeed, you are like Blaize. Once he gets something in his mind, he will not rest or change his mind until that thing is done. That is why I was surprised—delighted, of course, but still surprised—when he agreed to have a library in his house. Especially since he was so opposed to the idea at first."

Recalling the earl's comments about the value of books, Diana murmured, "I wonder why."

"Lionel is a man of action," Miss Flor said fondly. "He always was. When he was just a little lad, he was fearless. Did you know that he held the rank of major during the war and was decorated for bravery?"

In silence, Diana digested all this information. Miss Flor resumed, "It was a great shame when he sold his colors after

Waterloo. But he had lost so many friends that he became disenchanted with a military life, and —oh, I *beg* your pardon. I should not have been so thoughtless as to mention Waterloo."

Miss Flor looked so distressed that Diana hastened to change the subject. "I saw Archie riding Midnight some time ago," she said.

"The day is fine. Could you not leave the books and ride with Archie?"

Startled at the suggestion, Diana glanced out of the window and saw how the late afternoon sunlight was sifting gold over the green fields. Beyond she could see the sweep of Iris Lake, which formed the northwestern border of the earl's estate. On such a day, it would be heaven to ride and ride

As if reading Diana's mind, Miss Flor said, "If you keep up this pace, you will make yourself sick, and then where will you be?"

Sick underlings would surely not be welcome at Blaize Manor. Diana registered the fact that her back ached, her neck felt stiff, and that her head throbbed. She looked at the gold-and-green outdoors again.

"There is a dear little mare in the stables. Lady Arabella rode it when she visited last with their graces of Naunce," Miss Flor coaxed. "Poor Firefly has not had much exercise lately, except at the hands of the grooms. Archie tells me that Firefly would so enjoy being ridden by a lady again."

Diana thought that maybe Archie had put Miss Flor up to this. "Perhaps you could ride the mare, ma'am," she suggested, but Miss Flor looked alarmed at the idea.

"Horses are so large, and I am not as brave as Lady Kerwinkle, Colonel Pratt's sister, who lives in London. She actually is courageous enough to ride to hounds, and the colonel says—"

Miss Flor pinkened, broke off, and added hastily that it was Diana she wished to discuss. "If it is simply a matter of suitable clothing, there is no problem. Lady Arabella is about your size and height, and she always keeps a riding habit here." After a pause she added, "How delighted she would be if you exercised Firefly for her."

Diana gave in to temptation. A short ride with Archie would

not hurt anybody, she reasoned, and she could return to her work refreshed. Ten minutes later, dressed in Lady Arabella's flowing habit of emerald green velvet trimmed with golden frogs, Diana left the manor house.

The habit was much too grand for her, and Diana felt decidedly uncomfortable as she waited for Firefly to be brought around to the house. But her apprehensions disappeared into pleasure when Urse led out an elegant white mare, who fairly danced along and tossed her milky neck in anticipation of a ride.

Urse told her that Archie might be riding the trail by the lake and gave her directions. As Diana rode down this path, the scent of late summer flowers mingled with newly cut grass, and a bright blue butterfly danced ahead of her. No wonder, she thought, Archie loved this place. Though nothing like Somerset, there was some quality about Blaize that reminded her of home.

Her thoughts broke off as she glimpsed a rider ahead of her. She called a greeting and found herself face to face with his lordship of Blaize.

He was the last person she wanted to see. Diana would have happily turned tail and slunk back to the library, but it was too late. Halting his handsome bay gelding, he demanded, "Why are you here? Has something happened?"

Wind ruffled through his tawny hair making him look more leonine than ever. Swallowing a sour lump that had worked its way into her throat, Diana explained, "I intended to work all day, but Miss Flor insisted I ride Firefly for a little while. She said that the mare needed exercise."

"It was Guenevere's idea, was it?" the earl asked.

Diana felt her cheeks turn hot as she saw his eyes flick to her habit. Naturally, he would recognize it. "Miss Flor offered me the use of your sister's riding costume," she explained miserably. "I—I was just returning to the house."

"Nonsense. It's too fine a day to be closeted indoors with cobwebs and books."

Blaize looked hard at his librarian, who seemed poised to take flight. There was doubt in her eyes, and her cheeks were flushed with mortification. The effect, Blaize had to admit, was quite charming. And his sister's habit looked far better on Diana Gardiner than on Arabella, who was too pale to wear such dashing colors.

In spite of her stand on those tiresome books, Blaize owned that he was pleased with her company. "Let me show you Iris Lake," he said. "The view from the eastern side is better than this."

She was so grateful that Lord Lion had not sent her packing out of hand that she would have gladly ridden anywhere. But she was too tense to pay attention to her surroundings until he said, "This is the view from the east."

An incredibly beautiful vista lay before her. Diana forgot her anxieties as she gazed at the mountains. They were so close that their green slopes seemed to slide into the silver-blue waters of the lake. The lake itself was studded with water lilies of every color. Dragonflies and butterflies darted across the lily pads and then disappeared into the golden haze of the afternoon sun.

"Pretty, isn't it?" Blaize had turned in his saddle to watch her reaction. "My great-great-great-grandfather built the house here because his wife fell in love with the view. In the spring, the shore is covered with iris."

"Archie had told me about the lake, but I had no idea it was so lovely." Diana drew a breath of the golden air and found the courage to meet Lord Lion's eyes. "My brother thinks he is in heaven, my lord. Thank you for letting him run tame in your stables and for allowing him to ride Midnight."

He shrugged aside her thanks. "He is training that horse better than ever I could. He earns his keep, believe me. Archie knows more than any starched-up scholar buried in useless books."

The contempt in his voice recalled the scene in the library. Diana gulped once and said, "I am sorry if—this morning, I overstepped my bounds and spoke too freely. I apologize, my lord."

"No apology needed. It's simply that I have no use for books. At one point I wanted nothing more than to follow the drum. What use is a book to a soldier?"

"A soldier needs to read about military strategy," Diana could not help pointing out.

He shot her a scornful look.

"One engagement with a real enemy teaches far more than a stack of tomes. I didn't need what's written in books to keep my men and myself alive at Waterloo."

He broke off suddenly, and for the space of a second there was silence. "Dracot was a good man, and a good friend."

A wind ruffled the mirror image of the mountains reflected in the lake, then brushed through Diana's hair like a living hand. "I know that he valued your friendship, too," she said quietly.

"What did he say about me?"

Taken aback by the sharp voice in which that question was put, she stammered, "Not very much. Only that you were a true friend and not afraid of anything."

A brace of kingfishers had landed near the lake's edge. With his eyes on the birds, Blaize said, "Everybody's afraid of something, Miss Gardiner."

"Dracot believed that you were not." He smiled at this, and she was emboldened to add, "You are very different from Dracot, my lord. How did you and my cousin come to be friends?"

The earl shrugged his broad shoulders. "Bullies made fun of Dracot when he first came to school. I suppose I protected him from them."

"That was kind," she exclaimed.

"I didn't do it to be charitable. I abominate bullies. Sadistic brutes—but they didn't bother your cousin—or me."

He spurred his horse forward, and Diana followed while thinking of Dracot at school. Her mind drifted so that she did not immediately realize how the landscape had changed. Instead of the sweep of lake and mountains, here was a lush green field which ended at the base of a sheer rock cliff. The cliff was garlanded with flowering vines, and at the top stood a lone pine tree that had apparently grown out of the rock itself.

"*Natura genetrix*," the earl commented. "I always think that when I come here."

Nature is our mother.

Diana was surprised again. It seemed such an uncharacteristic thing to say, especially since he had just finished reviling books and learning. But she supposed he had picked up the Latin tag somewhere.

He must have read her thoughts, for he said, "Since your cousin *spoke* of me so often, he doubtless told you that I didn't cover myself with glory at school."

She could not imagine this vigorous, vital man ever being surly or lazy. "Was it so important to cover yourself with glory?"

"To Naunce it was. Perhaps that's why I didn't apply myself." He gave her a sudden, self-mocking grin. "Guenevere will tell you that even in leading strings I was a rebel. I received many canings because of my curst obstinacy, but so, probably, does any child."

Diana winced at his matter-of-fact tone. "Papa did not believe in beatings," she replied. "He was the gentlest of men. Both he and Mama would weep at the sight of a fallen bird."

"You had an unusual childhood, Miss Gardiner, believe me." The earl's lips curved in a dry smile as he added, "Naunce didn't believe in sparing the rod. My brothers and sisters toed the mark, but I—"

The shrug with which he ended the sentence was eloquent. Diana felt a rush of sympathy for the earl, who had been caned and reviled as a child.

"I'm sorry," she murmured.

He looked at her in surprise. "Why? It's the way of the world. Follow the sheep—or be prepared to deal with wolves."

He touched his spurs to his gelding and trotted ahead of her into the green clearing, and she followed thoughtfully. The earl, apparently, had decided to face the wolves.

Blaize was glad of his librarian's silence. He was astonished at himself for talking so freely to Diana Gardiner or that he had even invited her to ride with him. Memories of Dracot and those wretched school days had overtaken common sense. But enough was enough. Diana Gardiner was no friend of his, and if not for those curst books, she would not be here at all.

As the thought touched his mind, she remarked, "Someone is nearby, my lord. I hear a dog barking."

"Out here?" The earl looked astonished. "No one trespasses on my land with or without their dogs. They know better."

But now the wind definitely carried the sound of a dog's yapping. "I believe that is Claude," Diana exclaimed.

As she spoke, the little dog came bounding out of a clump

of bushes. It jumped about, barking and whining in an agitated way, then began to run back the way it had come. "Where is Archie?" Diana asked, suddenly fearful.

Just then there was the sound of an angry cawing, and Blaize exclaimed, "The young fool!"

He spurred forward and, with Diana close behind, rode after Claude. As they followed the curve of the hill, the gelding threw back his head and whinnied. An answering whicker came from nearby.

"Midnight! But where is—oh, dear Lord!"

Diana choked back a scream as she saw her brother clinging to the rock face about a hundred feet above the ground. Dark, winged forms were circling around his head.

"Ravens. They nest on top of that cliff," Blaize explained grimly.

Suddenly a large black bird came diving down over Archie's head. Diana screamed. The earl swore, wheeled his gelding around, and began galloping toward the rock face.

As Diana spurred after Blaize, she saw more ravens swoop about Archie's head and slash at him with wing and talon. Now that they were closer, she could see that he was clinging to the roots of a tree that grew in the rock face.

"He's going to fall," she gasped.

"Not if I can help it." Dismounting, Blaize commanded, "Don't call his name or frighten him in any way, do you understand? Stay here with the horses."

"What are you—" she began to ask, but he was already pushing his way through the bushes that grew at the base of the rock. Diana watched with her heart in her mouth as he began to climb the rock face.

Now the birds were attacking the earl as well as Archie, who turned a tortured face to look down at the man who was coming to his rescue. "Steady, lad," Diana could hear the earl call. "Hold fast."

Frantic, Claude darted in and out of the bushes. He barked and barked as more ravens swooped down to attack Archie. Diana couldn't keep back a scream as punishing wings dashed against her brother's face.

"I can't—hold on," he wailed.

Scrambling down from the saddle, Diana gathered up her

skirts and ran to the cliffs. "Be damned to that," she heard the earl say grimly. "Screw up your courage, boy, and stay where you are. I'm coming for you."

"I'll—I'll try—" Archie's voice ended in a scream of pain as an enraged bird struck him full in the face. Then he shrieked again as the root he had been clinging to came away in his hands and he fell backward while Claude barked hysterically. Diana screamed, too, until she saw Blaize's arm shoot out and grasp her brother in midair.

"I have you," the earl gasped.

It was an unbelievable feat, incredible really. But it would do no good, for how long could any man hold on to that sheer rock face with one hand? Hardly knowing what she did, Diana raced up the rock face and stood underneath, her arms outstretched. If nothing else, she could try to break Archie's fall.

But he did not fall. Diana held her breath and even Claude was still as, holding to Archie with his left hand and to the rock face with the other, the earl began slowly to descend. Eighty feet—sixty—forty—twenty—

Out of the corner of her eye, Diana saw the raven's plunge. But even before her words of warning were out, the bird had hurtled downward, its talons outstretched, and had torn at Blaize's right hand. Yelling, the earl let go of the rock and the two fell into some bushes at the base of the cliff.

Diana had no breath left even to scream. She pushed aside the bushes and knelt beside her motionless brother. Claude was whining and licking his face, but he lay so still and looked so white. "Oh, Archie," she whispered.

"D-di." To Diana's eternal gratitude, her brother opened his eyes and blinked at her. "Is the fledgling all right?"

Relief made her so weak she could only stare.

"The fledgling," Archie repeated. He struggled to a sitting position and gathered Claude close to him as he explained. "The little raven had fallen from its nest and Claude found him. I had to put him back into the nest or a fox or owl would have got him."

"And who are you to interfere with the laws of nature?"

The earl, too, sitting up amongst a tangle of branches, disentangled himself and got to his feet as he added, "Your motives may have been good but that was a bacon-brained thing to do."

"I'm sorry, sir." Archie put down his dog and, getting shakily to his feet, approached the earl. "Are you all right? I fell on top of you. Are you sure you are not hurt?"

As he listened to the worried young voice, Blaize recalled the day when he himself had climbed these rocks as a boy. He had fallen so heavily into these same bushes that he had knocked himself half-unconscious. His brothers had run back to the house for help, and when the servants had helped him back to the manor, his father had punished him for tearing his clothes.

Blaize turned away from that memory and said, "No harm done. Where the devil have the horses got to?"

"They were probably scared off by the birds. I'll get them." Archie whistled for Claude and hurried off as the earl turned to Diana.

"I *thought* I told you to stay with the horses."

She ignored this. "There is blood on your arm."

In her anxiety, she caught his arm and turned it over to examine it more closely.

"It's nothing—a mere scratch."

Blaize found he could not speak without difficulty. For the second time that day, Diana Gardiner was standing so close to him that her soft hair grazed his cheek. The scent of her hair reminded him again of roses and honey, and her fingers, as they brushed the tear on his coat sleeve, evoked a rush of now-familiar emotions.

Through the earl's rent sleeve, Diana could see an ugly gash. The sight of it made her realize just how close Archie had come to falling to his death and how the earl had gone to his rescue.

"Thank you," Diana whispered. "Thank you for saving Archie—and for not being angry at him. He thinks the world of you, and—and he means more than the world to me."

She looked up at him, and in the speaking depths of her coal black eyes, Blaize saw his own reflection edged with little golden flecks of sunlight.

He had not meant to take her in his arms, but now all rational thought deserted Blaize as all the pent-up desires he had felt in the library imploded through him. In this fantasy turned reality, Diana's lithe body nestled against his, and her lips tasted as sweet as honeyed wine until the world dissolved and disappeared and there was no reality except this, except the woman in his arms.

Diana, too, forgot the world, forgot even Archie's recent danger, forgot everything except the strong arms that held her so close. The ground on which she stood felt unsteady, and she could hear nothing except the drumming of her heart.

And then the drumbeat became something else. *What are you doing*? a voice screamed in her mind. Barely a week ago Lord Lion had roared at her and threatened to throw her bodily off his property. And yet now she was allowing him to kiss her.

Diana tried to pull free of the earl's arms, but he would not let go. Panic suddenly filled her and with it the memory of her uncle Radley's voice. *Perhaps he saw the chit somewhere and fancied her*. And if he did, who would come to help her? Who would stop the earl from doing exactly what he wanted?

She was a female without money or connection. No doubt the earl's kiss was a prelude to his giving her a slip on the shoulder. Worse, she was giving him every encouragement by kissing him back. Diana gave a little gasp as the horror of this other reality caught hold.

Blaize felt the warm, supple body in his arms suddenly stiffen and tense, and a cold wind of sanity cleared the fog in his mind.

What in thunder am I doing? the earl thought.

Abruptly, he drew away and regarded Diana. She was breathing hard and looked frightened. When he dropped his arms from around her, she took several steps backward as if she were ready to run away.

He had to say something and quickly, but his usually quick wits had taken French leave. "I beg your pardon," he finally managed to stammer.

His discomfort served to reassure her. So did the expression in his eyes. The earl was not about to give her a slip on the shoulder, Diana realized. He was fully as horrified and as surprised as she.

With an effort, she managed to say, "I—it was my fault. I was so grateful to you that I—that I forgot myself."

Blaize did not answer. He did not have the words because he was too appalled at his own reaction. Quite apart from the fact that it was unconscionable to take advantage of a female's distress—and that female being Dracot Gardiner's cousin into the bargain—he did not wish to become emotionally entangled with any female at this time of his life.

To give heart and soul into a woman's keeping was a dangerous thing for any man. It exposed his weaknesses, rendered him vulnerable.

No, Blaize thought.

He had merely hired the woman to put his library to rights and he had no interest in her besides that. Any thoughts he might have had about her beautiful black eyes were passing lunacy, probably occasioned by the excitement of the boy's rescue.

"The fault was all mine," he managed to say. "Danger affects people in different ways. After a battle, even seasoned soldiers are carried away by joy and the relief of having escaped a great danger."

He paused, cleared his voice and added in a firmer tone, "My own men behaved like schoolboys after Waterloo. One of the young lieutenants in my regiment actually forgot himself so far as to kiss the gunnery sergeant. Naturally he apologized later."

"Naturally," Diana murmured.

"You can see how crises can bring about a kind of temporary insanity."

Diana felt close to tears. No doubt they were tears of relief because the earl had come to his senses, and no doubt relief *had* made her throw her arms about the earl and press her lips to his. That was logical. Reasonable. What was neither reasonable nor logical was that the memory of Lord Lion's kiss still evoked sweet tendrils of madness.

Sternly, Diana scotched such dangerous lunacy. She had come to Cumbria to make a life for herself and Archie. By a great stroke of fortune, she was now able to earn her keep as Blaize's librarian. She must never forget that this was her sole, her only function at Blaize Manor.

5

"Have you ever seen such colors, Diana?"

Beaming with satisfaction, Miss Flor snipped a bronze chrysanthemum and laid it tenderly in her garden basket.

Diana nodded absently. "Your mind is not on the flowers," Miss Flor commented. "You are so dedicated to your work."

This morning Diana had misplaced a costly Herodotus, upended a collection of poems, and dropped a translation of Antoine de Rivarol into a tub of paste.

Since that afternoon by the lake she had gone out of her way to avoid the earl, yet he was on her mind too often. Even though that devastating kiss had been explained away, she could still recall the feel of Blaize's lips and her own tumultuous feelings.

Bird-witted, Diana called herself, as she turned her attention to Miss Flor, who was explaining how she had grown her chrysanthemums from cuttings and seeds.

Miss Flor was in high spirits this morning. Dressed in an old day dress, a voluminous apron, and muddy boots, she had been working in her garden for hours. In spite of her untidy hair and the streak of mud on her nose, she looked happier than Diana had ever seen her.

"Do not think me goosish, but these flowers are like my children," she confided. "Look, Diana, here is a pretty bloom for your wonderful new library."

"It is hardly wonderful," Diana murmured. She was trying to remember where she might have put the Herodotus.

"Oh, but it is. Lionel is right in feeling that you and Archie have brought light into his house." Diana stared at her in disbelief as Miss Flor continued, "He did not say so in so many words, but that is what he thinks."

"Hoy, there—anyone home?"

As the booming masculine voice shattered the peace of the garden, Miss Flor went rigid. "It is he," she gasped.

A stout, elderly gentleman in a red coat and dark pantaloons was marching toward them. He had a large, square, florid face truncated by bristling gray mustaches and heavy eyebrows that sat low over his eyes. Scanty iron gray hair hugged his bullet-shaped head.

As the red-coated individual raised a quizzing-glass to one eye, Miss Flor exclaimed, "I cannot let him see me like *this*!" and then picked up her skirts and fled. Her eyeglasses flew one way, and the chrysanthemums she had been gathering bounced out of her basket and scattered all over the lawn.

Bewildered and somewhat frightened, Diana stood her ground as the mustachioed gentleman now turned to her. "The footman said that Blaize was hereabouts," he said.

"I have not seen the earl all morning," Diana replied.

"Egad! Most inconvenient. Dashed irritatin', in fact. Where is he?"

He stared through his glass at Diana, who was also beginning to feel irritated. "I have no idea," she replied shortly. "Perhaps you had better ask the servants."

She curtsied and was about to exit when the gentleman behind her said, "Don't you run off too, ma'am. Forgot my dashed manners for a moment. My name's Horatio Pratt—*Colonel* Pratt, late of His Majesty's service. Most obedient servant."

He had a deep, booming voice and Diana realized that this was the hunt-mad neighbor who considered himself to be the earl's adopted uncle. Curious, she scanned Colonel Pratt more carefully and saw that his brown eyes held a penitent look.

"Didn't mean to scare Miss Flor," the colonel said. "I keep forgettin' how timid she is. Always was a shy slip of a thing, even in the old days at Naunce."

He tugged at one end of his mustaches in a perplexed way. "Dashed awkward thing, but there it is, but *you* won't bolt from the looks of you. Look as though you have good bottom, Miss, er—?"

Though tempted to laugh, Diana thanked him, introduced herself, and explained her presence.

The colonel looked thoughtful. "Heard that his cousin cocked up his toes and left him a collection of books. Astonishin' thing, that—Blaize's no bluestockin', never was. Man's too dashed good a horseman for that. Not," he added hastily, "that a library ain't a fine thing. Meant no offense."

He broke off and peered nervously at her. Perceiving that the colonel's bark was far worse than his bite, Diana assured him that no offense was taken.

"Knows his horses, does Blaize," the colonel resumed. "Was away in London visitin' my sister—noisy, rackety, crowded place, London—and just got back. Came to look at the black stallion he wants to sell me."

"I've changed my mind about the stallion," said Blaize, who had just stepped into the garden. "It's not for sale at any price." He shook hands with the colonel in greeting and added, "I'm glad you're here. I'd like your opinion on Midnight."

The colonel chuckled. "Me give you advice on cattle?" Then he grew somber. "Pity you won't sell that black stallion, though. He'd have looked good on the field once he'd been tamed. Horse like that'd knock my dashed brother-in-law's eyes out."

Diana gathered that the colonel was talking about his annual hunt. "He's always showin' off his horseflesh," he added bitterly. "Pudgy Kerwinkle was always a rabbit-sucking toad. Don't know why my sister married him."

The earl pointed out that the colonel's brother-in-law was well thought of in the House, then the colonel snorted and vigorously entreated Blaize to take a damper.

"Pudgy's a here-and-thereian, always was, but he has connections. It's who you know, not what you are. Take your brothers, Blaize—they know how to get things out of people. You're a dashed better man than either of them, but Naunce don't see that—"

"I'm obliged for your good opinion," Blaize interrupted.

"But do you or don't you want to see the horse?" He was smiling, but Diana had the feeling that he was not pleased.

"Egad, that's what I came for."

After the colonel bowed to Diana and marched off toward the stables, Blaize turned to Diana and directed a long, searching look at her. He said nothing, but that look and the slight bow he gave her was enough to bring heat to her cheeks and dismay to her heart. His lordship, Diana knew, had not forgotten a second of their indiscretion at the cliffs.

And neither had she. Deeply disturbed, Diana picked up Miss Flor's glasses and flowers and went in search of her. Miss Flor was in the morning room and Diana noted that she had washed the mud from her face and changed into a pale green cambric morning dress that was at least a size too large for her.

"Where—where is the colonel?" she asked in a tremulous voice.

When Diana explained, the little lady sighed so deeply that the green ribbons in her cap quivered. "He must think me such a fool," she said. "I wish I had not run away like a pea-goose."

Diana noted the color in Miss Flor's usually pale cheeks and suddenly understood. The little lady had a tendre for Colonel Pratt.

"What made you run away, ma'am?" she asked, gently.

"I did not want the colonel to see me in muddy boots." Miss Flor said. She fingered the buttons of her dress as she added, "That is how I looked the first time I met him."

Miss Flor explained that she had been weeding the rose garden at Naunce the first time the colonel stopped by to see the duke.

"I was having trouble with a stubborn weed, and he pulled it out for me. He admired my roses and sampled my strawberries and said they were the sweetest he had eaten."

Miss Flor's eyes took on a nostalgic glow which faded abruptly as she added, "But of course he was merely being kind. When I saw him next at Lady Ormsford's crush, he did not even remember me."

"I am persuaded you are wrong," Diana protested, but the elderly lady just shook her head.

"I am not important enough," she said simply.

As the colonel had stated, who you were mattered less than who you knew. Feeling depressed, Diana returned to her library where she worked steadily through the morning. But thoughts of Miss Flor kept intruding.

"It doesn't seem fair," she murmured.

"Talking to yourself?"

The deep voice startled her and she turned to see the earl walk into the library. In answer to Diana's look of surprise he explained, "Guenevere suggested it was time I admired your handiwork."

She stood aside so that he could see for himself, and he looked about him at shelves neat with books. Most of the crates had been unpacked, catalogued, and arranged. "Incredible," the earl exclaimed.

"There is much more to be done." Diana kept her voice studiedly formal. "As you see, I have started compiling a list of all the books in the library."

He took the list from her and glanced idly at it before handing it back. The list represented hours of work, and Diana felt a twinge of irritation.

"When all the books have been arranged according to category and author," she said in a cooler voice, "you will see that you have an exceptionally fine collection of books."

"I'll take your word for it." The earl nodded at the transformed room as he added, "You've done well, Miss Gardiner."

"I'm glad you're satisfied, sir."

"I am. I hadn't thought there was anyone alive who could make order out of that shambles." There was a little pause, and then the earl added, "Thank you for coming to Blaize."

More unexpected than those words was the softening in Blaize's tone. Diana caught her breath. He sounded as he had done that afternoon by the cliff, when—

"And for bringing Archie with you," the earl finished.

Diana was disgusted with herself. For just a second her defenses had come tumbling down like the battlements of Jericho, and she had allowed herself to remember how it had felt to be held in the earl's strong arms. She had recalled every nuance of Blaize's kiss.

She turned her back on the earl and began to straighten a

row of books. "What did the colonel think of Midnight?" she asked.

"He wanted to ride him, but first Archie said he had to get Midnight's permission. You should have seen Pratt's face when he heard *that.*" Blaize grinned suddenly. "After his ride, he offered me a huge sum—which I refused. Archie would have never forgiven me if I'd sold that horse." He paused and then said, "In fact, Pratt was so impressed with your brother that he offered to hire him on the spot, but Archie declined. He said that both Midnight and I definitely needed his help."

"I am sorry if he was impertinent." Diana looked so concerned that Blaize felt an almost irresistible need to put his arms around her and comfort her.

"No, Archie was right. I do need—him." He had checked himself in time. He had almost said, "I need *you.*"

She was needed to finish the confounded library of course—there could be no other reason, Blaize assured himself. But her lips were so close to his, and the feelings that those soft lips evoked had nothing to do with stacks of desiccated tomes.

Desperately, he tried to get his wandering mind back on track. "Pratt looked so blue-deviled that I suggested a compromise. I told him he could have the pick of the colts Midnight eventually sires."

"That was kind," Diana exclaimed. "No doubt the colonel's brother-in-law would not laugh at one of Midnight's colts."

She broke off as she realized that the earl was watching her. His eyes held hers with such unsettling intensity that she had trouble catching her breath. The ground beneath Diana's feet suddenly seemed to rock, and her heart was hammering as though she had been running for miles. She knew that she should turn away from the earl's green gaze but could not do so.

He took a step toward her just as she swayed closer to him.

There was an apologetic cough behind them and Diana started violently. The earl took several steps backward and fetched up against one of the shelves.

"What *is* it, Molhouse?" he demanded angrily.

"That new curate from the town, that Mr. Petty, is 'ere

to see you, me lord. 'E says that hit's important 'e talks with you."

The earl frowned. "I've given the man's church enough money to gild his steeple. Does he think I'm a bottomless pit? I won't give him another penny."

"Very good, me lord. Shall I tell 'im so?"

The earl considered. "No. Send him up here. I'll tell him myself."

As Molhouse left, Blaize walked away from Diana to stare out of the high oriel windows. He was not sure whether he was grateful for his valet's inopportune entrance or whether he wanted to strangle the man. One moment longer, and he and his librarian would have been locked in a passionate embrace.

"Thunder and hell," he muttered.

"Er—my lord earl?"

Blaize turned to see the new curate standing inside the library, blinking and smiling like a self-important goldfish. He bowed first to the earl and then to Diana whilst offering them the blessings of the morning.

Blaize cut short the benedictions. "I suppose you're looking for money again," he began abruptly.

A beatific expression filled the curate's face. "I have come, my lord earl, to petition your generosity for the deserving poor."

The earl remained ominously silent.

"As the scripture says, 'God loveth a cheerful giver'—Second Corinthians, 9:7. As your lordship yourself must know. Those of us who have been blessed with position and birth must be generous in this world in order to be blissful in the next."

"No more money," the earl said.

Diana saw an obstinate look steal across the curate's face. Looking more fishlike than ever he pointed out, "I am here to do the Lord's work, sir. The money is needed for the poor widows and orphans in the area—"

"I take good care of my tenants' widows and orphans," the earl said firmly. "I've already given you money, Petty. Ten pounds five months ago, five three months ago, another ten last month for a new steeple for your church, and ten pounds two weeks ago to the day because you needed to mend the church bell."

"You are to be blessed for your philanthropy, my lord. 'Yea, cast thy bread upon the waters,' Ecclesiastes, 11:1. But the widows and orphans—of *other* areas need help. Suffice it to say that your name will be entered amongst the lists of the many generous persons who have contributed to this worthy cause."

The curate whipped out a sheet of paper and held it out to the earl. "If my lord will be so kind as to read this, he will see that there are many who see that it is more blessed to give than receive."

The earl's green eyes narrowed. One booted foot had begun to tap impatiently as he said in a firm voice, "I've made up my mind."

But Mr. Petty's vanity had been pricked by the earl's cavalier attitude toward his beloved list. He had worked hard to gather together a group of the noble and the great, and he felt sure that it must impress everyone—even the earl of Blaize.

He put the list away and produced another paper. "Pray, my lord," he said somewhat huffily, "if you will but look on this."

He nearly shoved the second paper into the earl's hands. Blaize glanced at it and then barked, "So?"

"But—but, my lord, surely you can see that the duchess of Naunce is one of our patrons. Surely you cannot help but be moved by my lady's endorsement of our charity. When you read her moving words, your heart must soften!"

"Thunder and hell—do you dare to tell me what to do in my own house?"

The earl's snarl fairly shivered with menace. The curate's eyes went wide. He tried to say something but could not get the words out.

"Get out or I will throw you out myself," the earl went on in that same menacing tone.

The curate did not move. He seemed rooted to the spot. "M-my lord," he babbled.

The earl took a step closer.

"P-please, your lordship!"

The terror in the curate's voice reminded Diana of a rabbit squealing in a trap. "My lord, Mr. Petty means no harm," she said in his defense. "I pray you, consider what you are about to do."

Seeing that he had an ally, the curate took heart. Stubborn to the end, he bleated, "If you would only r-read the list, my lord, you will understand why I—"

"Get *out*!"

This time, Lord Lion's roar reverberated down the hall. Dropping his precious list, the curate fled. "Damned idiot," the earl said with a growl.

Logic told her to hold her tongue, but Diana was too upset to be discreet. "The man truly meant no harm. He was persistent, truly but—"

"Stop," he said curtly. "This has nothing to do with you. That officious fool deserved to be taught a lesson."

"You more than taught him a lesson. You terrified him! You—you browbeat him."

"You've said enough."

Voice silky smooth, eyes flashing green fire—danger signals all—but she ignored them. "You said you hated people who bully those weaker than themselves. It would appear you don't take your own advice, my lord. That wretched man wouldn't have dared to stand up to you, and you knew it."

There was the sort of ominous silence that presages an electrical storm. She had gone too far, Diana knew, but there was no way to unsay those words or to apologize—if indeed she wanted to apologize for telling the truth.

"If you want to continue in my employ," he told her coldly, "learn to keep your place. I won't have intefering chits working for me."

Then he turned on his heel and walked out of the library. Diana stood where she was. There was a cold knot in her stomach and her cheeks felt hot with humiliation. *Interfering chit* the earl had called her—and perhaps that was what she had been.

Then, anger stiffened her spine. How dare he speak to her in that way? It was he who was wrong, not she. Her only fault was in forgetting that, like the footmen and Molhouse, she was little more than a servant in Lord Lion's eyes.

* * *

After the tempest of the morning, an almost unearthly quiet blanketed Blaize Manor. No underling dared to make a sound for fear of upsetting their lord. Miss Flor penned herself up in her room and Diana, too, repaired to her chamber, where she pondered her next step.

She knew that she could not hide for very long. Indignation was not a luxury open to her. If she could have done so, she would have left Blaize Manor, but there was nowhere else to go. Though she winced at the memory of what had happened that morning, she knew that she must eventually put her pride in her pocket, apologize most humbly to the earl, and return to work. If, indeed, Lord Lion did not dismiss her out of hand.

After a while the funereal silence grew too hard to bear, so Diana returned to the library. On her way, she encountered Molhouse in the corridor, and the valet bowed wordlessly. This was so different from his usual cheeriness that Diana felt even more cast down. She was now persuaded that the earl was going to dismiss her.

In the library, she fairly drowned herself in work. But she could not escape her thoughts. *How* could she have been so insane as to allow her temper to get the better of her? She, who had held her tongue during the terrible days at Radley Place, had forgotten herself. But at Radley Place she had known herself to be an outcast, unwanted and shunned, while here—

Here she had been almost happy. Impatiently, Diana slammed down a volume of Voltaire. "I wasn't hired to be happy," she muttered.

"What was that, Di?" Archie had popped his head around the door. "I've been exercising Midnight. He's such a champion goer, I don't wonder that Colonel Pratt wants him."

He came into the library bringing with him the cool freshness of the outdoors. His cheeks glowed with exercise, his eyes were sparkling, and he was tapping a riding quirt against his leg.

Diana looked hard at her brother. Gone was the frightened, nervous youth of a mere fortnight ago. "I don't remember seeing those riding clothes before," she exclaimed.

"Lord Lion gave them to me," Archie said. Then, noticing

the stern look from his sister at the use of the earl's nickname, added earnestly, "He doesn't mind, really. It slipped out once, and I apologized, but he said that since I liked animals so much, 'Lord Lion' was probably a compliment." He paused. "He's champion, isn't he, Di? And he's got such a light hand with the horses. You can't fool Lord Lion—he knows just which one is a windsucker and which one is a bang-up bit of blood and bone."

Since coming to Blaize, Archie's conversation had become peppered with Urse's Yorkshire expressions as well as slang picked up from the grooms.

"You are back early from your ride," Diana commented.

"The colonel asked me to ride Midnight down to Pratt House. He's a nice man, the colonel." Archie paused. "I thought I'd stop in to see how you were doing before I left."

As her brother whistled himself away, Diana resolved that she would apologize to the earl without delay. *Whatever he thinks of me, the earl seems fond of Archie. Perhaps he will accept my apology.*

She girded herself up for this grim task, but dinner did not produce the earl. Miss Flor presided over the meal that was served by nervous servants. Noting that the footmen started whenever there was a noise, Diana knew that everyone was dreading the angry lion's return.

So was she. She hardly touched her plate and, immediately after dinner, went to her room. No comfort awaited her there. In the ominous silence, the painted faces of Naunce's children seemed to mock her from the wall.

Restless, far from sleepy, Diana first attempted to read, then tried her hand at some mending. Nothing engaged her attention. Finally recognizing that only one thing would help, she picked up her shawl against the chill of the evening and returned to the library.

The house was settling down for the night, and only the ticking of the clock on the staircase landing accompanied Diana as she went downstairs to the first floor. At the library door, she hesitated, when she noticed a light burning inside.

She must have forgotten to blow out the candles, Diana thought. But when she opened the library door she saw the earl standing near the oriel windows.

His back was to her, but she could see from the condition of his mud-splashed boots and clothes that he had just returned. When had he come in, and what was he doing *here*?

From the tension in his broad shoulders and his combative stance, it was clear that the earl had returned in no friendly mood. In fact, he was probably recalling each insult she had leveled at him. Diana's first impulse was to tiptoe away before he saw her, but she dismissed this hen-hearted thought.

Taking in one long, prayerful breath, she stepped into the library, but her brave resolve went to dust as the earl half turned. Diana clenched her lower lip between her teeth as she saw that Blaize was holding Mr. Petty's wretched list.

She watched in horror as his frown became blacker. At any moment, he would roar for her and dismiss her—but as she thought this, the earl shook his head in a baffled way. "Thunder and hell," he muttered.

It was not the raging of an angry lion. The earl sounded perplexed and frustrated. His lordship's frown was more a frown of bewilderment than of irritation, Diana saw his lips moving. Moving as she had seen Archie's lips move when he was very young and she was teaching him how to read.

Realization burst upon her. No wonder the earl had no use for books and libraries. No wonder he had loathed school and had been no scholar even though his father had beaten him—

Diana's thoughts faded away as she saw that the earl had looked up and seen her. His green eyes had never been less friendly, but surprise had taken her fear away.

"It was not because you were lazy and rebellious," she whispered. "It was not that at all. How terrible for you, my lord—you *couldn't* do the schoolwork because you were unable to read."

She knew. Anger and frustration flared within him, and he snapped, "What in hell are you doing here?"

"I came to work," she said. "When I saw you, I decided to apologize—"

Her words trailed away and she prepared herself for an outburst that was sure to come. Instead, he turned his back and said, "Get out."

"Get out of Blaize Manor, do you mean?"

He said nothing.

"I am sorry for everything I said," Diana went on, gently. "I mean that all the more now that I—"

"Now that you *what*?" His anger had drained away into a bitter resignation. "You're a clever woman, Miss Gardiner," he said, still with his back to her. "You've succeeded in guessing what no one else knows—except for Molhouse."

"I didn't mean to." She watched him swing around to face her, and it took all her courage to stand firm. "It was just that now, when I saw the way you were looking at that dreadful list and moving your lips, I remembered what Papa told me about a friend he knew who had this same problem. Tell me, how did you manage at school?"

"Not very well. My masters as well as my parents thought that I was lazy or a rebel."

"So your father beat you."

He shrugged.

"But could not your mother protect you?"

"She tried, but she is not a very brave woman and Naunce was sure he could cure me by breaking my spirit with his cane."

His smile was dry, but his carefully casual voice concealed such anger and pain that it hurt her physically. With the hard, dry knot growing in her throat she managed to say, "Still, you passed your courses at school. How?"

"I have a good memory. I memorized the lectures and gave them back. My teachers thought that since I performed well in the oral part of my schooling, I was being worse than lazy when I didn't even attempt my written exams. Sometimes I bribed some bluestocking to write essays for me. I would pretend I'd hurt my hand and couldn't write. Of course, I paid him for his trouble."

He took a turn around the room and stopped in front of Diana. "Dracot's coming to school changed all that. I never offered him money—he would have been insulted if I'd suggested such a thing. He was my friend. Eventually he learned what was wrong with me."

How had the proud man before her felt when he confessed his weakness? "It must have been so hard to tell him," she murmured.

"I didn't have to. He guessed as you did." Blaize paused to explain, "Naunce had beaten it into my head that I was an imbecile who would never amount to anything. I had grown up believing that anyone guessing my—inability would shun me. But when Dracot found out, he wanted to help."

Dracot had read every lesson to his friend. He had painfully written down every assignment in Blaize's own words.

"But the examinations?"

"I broke my right hand," he said indifferently. But Diana winced and clasped her own hands tightly. "The headmaster allowed me to give oral answers, so it was easy." He smiled his dry smile again. "My father was astounded when he heard how well I had done. He said that he knew that I had been slacking all those years."

"No praise?" Diana exclaimed indignantly. "Not even when you had succeeded at such cost?"

"You don't know my father." Blaize's smile was bitter. "He wanted me to go into politics like my brother, but instead of going to Oxford, I bought my colors. Pratt helped me to do so."

He paused and added in a softer voice, "I wanted to do something for Dracot, but he wouldn't let me. In his own way he was just as proud. We swore we would keep in touch, but—"

He shrugged.

Diana guessed that in his heart of hearts the earl was not sorry to part company with the only man who knew his secret. "Life is like that," she agreed. "But you must not think you are the only person who cannot read his letters, my lord."

He turned back to the window. "Like your brother, you mean."

"Not really. Archie had no interest in learning his letters. You, I think, have a different problem. The 'p' and the 'q' look the same to you, for instance. Words reverse themselves or become hopelessly scrambled. When you try to write, letters often come out backward."

Rounding on her, Blaize regarded her in astonishment and suspicion. "How do you know this?"

"As I told you, Papa had a friend who also had trouble recognizing certain letters. 'Word blindness,' he used to call it." Diana added hastily, "It has nothing, *nothing* to do with intelligence, my lord. My father said that his friend was quite brilliant. He must have been, because he taught himself how to overcome his problem."

Now the green eyes were watching her intently. "Cured himself, you mean?"

She hated to dampen his hopes, but she knew she must be honest. "I do not think there is a cure as such, but Papa told me how his friend taught himself to read." She added eagerly, "He discovered that if he concentrated on one word at a time, he made progress. I could try and remember all that he told me—if you would let me help you."

"I don't need your help, Miss Gardiner," he said, curtly. "Or your interference. I told you merely because it is better to know the whole truth than to guess at half-truths."

"I don't mean to interfere," she said, earnestly. "It only seems that you are a brave man—"

He had started to leave the library. Now he turned to look at her quizzically.

"You are a decorated soldier and everybody says you fear nothing. You have borne this painful secret all this time, alone. So why not be courageous enough to try and see if you can beat your enemy?"

When he started to refuse she pleaded, "Please, my lord. Let me help."

She looked nothing like her cousin Dracot, but there was something in her eyes and voice that made him remember the friend of his student days. Blaize suddenly recalled that afternoon when both of them sat under the oak tree at the edge of the cricket field, and Dracot had looked up at him and said so simply, "Lion, can't you read?" and then— "How can I help?"

Blaize crossed the room and looked down into her upturned face. Black eyes, earnest and clear, met his.

"Let me help," Diana repeated. "You have been so kind to Archie. *Please* let me repay that kindness. No one need know about the lessons. And you have already trusted me with the truth. You could tell Miss Flor that you have asked me to put together a—a genealogical chart of your family."

What would one or two lessons matter? Blaize asked himself. But it wasn't the lessons, really. As Diana Gardiner had said, it was a matter of trust. Either he trusted her or he did not.

His eyes were full of shadows and an odd expression that she thought she understood. The earl had suffered so much because of his affliction; he had been called lazy and stupid. To admit that he needed her help was to expose himself to further pain.

"I will not betray you," Diana vowed. "I promise that I will keep your secret."

He remembered Dracot's words: *This is between us—our secret.* But this was not Dracot who looked up at him. Blaize hesitated. It was hard to break the habit of a lifetime.

Then he remembered that day when Diana had stood underneath the cliff to try and break her brother's fall. She had not feared for herself, only for Archie.

She had courage and resolve and her lips were very close, close and soft and curved in an eagerness to help. Blaize felt as though the wall he had built around himself, the impenetrable wall of secrets and shame and subterfuge had suddenly developed a chink.

He had to clear his throat before he could say, "We can try."

6

"'Ave a good ride, me lord," Molhouse said.

He cocked an approving gray eye in the direction of Miss Gardiner, who was talking to her younger brother on the steps. It was gratifying to know that he hadn't been wrong about that young lady. Since she'd arrived at Blaize, she had not only accomplished miracles with the library but with his lordship as well.

Never before had the earl been in such high tweak. Of late he had lost that brittle tension that had sent his underlings scurrying for cover, and when that fool Witton had dropped the mutton whilst serving it for dinner last night, his lordship had merely commented that mutton had never been his favorite dish.

Molhouse watched the earl helping Miss Gardiner into the saddle and began to hum under his breath. No, the lion had not roared for some time, and he, Molhouse, was the one to thank for it.

"Have a *lovely* ride, my dears," Miss Flor called shyly from the step above Molhouse. She was congratulating herself on doing something right for once. After all, it was she who had suggested that Diana exercise Firefly, and this had started a chain of events which had led to Diana and Lionel's riding out together every single day.

Dear Diana was looking so much happier these days. She was doing fine work in her library, and now Lionel was actually helping her to put together a full genealogy of his family. As for Archie, he had put on weight and seemed quite content. Miss Flor, who understood only too well what it was like to be a poor relation, felt her own heart swell with pride at the thought of her young friends' triumph.

But Archie, while he waved his cap after his sister and Lord Lion, was actually supressing a twinge of hurt that they had not asked him to ride with them. For full ten days now they had gone junketing off together in the afternoon to write some tiresome genealogy, the use of which escaped him utterly. It was true that he'd wanted Di and Lord Lion to mend their fences, but he couldn't help feeling a little left out.

As Blaize and Diana trotted down the path toward the lake, Blaize remarked, "Your brother's not happy."

"His nose is out of joint," Diana agreed. "He wanted to come with us today, and I had to put him off. Naturally, I could not tell him the real reason why you and I needed to be alone."

"No doubt they all think we desire to be together." Blaize gave her a sidelong glance. "The thought has its merits."

He saw her color mount at his provocative remark, but she made no reply. A gentle wind was playing with the rather bedraggled feather that ornamented her bonnet, and sunshine was turning her dark hair to bronze.

To distract him, Diana gestured to the book concealed in the large satchel attached to her saddlebag. "I have brought a new book," she said. "I am persuaded you will enjoy it."

Blaize did not answer. He had started these sessions with many misgivings, and memories of his past humiliations had kept him tense and unreceptive during the first few sessions. But Diana had been so patient, so encouraging, so genuinely delighted when he made any kind of progress, that he had begun to relax and even to look forward to their meetings.

"Are we not going down to the lake today?" Diana asked.

Blaize saw that her dark eyes were eager and, with an unaccountable lift of heart, realized that she was looking forward to the day as much as he was.

"I'm taking you up to the top of Peavey Hill," he said. "You'll like the view."

His smile was warm and relaxed. This was not the Lord Lion she had met, Diana thought, all tense and ready for attack. "You have so many lovely views on your estate," she said aloud. "Of course I will like it."

In companionable silence they began to climb a gentle incline. The sides of the hill were thick with ash and oak, and as they rode higher the trees formed a lacy canopy through which sunshine filtered like gold dust. Birdsong mingled with the rustle of branches, and the air was fragrant.

"How wonderful to have a hill of your own," Diana exclaimed. "Dracot and I had to make do with the little knoll at the end of Mr. Sparvin's sheep farm. We used to pretend it was the top of the world."

Blaize started to ask a question, then saw how Diana's face reflected the dappled sunshine and forgot what he'd wanted to say.

"Do you miss being in Somerset?" he asked finally.

Before she could answer, the woods thinned, and the slope leveled into a summit strewn with moss-covered rocks and autumn wildflowers. From this vantage point they could see all around them—the rolling green countryside to the south and west, Kernston-on-Stream to the east, and to the north the sweep of Lake Iris, with the mountains at its back.

Blaize pointed these giants out as if they were old friends. "There's Great Gable, and Scafell, and Scafell Pike. Locals call them the Roots of Heaven."

"I can see why. This *is* the top of the world." Diana tried to focus her attention on the magnificent view and failed. Doubtless because he was enthralled by the landscape below them, his lordship had ridden up close to her. He was so near that their knees were almost touching.

His proximity brought disconcerting memories. Diana heroically resisted the urge to look at the earl and kept her eyes fastened on the Roots of Heaven instead. "Have you ever climbed those mountains?" she asked.

"The last time I went up Scafell Pike, it was in the dead of winter." Blaize heard his own voice describing that climb, but it was hard to concentrate. She was so close to him that if he reached out, he could touch the warm peach-bloom of Diana's cheek.

Abruptly, Blaize swung down from Sultan and announced, "Here's as good a place as any to face my enemy."

To keep her mind from dwelling on the strong hands that helped her down, Diana looked about her at the hill. She saw that between the Michaelmas daisies and the last of the wild roses lay a tangle of blackberry bushes.

He had followed her glance. "The sun makes the berries sweet," he began, then checked himself. He had almost said, "We can come here again next summer."

Would Diana be at Blaize next summer? By then she would have finished her work at the library. She would have collected the handsome salary he had promised her and doubtless gone on her way. That logical thought brought sudden and inexplicable pain, and the earl did not know what to do about it.

In an attempt to rid himself of that pain, Lionel focused on the task at hand. "What is today's lesson?" he asked.

Diana seated herself on a mossy stone and brought a book out of her bag. "This book is about horses."

In silence Blaize deposited his long length on the grass. But as he took the book from her, he felt the old, familiar panic stir within him. He put the book down on the ground and said, "It's too nice a day to bleed from the brains."

Diana held back a sigh. These reading lessons had not been easy. Though he seemed more relaxed these days, he had not made much real progress, and every failure had driven him to frustration, even to the brink of despair.

But Diana was determined not to let him despair. With a renewed sense of hope she opened the book and handed him a paper marker. "Pray begin, my lord."

Blaize looked down at the book and saw a meaningless jumble of letters and words. Into his mind came a harsh voice which snarled, *You are an idiot, a lazy dolt who can't even make out his letters. You're no son of mine.*

"Look," he said, "there is an eagle. He looks as if he's admiring the view."

Indeed, a majestic bird was soaring through the blue sky and then across Iris Lake, which sparkled a lazy amethyst. "This is not a very good classroom," Diana protested. "It is much too beautiful for anyone to *want* to do any work. But that is what we have come for."

She picked up the marker again, but once again Blaize forestalled her. "Stop a moment. The eagle's getting ready to hunt."

Mentally, Diana reviewed the ways in which she had attempted to deal with the earl's problem. She had gone over the alphabet with him and realized that though he reversed some of them, he knew his letters. He had a phenomenal memory and could identify phonetic sounds. Theoretically, he had all the tools with which to read, but the "word blindness" held him back.

Diana's father had told her that when his friend looked at a page of writing, his eyes would skitter from one line to another, picking up a word here or there at random. Recalling how he had trained himself to make sense of this confusion, Diana had taken a sheet of blank paper and cut a narrow window into it. When this "marker" was fitted over a page, the earl could see only a few words at a time and was thus forced to concentrate on them alone.

It was laborious, tedious work, and Diana worried that the earl was losing interest. Between lessons, she racked her brains thinking of different ways to help him. She had no idea how much she could accomplish, but when she looked at the majestic golden eagle, she knew that somehow she must find a way to make the earl soar.

"There's a butterfly sitting on your shoulder, Miss Gardiner."

He was leaning on one arm and looking up at her with a smile. Though she knew that these were merely delaying tactics, she could not help returning that smile.

"Papa used to say that butterflies were flowers with wings," she commented.

"Dracot didn't tell me much about your family, but he said that his own father was fond of gaming. Is that true?" When Diana nodded he continued, "He said that his father had been knocked into the horse stalls more than once before trying his hand on the exchange. He didn't say whether or not he fared better there."

"Uncle Thomas was—adventuresome in his speculations."

Which meant that the man had made a mull of his investments, too, Blaize realized. "What about your father?" he asked.

Since he had told her a great deal about his own family, turnabout was fair play.

Diana said, "Papa lived in a world of books and gardens. He knew very little else. Uncle Thomas was much more worldly. Even so, they were close friends. They would have done anything for each other."

No doubt the bluestocking had franked his "worldly" brother more than once. Blaize's cynical thought was so well reflected in his expression that Diana felt the need to protest, "It was not that way at all."

Blaize raised his eyebrows in doubt.

"We were *close*," Diana repeated. "Our families lived on adjoining estates, and we were always coming and going between the houses. I called Dracot's home 'the other house.' Dracot and I grew up more friendly than most brothers and sisters." She chuckled suddenly. "And there was also Signor Alfonso."

At his quizzical look, she explained, "Mama wanted me to learn the social graces, so she hired a dancing master. He was a small, droll little man who always looked as if he were ready to cry. Dracot and I would practice dancing together—and I suppose we were really abominable. Signor Alfonso called us the dancing bears."

What would it be to hold Diana Gardiner in his arms again? To dance with her? The desire that shivered through Blaize was almost painful. Intently he watched Diana. With her black eyes full of memory, her mouth soft, and the golden sun turning her eyes to warm black velvet, the woman was beautiful.

Blaize suddenly realized that he envied poor, long-dead Dracot. "What happened to this halcyon existence?" he asked.

"It is a sad and familiar tale, I am afraid. Both Papa and Uncle Thomas had comfortable livings until Uncle Thomas—but Dracot told you that he was most unlucky. In a desperate move to recoup all he had lost, Uncle Thomas had decided to become a soldier. He thought that if he fought Napoleon, he would cover himself with glory and the good days would return. Dracot could not let his father go alone," Diana went on sadly, "so Papa bought their colors. When they did not come back, Papa became sick with grief and blamed himself. He caught the grippe that winter after Waterloo and died. Mama followed soon after."

"And your father's living died with him, of course." Blaize's voice had an edge to it. "He should have thought less about others and more about caring for his own family."

There was a small silence. Then Diana said in a subdued voice, "That is enough ancient history." She took her marker and laid it over the page again. "Please, my lord, begin."

Reluctantly, Blaize picked up the book and looked down at the words before him. Once again, the letters converged into a tangled mass. Once again, Naunce's voice clamored in his mind. He thought of his father's contempt and fury, his mother's tears.

"It is not easy, I know." Diana could not tell what battles raged within the earl, but she was familiar with the set line of his mouth. "Please," she said, gently, "try to forget what has happened before. *Now* is the only thing that counts." When he still did not move she added, "There is never any shame in trying, my lord."

"I would rather face Napoleon's cannons," Blaize said, honestly.

"I understand. I am sure that is the way I would feel too. You are very brave to try."

With an effort Blaize took the marker in his hand. Forcing himself to concentrate on one word at a time, he read, "'Ha—has-ros-' what is this damnable word?"

He broke off. "It's no use. I can't do it."

Diana caught his hand as he put down the book. "You must try again." His eyes met hers, troubled, angry. "We are facing the cannons together, you and I," she told him. "You are not alone, my lord, and I believe in you."

"Your belief may be ill placed." Nevertheless, he lifted the book again, took a deep breath and said, "'Ha—' no, 'Horses.' "

"Go on," Diana breathed.

" 'Horse have de—no, have *been* on the earth since—aunt—no, since *ancient* times.' " He heard the inrush of her breath and asked sharply, "Am I wrong again?"

"No, you are correct—quite correct," Diana cried. "Pray continue—what comes next?"

" 'The aunt'—no, that's *ancestor*, isn't it?—'of the horse was a small pard—no, that is *quadruped*,' " the earl read. He looked up, astonished green eyes meeting hers. "Is that right?"

"Wonderfully, marvelously correct!" Hardly able to contain her excitement, Diana clasped both hands over the earl's arm and held on tightly. "Do not stop now—oh, please, do not stop! What comes next?"

She held her breath as Blaize read the next sentence. He read haltingly, slowly, with many mistakes, but what he read made sense.

He put the book down and they looked at each other in dumb wonder. "You have done it," she whispered. "You have conquered the 'word blindness.' "

Tears of joy filled her eyes and blurred his image as she exulted, "You have beaten your enemy, my lord. I am so happy, so—oh, I knew you could."

Blaize shook his head. "I didn't share your confidence," he said in a shaken voice. "I was sure I'd fail."

"What matters is that you *tried*." Passionately, Diana added, "If someone had given you the confidence to do so, you would have tried years ago."

She brushed the back of her hand across her eyes. Blaize felt even more shaken. Grief or happiness, her tears were all for him.

"Diana," he said.

His voice was husky, and her name sounded so sweet on his lips that Diana caught her breath. That was all she had time for before he drew her into his arms and kissed her.

The sun-dappled hillside, the lake below, the world itself shivered into nothingness as Blaize's arms enfolded her. Diana felt as if she, like the golden eagle, were soaring in the sky, winging into the sun.

In Lord Lion's arms, there was no sorrow, no loss, no loneliness. His lips were familiar now, and her own mouth welcomed back their sweet, cool texture. She clung to him as if he were the only solid thing in her universe.

Blaize felt a welter of emotions as he held Diana Gardiner. He felt triumph, and joy, passion mixed with a sense of warmth and homecoming. But as he held the warm, lithe body in his arms, the cold wind of reason intervened.

She had just told him about her closeness and love for Dracot. Yet now, when she had done him an unbelievable favor and had given him an incredible gift, he was treating her like some lightskirt.

With an effort that was almost physically painful, Blaize loosened his arms around Diana. When she remained nestled against him, he took her gently by the shoulders and put her away from him.

"I can't thank you enough," he said, huskily.

Diana's heart suddenly stopped soaring. The glorious dazzle in her mind began to drift away as she realized that Blaize was no longer holding her in his arms. He was *thanking* her. For a moment she could only blink up at him, and then comprehension came.

But of course he was grateful to her. She had helped him to conquer the "word blindness" and elation at their mutual victory had made him embrace her. That was the explanation, the *only* explanation.

She withdrew still farther and tried to compose herself, but she still felt light-headed. Her heart was pounding, and it seemed as if her bones had gone soft. When she tried to restore her hat, her hands shook.

Blaize saw them shake and wondered if he had insulted her beyond all hope. "You've just given me something no one could," he said. "You can command me in anything, Miss Gardiner. I respect you. I—I honor you."

Honor. Respect. The words plunged down to lie like cold stones in Diana's heart, but she forced a smile. "I am so glad for you. We—we went a little mad, I think. It is understandable."

Blaize nodded. "Exactly so."

He himself knew that this was not the whole story. Even now, remorseful as he was, he could not help wanting to gather Diana to him and kiss her again.

Madness, Blaize thought.

He got to his feet and declared, "That's enough for today. It's time to return to the house."

Now that Blaize had learned how to breach his enemy's fortress, he mounted a relentless campaign. He worked so hard and practiced so arduously that Diana was astounded by her student's progress.

One morning while they were all in the breakfast room, Molhouse brought in a letter on a silver tray and presented it to the earl. "From Colonel Pratt, sir," he said.

As Blaize slit the envelope, Diana saw Molhouse position himself so that he could discreetly interpret the letter for his employer. But after several moment's concentration, the earl exclaimed, "Confound the man. He's invited us to a dinner party."

"Sir Ogden and Lady Kerwinkle must have arrived from London for the annual hunt," Miss Flor began, but she got no further.

"Oh, gorblimey!" Molhouse gasped. "But, me lord, 'ow could you 'ave possibly—"

He encountered his employer's glacial eye and made a superhuman effort to swallow the rest of his sentence. "Hexcuse me, me lord," he choked. "I beg you won't pay hattention. I was thinking of somethink else. Hit won't 'appen again, sir."

"It had better not. If I didn't know better, I'd think you were in your cups." The earl turned his attention back to the sheet of paper in his hand. "You're right, Guenevere. Pratt's sister and husband and some of their friends have arrived at Pratt House. The plaguey dinner will be held on Thursday, it says, but I'll cry off. Kerwinkle's the biggest bore in England."

Molhouse threw up his hands as if to give silent thanks to the Almighty, then recalled himself and pretended to be swatting at a nonexistent fly.

Meanwhile Archie commented innocently, "But Miss Flor will be disappointed. She wants to go to the colonel's party."

Miss Flor, who had been nibbling on her toast, promptly choked and went into a paroxysm of coughing through which she wheezed that Archie was mistaken.

"Oh," Archie said, and began to eat his boiled egg.

"In that case, I'll send my regrets." With an air of relief, Blaize directed Molhouse to have Sultan and Midnight saddled and brought around.

The valet pulled himself together sufficiently to leave the room with some semblance of dignity, but immediately thereafter there was a scuffling sound in the hallway that sounded as if someone were dancing a jig.

"Then we are not going to the party," Miss Flor murmured.

Blaize looked bewildered. "I thought you loathed parties, Guenevere. The last time we went to Pratt House, you told me that nothing would induce you to spend another evening with Kerwinkle and his rackety crowd."

"Oh, I was not thinking of myself." In a voice raspy from so much coughing Miss Flor explained, "I merely ask because it might be of interest to dear Diana. A—a distraction, as it were. It must be dull for a young lady here in Cumbria." She broke off, shifted in her chair, and clasped her hands tightly in her lap.

"*Would* you like to go, Miss Gardiner?" the earl asked.

Seeing the almost painful blush that stained Miss Flor's cheeks, Diana said, "I would gladly go to keep Miss Flor company."

"Oh, but —oh, but really, I could not venture to—there will be so many people at the party," the little lady faltered.

She looked so distressed that Archie came to her rescue. "Don't worry, I'll be there, too, ma'am," he comforted. "We'll be all right and tight if we have each other."

If we have each other.

Diana looked up and saw that the earl was watching her. She dropped her eyes hastily but not before she had seen something flicker in those green depths.

"In that case we'll all go. I suppose I can endure one evening with Kerwinkle for Pratt's sake." With the air of one who has made a supreme sacrifice, Blaize excused himself from the breakfast table and left the room. Archie followed him.

Miss Flor clasped her hands in her lap. "I wish I had not spoken," she murmured. "I am persuaded that I will disgrace Lionel amongst Lady Kerwinkle's clever London friends."

"I am sure you are wrong," Diana said gently.

"Oh, Diana, you do not know what a ninny I am. Last year when we were invited to Pratt House, I did not speak to a soul the entire evening."

"You mean that those people ignored you?" Diana asked, indignantly.

"Lady Kerwinkle tried to be kind, but she is a strong personality, Diana, and I could think of nothing to say. And later, I heard Lady St. Aubrey remark to Sir Rupert Grue that I was just a dowdy old frump without two words to rub together."

She began to crumble her toast on her plate. Watching her, Diana thought of the ugly dresses that Miss Flor always wore. "Supposing you were to go to the colonel's party," she prodded gently, "only *supposing*—what would you wear, ma'am?"

With many protestations and palpitations, Miss Flor conducted Diana to her chamber. Here, she displayed an ugly polonaise with tobine stripes, a plain round gown fashioned from a bilious yellow French cambric, and a dress of deep blue crepe with a long train guaranteed to trip its owner up at every step.

"*Where* did you find these, ma'am?" Diana had to ask.

"Lionel has my garments sent from London," Miss Flor explained. "The sister of his man of business resides there and kindly selects suitable items for me."

The lady obviously had execrable taste. Thoughtfully, Diana held up the blue crepe dress. Then, to Miss Flor's astonishment, she removed that lady's spectacles. "That is much better," she exclaimed. "Now, the color of the dress brings out your eyes."

"But, Diana, I can hardly see without my spectacles!"

"What is important is that *you* be seen." Diana smiled down into Miss Flor's astounded face. "May I take this dress apart and show you what I mean?" When Miss Flor protested that she could not make additional work for her friend, Diana added bracingly, "Remember what you said to me on that first night at Blaize. We 'mice' must help each other."

With the help of one of the housemaids, who was gifted with the needle, Diana made over the blue dress. Miss Flor's protests dwindled into admiration when she saw the speed and skill with which this garment was taken apart, pressed, and cut to a modish new pattern.

"It is remarkable. Truly astonishing," she exclaimed. "I would not have believed it possible. Oh, but the *neck*, are you sure that such boldness is the fashion?"

Diana had raised the neckline, looped a fringed trim to give an illusion of bust, and caught up the hemline with smart velvet ribbons. She had found some silver shoes languishing at the bottom of Miss Flor's old trunk and had them cleaned and polished.

But even Diana owned herself surprised when Miss Flor faced the mirror on the night of the colonel's dinner party. Her small friend looked twenty years younger. Her abigail had arranged her silver hair into curls swept up on her head, and her blue, sparkling eyes, divested this evening of the ever-present spectacles, sparkled like sapphires.

"You will be the reigning beauty there," Diana declared. "No one else can touch you."

Miss Flor peered at her reflection in the glass. "That is a great whisker. But, my dear, I confess that you have worked a *miracle*. I wish I could thank you somehow."

"You already have." Smiling, Diana touched a cluster of bronze chrysanthemums which she wore in her hair.

Miss Flor sighed. She had carefully selected her choicest blossoms, and she was pleased to note that the flowers were the exact shade of Diana's dress. But her young friend's amber gown was not in its first blush, and Miss Flor knew from sad experience that its one band of lace concealed a tear or a burn.

"How I wish that Arabella had left one of her lovely gowns behind," she sighed. "She had hoped there would be a party when she and their graces last visited Cumbria, but instead Lionel and his father had one of their infamous brangles."

Diana, who had been rearranging a flounce in Miss Flor's dress looked up at this. "Why did they quarrel?"

"I don't remember, but it was probably something inconsequential. It usually is. The duke was sarcastic and Lionel lost his temper." Miss Flor added unhappily, "That is always the way it happens."

Would history repeat itself when next the duke came to call? Diana set the thought firmly aside. It was no concern of hers.

She had been hired to organize the earl's library. She had discovered his secret and helped him deal with it. That was the sum total of her involvement with the lord of Blaize. That was *all* there was and, given the disparity of their stations in life, that was all there could ever be.

I respect you. I honor you . . .

Resolutely, Diana pushed from her mind the remembered sweetness of the earl's lips. Determinedly, she rejected the memory of his arms about her. "Are you ready to go down, ma'am?" she asked.

Miss Flor slipped her tremulous arm through Diana's and walked with her onto the staircase landing. "I am all aquake," she confessed. "Suppose Lionel does not like this dress? Supposing Lady St. Aubrey and Sir Rupert Grue laugh at me again?"

"They would not dare." Diana would have added more had she not looked down just then and seen the earl waiting at the foot of the stairs.

Tonight Blaize was dressed in unexceptional gray. There was nothing remarkable about his well-cut gray cloth evening coat, or the matching breeches which fit his muscular thighs to perfection, or his waistcoat with diamond studs. Even his neckcloth was simply arranged. Yet the man had presence. Simply by standing there with the candlelight glinting against his tawny hair, Lord Lion was able to wipe out every other thought in Diana's mind.

"Miss Flor, what have you done to your hair?" Diana had not heard her brother come up behind them. "You really look champion."

The earl looked up at the sound of Archie's voice and stared openly at Miss Flor as she descended the stairs. "'Champion' indeed. Cousin Guenevere, you're a diamond of the finest water."

The earl kissed his blushing cousin's hand. Then, as she and Archie walked past him toward the door, he turned to Diana. "How did you pull off this miracle?"

"No miracle," Diana smiled. "Miss Flor is really very pretty. She only lacked the right clothes."

"The effect is wonderful."

But as he looked at Diana rather than his cousin she wished, suddenly and painfully, that she was wearing something other than a well-worn dress and a few flowers in her hair. Then, in the next thought, she rebuked herself. She was, after all, only going to Pratt House to give Miss Flor moral support.

She was hard-pressed to keep her small friend's spirits up during the short journey to the colonel's house. Miss Flor's stock of courage wilted with the miles, and she fairly blanched as the carriage drove into the large courtyard.

"Just *look* at all those carriages!" Archie exclaimed. "The colonel must've invited everybody he knows to his party."

The courtyard seemed full of carriages, buggies, curricles, traps, and other conveyances. Miss Flor clasped both hands to her fringed bosom and murmured that there could not be so many people in all of Cumbria.

With a supreme effort, Miss Flor tottered down from the carriage and, leaning on Blaize's arm, walked toward Pratt House. This was an interesting structure since, apparently, it had not been built in any given style. The general shape was Jacobean, but it also had a roof with gable ends, small pinnacled turrets at four corners, and parapeted bay windows. On each side of the door stood a ferocious stone lion.

Archie eyed them askance. "I'm glad Claude couldn't come to the party," he whispered to Diana as they walked arm in arm up the stairs. "He wouldn't have liked the look of those lions."

Inside, an orchestra was playing on the staircase landing and sounds of dancing and laughter emanated from the first floor. The colonel, dressed in a coat of military cut, stood in the hall and greeted his guests. "Glad to see you, Blaize," he boomed. "And young Archie, too. Yes. Miss Gardiner, your most obedient. Ma'am—oh, egad! It can't be—"

"Don't you recognize my cousin, Pratt?" Blaize asked as the colonel stopped in midsentence.

Colonel Pratt goggled at Miss Flor, who blushed to the roots of her hair. "No," he said, faintly. "You can't mean that this lady is your cousin? Miss Flor?"

"Good evening, Colonel Pratt," Miss Flor murmured. She looked ready to take flight, but Blaize held her arm, preventing escape.

"Who'd have thought it?" the colonel mumbled. "Yes. Miss Flor, your most obedient—"

"There you are then, Blaize."

A tall, spare gentleman with very little hair and what seemed to be a permanently disgruntled expression, was introduced as Sir Ogden. He had come up beside his brother-in-law, Colonel Pratt, bowed perfunctorily over Miss Flor's hand, dismissed Diana with spartan courtesy, and then turned to the earl.

"You'll be riding Sultan for the hunt, of course. He's a goer, Sultan, though he don't compare to my new chestnut gelding. Mean to show what Lancer can do, by Jove. He'll dance rings around Horatio's puffer."

Colonel Pratt growled that they would see about *that*. He linked an arm through the earl's and, looking resigned, Blaize allowed himself to be led away. Sir Ogden and Archie followed.

"Good evenin', good evenin'!"

Diana looked up to see a large blond lady in an emerald green gown bearing down upon them. "There you are, Miss Flor," she called. "Lookin' in plump currant, I see."

Faintly, Miss Flor pronounced herself delighted to see Lady Kerwinkle and introduced Diana, who found her hand taken and gripped most heartily.

"Horatio and Kerwinkle are as bad as schoolboys," she declaimed. "Hunt mad, the both of them, and determined that each will outdo the other. Ha! M'brother never forgave Kerwinkle for showing him up last year when we rode to hounds. Called him a laggard, then, and Horatio's goose was pissed!"

Diana commented that she had heard that Lady Kerwinkle also rode to hounds.

"Fact! Better to be on a horse takin' a stitcher of a fence than sittin' on one's rump doin' deuced embroidery."

Linking arms with both ladies, Lady Kerwinkle drew them into a large room where a number of ladies and gentlemen were either conversing, dancing, or helping themselves to the viands carried about by servants. "Tell that to m'friend Marion all the time—but she don't ride or hunt. Ha! All she does is dance."

She nodded to an auburn-haired lady in a dress of garnet taffeta who was leading a beefy gentleman onto the floor.

"Colonel Pratt," Miss Flor exclaimed faintly.

"Marion ain't a bad-looking gel," Lady Kerwinkle said, tolerantly. "Widow, don't ye know, but then St. Aubrey was old enough to be her father. High-spirited. Likes to kick over the traces when she can. Thought it would be dull for her out here, but Horatio seems to have taken a fancy to her. Look at him prance about."

The colonel was dancing with all his might. When the candlelight fell full on him, Diana could see that he was perspiring.

Lady Kerwinkle's eyes glinted. "As I told Kerwinkle, maybe Horatio's ready for the parson's mousetrap after all these years."

When she saw a latecomer walking in to the party, she excused herself and trundled off.

"I wish I had not come," Miss Flor murmured. She peered at the dancers and then turned her head away.

Diana did not know what to say. She looked about the room for Archie and Blaize, but they were nowhere to be seen.

Another loud hoot of laughter signaled that Lady Kerwinkle had returned. With her was a pale gentleman of indeterminate age. His padded coat of bottle green superfine, elaborately tied neckcloth, and yellow pantaloons proclaimed him a tulip of the ton. He compensated for his lack of inches by wearing shoes with impossibly high heels.

"Thought I'd make Sir Rupert Grue known to you," Lady Kerwinkle boomed. "Miss Gardiner, Sir Rupert. He's Marion's friend. Sir Rupert, you already know Miss Flor."

Sir Rupert, who had been eyeing Diana through his quizzing-glass, transferred his attention to Miss Flor. He stared for several moments before bowing so deeply that he creaked.

"Cherished madam," he said in an affected voice. "Enraptured to cast my eyes upon you once more. Flower of beauty in the wilds of Cumbria, give you my word. You are radiant, ma'am. Radiant."

As the gentleman seized her hand and bowed over it, Miss Flor stammered that she could not stay to talk. "Diana and I must—we are to meet—er, meet my cousin," she said in an attempt to escape this fop.

"But I cannot allow you to escape. Pray vouchsafe me the honor of this next dance. It is, I believe, a country dance. Most invigorating."

Miss Flor faltered that she could not dance. "Very well. May I sit with you and converse for a little moment?"

Sir Rupert Grue waved a hand toward two chairs set close together and attempted to lead Miss Flor toward them. The little lady sent Diana a look of such profound distress that she felt honor bound to do *something*.

She suggested, "Perhaps, sir, you will teach *me* the steps? I have never danced a country dance before, but I am sure I could with such an excellent teacher."

Sir Rupert Grue blinked twice. "Er—of course, ma'am?" he said in an astonished voice, before helplessly leading Diana to the floor.

Diana felt as if she were a sacrificial lamb being taken to slaughter. She tried to remember how a country dance was danced. Perhaps if she cleared her mind and let her feet move by themselves—

"Ouch," snuffled Sir Rupert. "Oh, I say. Er—not that way, ma'am. Supposed to use the left foot. *Left* foot, ma'am."

"I beg your pardon." Diana winced as she trod on her partner's foot again. He looked pained as they parted and went down the line.

"Don't look down at your feet. Look up at me."

It was not Sir Rupert's voice. Diana looked up and saw Blaize smiling down at her.

"Just keep going, that's the girl," he encouraged.

Diana looked around and saw Sir Rupert Grue limping away from the dancers. He wore a look of almost pathetic relief.

Diana heard Blaize swear under his breath when she stepped on his foot again. "I told you I could not dance," she exclaimed. "Why did you take his place?"

"What possessed *you* to stand up with that rackety little pigeon fancier?"

Blaize whirled Diana around until she felt giddy. "I did it to save your cousin," she sighed. "That odious man pretended to be smitten by her and would not leave her alone."

"Grue's a gazetted fortune hunter on the make," the earl commented. He swung Diana around and remarked, "But

Guenevere certainly looks pretty tonight. Pratt couldn't keep his eyes off her."

When the county dance ended Diana felt a strange sense of regret as the earl withdrew his arm and led her from the floor.

"Aren't we rejoining Miss Flor?" she wondered.

"She is talking with Archie and Lady Kerwinke."

Blaize smiled at a guest, bowed to another, and led Diana firmly toward tall French windows where a servant was passing about drinks and eatables. "I lack the energy to listen to her. Besides, both of us need a drink."

Diana took the glass the earl handed her and sipped. It was more fiery than wine, but it felt good traveling down her throat. "I warned you that I could not dance," she said.

"I thought you were exaggerating."

They looked at each other and laughed. How easy it was, Diana thought, to feel happy at such a moment. The music began again, not as spirited as before but with a slower, lilting cadence.

"A waltz," she murmured. "Of all dances, I like it best."

"Then, perhaps you'll do me the honor?" the earl asked.

"I meant I liked to *watch* it. Beware, my lord. I dance the waltz worse than I do the country dance," Diana warned. "Dracot said I was abominable at it."

"I'm not Dracot," the earl reminded her as he whisked her through the French windows.

"What are you about?" Diana protested as the earl put his arm around her waist and took possession of her hand. "Really, my lord, this is not at all the thing. We should—"

"I'm about to give you a dancing lesson," he interrupted. "Pay attention! If you could teach *me* to read, I can certainly teach *you* to dance."

"Impossible," Diana exclaimed. She trod on the earl's foot and added, "Now, do you believe me?"

"Nothing is impossible," the earl said with a determined smile. He whirled her around and swore when she kicked him in the shin. "It's simple. Just let yourself go. One, two, and—*damnation*!"

"I beg your pardon," Diana moaned. "Will you please let well enough alone?"

As she spoke, the moon sailed out from behind the clouds and shone down on her upraised face. Blaize stilled and looked down at her. He swore again—softly.

Diana knew that the earl was going to kiss her. She knew that she should break away from him, excuse herself, and walk back to the house. His arms about her held her loosely, and she could break that hold if she wanted to.

She did not want to.

Instead, she moved closer to the earl, lifted her lips to his, and heard him murmur her name as he leaned down to kiss her. Once. Again.

"I didn't intend to do this," Blaize whispered. He kissed her a third time. "We should go back into the house."

"Yes, we should."

Mutely Diana lifted her lips again. This time his kiss was like stormwind and fire. It seared her to the depths of her being until she could feel herself melting like candle wax. Nothing existed outside Blaize's embrace. Nothing.

Finally, dazed and breathless, they drew apart.

Blaize no longer blamed himself for allowing this moment to happen. It had been fated to happen, he thought. Since the first time she had defied him in the library, he realized that he had been falling in love with Diana Gardiner.

In her dark eyes he read emotions that echoed his own. There was no fear in her expression, and no hesitation. Blaize felt a rush of intoxicating joy. Whatever he felt for Diana, she felt for him as well. It was time, he thought, to give words to the question that had been in his heart.

"Diana," he began, "I must ask you—"

There was a rush of running footsteps, and a dark shadow came darting through the French windows. "Is that you out there, Di?" Archie demanded.

"What has happened?" Diana exclaimed.

It was hard to speak coherently. Her heart was still thumping like a kettledrum, stars still dazzled her eyes. Around her, Blaize's arms tightened fractionally and then dropped away as Archie hurried toward them.

"In the courtyard," he stammered. He was breathing hard and was almost incoherent. "C-come this way, Di, you'll see. *Come*!"

"Can't this wait?" Blaize demanded, but Archie had already seized his sister's hand and was dragging her down the steps into the garden. Reluctantly, Blaize followed. "Where are you going?" he demanded.

Without bothering to answer, Archie made his way around the house toward the courtyard. Here he pulled his sister over to one of the carriages. "Look, Di. Just look."

Diana could see nothing unusual about the carriage. Four horses were yoked to it, but there seemed nothing out of the way about them, either. "What am I supposed to see?" she asked in bewilderment.

Running forward, Archie caught the bridle of a gray gelding. "Don't you know this horse, Di?" he cried. When she shook her head he explained, "It's Gallant—the horse Dracot rode to war!"

7

Diana stared at the horse in the uncertain lamplight. At one time it might have been a fine animal, but those days were far behind. Standing still with head drooped, it appeared not to care much about anything.

"This can't be Gallant," she cried. "You are wrong, Archie. Gallant fell with Dracot—miles and miles away."

"This is Gallant," Archie persisted. "He *is*, Di. I'd know him anywhere, and he knows *me*."

He rubbed the spot between the gray gelding's eyes. The horse whickered softly and rested its head against Archie's shoulder.

Diana gave a little cry of surprise.

"That means nothing. Any horse will come to you," Blaize said sharply.

Archie was fumbling under the gelding's mane. "But this *isn't* just any horse, sir—it's Gallant. See, Di? Here's the spot where he was hurt. Remember, when he was just a colt and he cut himself so badly on that wire fence? And here is the mark which Uncle Thomas's groom put on all their horses."

Diana put her hand under the gelding's mane. The animal started to shy away, then paused at the sound of her reassuring voice. As if recalling something dim and far away, it whickered questioningly.

Under her fingers, Diana now felt the hard, knotted scar. Tears filled her eyes. "It *is* Gallant," she said in a low voice.

"I can feel the scar and—and here is the Gardiner brand, just as Archie says. Gallant—oh, poor Gallant, what are you doing here?"

And where is Dracot? The unspoken question hung in the chill air.

"Who owns this animal?" Blaize asked abruptly.

According to the driver of the coach, the conveyance belonged to Mr. Gerald McDermott, a friend of the colonel's who had driven out from Grassmere. Archie elected to stay with Gallant, while Diana and Blaize went back to the house where the dancing was in full sway. As they searched for Mr. McDermott, Diana glimpsed Miss Flor sitting with Lady Kerwinkle and her friend, the dashing Lady St. Aubrey. Colonel Pratt was with them, gesturing broadly as he told some story.

Though understandably astonished that the earl of Blaize had taken a sudden fancy to his horse, Mr. McDermott soon recovered and, protesting that his Rayvaynan was as superior an animal as he had ever bought from Harcom's Stable, settled down to bargain. Since Blaize was not disposed to haggle, they settled for a sum that was twice the animal's worth.

"My man of business will see McDermott tomorrow and arrange for the horse to be brought to my house," Blaize told Diana as they walked away. "Meanwhile I'll send Urse to Harcom's Stable in Yorkshire. They'll have a record of where they acquired Rayvaynan."

"*Revenant*." In a low voice Diana explained, "It's the French word for ghost—'the one who returns.' "

Blaize looked at her sharply. "Are you all right?"

"Yes—no—it doesn't matter." Diana moistened her dry lips. "Can it be possible that Dracot is alive, too?"

Blaize did not answer at once. He was thinking of how, not ten minutes ago, he had held Diana in his arms and felt happier than he had been in his life. He recalled that he had been on the point of declaring his love when Archie interrupted them.

Now, the equation had changed. Diana was promised to Dracot. She still loved him.

Very carefully, the earl took the small hand on his arm, held it for a moment, and put it down gently. "I don't know," he said, "but I am going to find out."

They left Pratt House soon afterward. Archie, who was not

happy about having to leave Gallant behind, was uncharacteristically quiet, and Miss Flor seemed far away. In that unnatural hush, Blaize considered what needed to be done and watched Diana's white face with increasing disquiet.

When they reached Blaize Manor, Diana pleaded a headache and went straight to her room. Here she lay awake all night until, at dawn, she heard Archie's footsteps in the hall. Then she dressed and went out to the stables where she found her brother grooming and talking to Midnight. Claude, curled up in a pile of clean straw, wagged his stumpy tail and barked a greeting.

"Look, Di—I've helped to prepare a stall for Gallant," Archie reported. "I can't wait until he gets here. I've been telling Claude and Midnight about him, and they're ready to be friends."

"I wish Gallant could tell us what happened to Dracot," Diana mused.

"I tried asking him, but it was all too confusing to understand." Archie gave Midnight another pat. "Don't worry, Di—Lord Lion will find Dracot. They were bosom bows, remember? Lord Lion's the kind of man who'd do anything for a friend."

Doubtless, Archie was right. But as Diana went back to the house, fearful thoughts nudged her mind. Supposing, she thought, Dracot had been sorely wounded but had not died. Perhaps he had lost his memory. That would explain why he had not tried to contact them all these long months.

Blaize was already up and finishing an early cup of coffee in the morning room when Diana came in. His eyes went swiftly to her face and read the trouble there, but he only said, "Urse has gone to Yorkshire. We should have some news by tomorrow at the latest."

He poured her a cup of coffee, but she could not drink it. Her throat had closed up at the thought that Dracot might have lived in poverty, perhaps even starved, all this time.

As if he had read her thoughts, Blaize said bracingly, "Heart up, Miss Gardiner. We'll ford our bridges as we come to them."

He broke off at the sound of a cheerful humming outside the morning room, and a moment later Miss Flor made her entrance.

"Good morning," she chirruped. "A lovely morning to all."

With uncharacteristic briskness she tripped over to the sideboard, where she fairly piled her plate high with eggs, bacon, kidneys, and toast. "I am so hungry this morning that I am persuaded I could eat a tiger," she exclaimed.

The earl grinned. "Tigers? I take it Pratt was bragging about his adventures last night."

"He did not *brag*," Miss Flor reproved. "He told Lady St. Aubrey and Lady Kerwinkle about his experiences in India. I—I was there, too." She paused and gave a nod that was vaguely defiant. "I collect that Lady St. Aubrey was not pleased about that, for she looked daggers at me. But I stayed where I was."

Even in her present mood, Diana felt like applauding. But before she could comment, there was the sound of running footsteps and Archie burst into the room. He was very pale, and his eyes were almost starting out of his head.

"They've come," he stammered.

Blaize looked surprised. "You mean to say that the horse has been delivered already?"

"No, it's *them*!" Archie gulped hard and shot a terrified look at his sister. "Aunt and Uncle Radley. They've come to take me away to the madhouse."

Miss Flor gasped while Diana rose so quickly that she overset her chair. Blaize also got to his feet exclaiming, "Thunder and hell, lad, pull yourself together. No one's taking you anywhere."

He strode out of the room and Diana followed immediately. A pale Miss Flor clasped Archie's hand reassuringly, and the two brought up the rear.

Diana had hoped against hope that Archie had been mistaken, but when they arrived at the staircase landing she saw three familiar figures standing in the ground floor anteroom.

"What can they be doing here?" she groaned.

Blaize crossed the landing and looked down at his uninvited guests. "Lord and Lady Radley, I believe?"

His voice was so unfriendly that the footmen so far forgot themselves as to cast apprehensive looks at each other.

Not so Lord Radley. "Quite right, sir, quite right," he said, his small, pink features alight with unaccustomed good cheer.

"Don't mean to impose on your hospitality, but we've come to look in on our niece and nephew." Then he rubbed his hands as if in delight.

His lady added mournfully, "It is *early* in the morning, I know, but *none* of us could sleep. It was *such* a long ride to Cumbria and so uncomfortable at the inn. And the conveyance we hired in town *bounced* so that Edward was almost sick. Weren't you, dearest?"

Blue eyes bright in a cherubic face, Edward nodded. "Hullo, Cousin Diana," he caroled. "Hulloa, Archie."

"Our favorite niece and nephew," Lord Radley interupted. "By my head—what's a man without his family?"

Diana was speechless. While Miss Flor squeezed Archie's hand.

"And you came all this way solely because of family feeling," Blaize suggested.

"Then you haven't come to take me to the madhouse?" Archie ventured to inquire.

Lord Radley gave vent to jovial laughter. "My boy—my dear boy, how could you have mistaken my joke in that way?"

He poked his lady in the ribs. Lady Radley gave a sound like a startled field mouse and recited rapidly, "We learned from Lady Silvers, in Sussex, who is connected to Lady Kerwinkle, that his lordship the earl had engaged you as his librarian. Dear Diana, we could not rest till we saw if you were truly well situated."

More to the point, they wanted an entrée into Blaize Manor, the earl thought grimly. "Are you staying in the area?" he asked aloud.

"At the Gable Arms," Lord Radley said. "We didn't want to be so rag mannered as to impose on you."

"Good," said the earl.

"You must not regard the problem," Lord Radley went on, waiting to see if anyone would take the bait.

"And what problem might that be?" Miss Flor asked after a strained silence.

"Nothing to concern you, ma'am," Lord Radley said in a way that plainly meant the opposite. "The inn had only one room. Cramped. Hey? My wife's abigail has to sleep in the kitchen on a folding cot. My valet's sharing quarters with the grooms. But it don't signify. It's a sacrifice we must make to be near our dear niece and nephew."

"And the food at the inn is horrid," Edward put in. "The porridge has lumps in it. The beef is as tough as an old shoe."

Diana at last found her tongue. "I am sorry that you are inconvenienced," she declared, "but Archie and I are, as you see, in excellent health and spirits. We thank you for your concern, but there is no need for you to stay in Cumbria."

And that, Blaize thought with grim satisfaction, was that. "If you don't have a carriage," he added, "I'll gladly provide you with transportation back to the Gable Arms."

Suddenly, Lady Radley moaned and crumpled to the floor. Edward let out a shout of, "Mama!" and ran to her side. Lord Radley got down on one knee and entreated his wife to be brave.

"It's her heart," he explained. "The long journey—too much for her. Drafty room at the inn nearly finished her off."

Affecting a look of great concern, he took hold of Lady Radley's hands and began to slap them. Edward broke into loud tears and begged his mother not to die.

During the commotion, Diana turned to Blaize. "I do not believe she is sick at all. It's a trick to force you to invite them to stay here."

"I'm sure you're right." Blaize watched the disgusting scene below and wished the Radleys to Jericho. But these people were Diana's relatives, after all. He could not very well toss them onto the street.

Meanwhile, Edward was appealing to Miss Flor. "It's really horrid at the inn," he implored. "Please, ma'am, can't we stay here with you?"

Miss Flor did not know what to say. On one hand, she remembered everything that Archie had told her about the Radleys. On the other, Edward seemed to be such a sweet child, and one could hardly blame a child for the sins of his parents.

She looked helplessly at the earl, who snapped, "Whitton, have them make up the north bedroom."

Diana saw a furtive smile quiver across her uncle's small, mean mouth.

"Not right for us to intrude on you," he said in a falsely humble tone. "If it weren't for my lady—but you see how she is. Not at all the thing, hey? In your debt, my lord earl. In your debt."

Lady Radley gave a feeble moan. Edward sniffled loudly. It was degrading. Hot with shame, Diana turned away.

Archie plucked at her sleeve. "Perhaps they won't stay long, Di," he whispered hopefully.

But seeing her uncle look around him with that satisfied gleam in his eyes, Diana knew better. Like birds of ill omen, the Radleys had come to roost.

"Magnificent, madam—mag-ni-fi-cent! By my head, I've never seen such flowers."

Lord Radley beamed on Miss Flor, who blushed and stammered that perhaps her flowers were not bad. "Not bad, ma'am?" Lord Radley exclaimed. "Not bad? By my head, you're more than modest."

Standing unseen at the door of the morning room, Diana writhed internally. Since he had arrived, her uncle had flattered everything and everybody. Words of unctuous praise rolled off his tongue like water off a duck's back.

She watched as Lord Radley hurried to his wife's chair and inquired solicitously as to how she felt. "Remember you're sick," Diana heard him whisper. "Help me flatter that old trout, now. We need her goodwill."

Diana felt that if she did not get some air, she would be physically sick. She walked out of the room and down the curving staircase to the ground floor. Here she paused to look about her just as she had seen her uncle look about him when he thought nobody was looking.

He had the air of a man taking inventory of what he possessed. Lord Radley had wanted his niece to gain entrée into high circles, and now he was here to reap the harvest. It was less than a week since he had inveigled an invitation to stay at Blaize Manor, but he already was acting as though this were his home.

The day after his arrival, he had borrowed the earl's carriage and gone visiting the neighbors. He had driven to Pratt House and flattered and oiled Sir Ogden Kerwinkle so that they were already bosom bows. He had danced attendance on Lady Kerwinkle and her friends. He had secured an invite to view the colonel's fast-approaching hunt.

Daily he flattered and deferred to the earl, but under all the compliments and the toad-eating, the meanspiritedness of the man was apparent. Diana had heard her uncle snarl at the housemaids and treat his underlings with contempt. She had watched him eye Archie with a cold and speculative look.

Diana's cheeks felt hot as she considered what Blaize must think of her family. But the earl had said very little of late except to relate the news that Urse had brought back from Harcom's stable. According to them, Gallant had been bought from a gentleman who lived in Sussex. Molhouse had subsequently journeyed to Sussex to see if he could learn more, but he had not yet returned.

Diana was thankful beyond words that so far the inquisitive Radleys knew nothing about Gallant or Dracot. They did not suspect the identity of Blaize's new gray gelding, and both Urse and Molhouse, the only people beyond the family who were in on the secret, were careful to keep their silence.

"Diana, my dear."

Lady Radley was descending the stairs. As politely as she could, Diana asked her how she felt.

"Poorly," Lady Radley sighed. "Still, I see *some* small improvement. This morning, at least, I feel enough *energy* to have a cose with my dear niece."

Diana misliked the syrupy note in her aunt's voice. "You must not tax your strength," she replied. "I will have one of the servants help you to your room."

Lady Radley clasped her hands, and gave thanks that her niece was so well situated that she could give commands to the servants of an earl.

"What a pleasant place Blaize Manor is," she went on. "Your uncle was saying last night that it is *most* aristocratic. And the earl—he is so *noble* in appearance and distinguished in address."

Almost desperately, Diana asked, "How long are you going to stay here?"

"I am not sure. Your uncle has not decided—I mean, I do not feel well enough *yet* for a journey." Lady Radley heaved a great sigh. "It was such a *long* journey. Cumbria is truly the ends of the earth."

"I am sorry you were put to such trouble on my account," Diana said. "But you must realize that the earl is my employer. It is awkward for me to have you impose on his hospitality."

Lady Radley tried to look wise and knowledgeable and only succeeded in looking sly. "The earl is unmarried."

When Diana did not comment she added, "Blaize is such a fine man, and kind to Archie as well. I am persuaded that there has been a great improvement in dear Archie. He appears civilized."

She then lowered her voice to a confidential whisper. "We *must* put our best foot forward, must we not?"

Speechless with insult, Diana stared at her aunt. In the same low murmur Lady Radley added, "It is the only way, my dear, believe me. Your uncle has his faults. I knew that when my dear papa gave his consent for Radley to pay his addresses to me. But I was not exactly *young*, you understand, and there was little chance of a better match."

Diana was surprised to see that the slyness in her aunt's eyes had changed to resignation. "Seldom is a woman granted the wishes of her heart. When I was your age I had dreams, but—" She broke off.

"What dreams, Aunt Hortensia?" Diana asked, astonished at this side of her aunt which she had never seen before. She was even more astonished when Lady Radley reached out and took her hand.

"Oh, the usual foolishness. Diana, I give you this advice not because of what your uncle wishes but from one female to another. A woman alone *cannot* hope to make her own way in the world. Collect that only through marriage can a lady be truly free. If Blaize is interested in you, *fan* that interest, or you may live to regret it."

Her aunt walked away then, and, hardly seeing where she went, Diana crossed the ground floor anteroom and went outside into the garden. Perhaps Lady Radley had indeed meant her advice kindly, but such advice was unwelcome.

Behind her she heard the front door open and Lord Radley's voice. Unable to bear the thought that she might have to speak to him, Diana walked even more rapidly.

"Infamous," she repeated. "I must get as far away as I can from him."

"What's that, ma'am?"

Diana realized that her rapid walk had brought her to the stables, and that Urse was watching her in some surprise. "Dosta want Firefly saddled?" he wondered.

Well—why not? she thought. She was not dressed for riding, but in her present mood this did not signify in the slightest, and riding might return her equilibrium. A few minutes later, mounted on Firefly, Diana was riding the path down to the lake.

But though the lake was as beautiful as ever, Lady Radley's words stayed with her. "What wicked nonsense," Diana said aloud. "The earl is simply my employer. Besides—besides, I was promised to Dracot and he may still be alive."

She tried to summon memories of her cousin, but his face seemed misty and far away. Too clearly, she saw another man—tall, tawny-haired, broad-shouldered.

"But I loved—I mean, I *love* Dracot," Diana protested aloud. "I would have married him."

But would she have married him because of love, or because their marriage had been arranged since they were in leading strings? But such questions were foolish. Diana reminded herself that marriage in their circle was usually a contract of convenience, and she and Dracot had thought themselves lucky because they liked each other so much.

Abruptly, she turned Firefly away from the lake. As she did so, she realized that she was no longer alone. Blaize was riding toward her, and at the sight of him, every nerve and fiber in Diana's body seemed to come alive.

And with this quickening of emotion came truth. She had loved Dracot, but she had never been *in* love with him. They had enjoyed each other's company, shared a deep and loving friendship, but never once had Dracot looked at her as the earl often did. And when he had kissed her, it had been a warm, pleasant, *friendly* kiss, not a cataclysm that turned her blood to honey and her bones to water.

"No," Diana protested, "I cannot be in love with Lord Lion. Aunt Hortensia has put that ridiculous notion in my head."

Affecting a calmness she did not feel, she waited for him to come up to her. He took one look at her face and asked, "Have your relatives been up to their old tricks?"

She nodded, ruefully. "My uncle smiles and smiles, my aunt complains, and Edward clings to Archie like glue. I am persuaded that Uncle Simon has ordered him to turn Archie up sweet."

"Let's not think of them anymore. Ride with me instead."

She could think of no good excuse to refuse. As she fell in beside him, Blaize resumed, "I have just come from riding with the colonel and his boring brother-in-law. Kerwinkle was showing off his Lancer and goaded poor old Pratt into challenging him to a race."

He was riding close to her—so close that if she reached out a hand, she could touch his arm. Diana forced herself to keep her eyes straight ahead and asked in what she hoped was an interested voice, "Did the colonel win his race?"

Blaize shook his head. "His horse stepped into a hole and stumbled, and Pratt went over his head. Worse, his horse went lame. Not badly—fomentations will heal the leg—but Pratt was beside himself."

"Poor colonel," Diana exclaimed. "And his hunt so close at hand, too. Does he have another horse to ride?"

"I've lent him Midnight. There seemed nothing else I could do." Blaize sighed. "Archie is out of charity with me. He told me to my head that he detests the idea of hunting foxes for sport. Finally, he allowed that since Midnight likes the colonel, it *might* be all right."

"Of course it is all right," Diana exclaimed indignantly. "Midnight is your horse, my lord, not Archie's." She paused before adding, "You are too kind to my brother, and—and in return I have foisted my relatives on you."

The tremor in her voice, and more so the shadows in her eyes worried Blaize. Those shadows did not merely come from distress over the Radleys.

"I know what you're thinking," he said. "But you must try not to worry. It's some distance to Sussex."

"It has been days since your valet left," she murmured.

"These things take time. Don't worry—Molhouse can pry loose secrets from the grave."

She winced at his choice of words. "I keep wondering," she said in a low voice, "what really happened to Dracot. While Archie and I have been fed and clothed, he may have been starving or in pain."

Her voice broke. Blaize felt an almost uncontrollable urge to put his arms around her and comfort her. He had to clear his throat before he could say, "There's no use making yourself ill. As I said, Molhouse has ways of learning things. If Dracot is alive, he'll find him."

He reached out to clasp her hand and then impulsively raised it to his lips. Diana felt the warmth of that small kiss travel all the way into her heart. She looked up into his green eyes and was lost.

"Diana," the earl said, "you must know—"

He broke off, and in the silence Diana knew that she had never really loved poor Dracot, not like this. What she felt for the earl was something incomprehensible, irreversible. Even now she wanted to be in Blaize's arms.

"You must know that I would do anything to keep you from being hurt," Blaize said in a low voice.

I am as shameless as my uncle Radley, Diana thought miserably. Aloud she said, "We had better go back to the house. I don't know what my uncle and aunt are up to there, my lord, but I don't trust them."

The trouble was that he no longer trusted himself. Blaize let go of Diana's hand and turned his horse's head toward the house. He knew that if he had stayed with Diana another second, he would have swept her into his arms and told her of his love. He would have betrayed his old friend without a qualm.

"Thunder and hell," the earl muttered under his breath.

He spurred forward up the lake path and was the first to see a familiar figure near the stables.

"Molhouse," the earl exclaimed and he urged Midnight forward, with Diana trailing behind. "Have you learned anything?" the earl demanded as his valet hurried forward to meet him.

Molhouse noted how Diana's eyes asked the same mute

question. He looked from his employer to the lady, both of them anxious and unhappy, and he regretted to give them news that would doubtlessly make matters worse.

"I'm sorry, me lord, madam," he said, "but there was little to learn."

When Diana gave a little, painful gasp, the earl said, "It won't do to talk about it now. Too many listening ears." He frowned hard at Edward, who was peering at them from behind a nearby bush. "Have something to eat, Molhouse, then come and report to me."

But there was not much to report. Later in the earl's study, Molhouse described to Blaize and Diana how he had visited the house of a Mr. Peter Ramsey in Folkestone, Sussex, and learned that Mr. Ramsey had indeed bought a horse called Rayvaynan.

"Mr. Ramsay was not at 'ome, me lord," Molhouse explained. "I talked to Mr. Ramsey's 'ead grooms. They didn't know much beyond the fact that their employer had bought the gray from a 'orse dealer. I found that dealer, 'oo said as 'e'd acquired Rayvaynan—Gallant I mean—from a Belgian while on the Continent. That's all 'e knew."

Molhouse glanced from the earl's unreadable face to Diana's white countenance. "It doesn't mean that Mr. Gardiner is deceased," he pointed out. "It just means that we've come up against a wall, like."

"Then you think there may be another explanation?" Diana could not help asking.

Molhouse glanced at the earl. "Say what's on your mind," Blaize ordered.

"The 'orse was bought from a Belgian, as I said. Mr. Gardiner is supposed to 'ave been killed in Belgium. I'm thinking that hit might be worth a look at the area near Waterloo."

The earl looked thoughtful. "Each regiment looked to its dead and wounded and the sound horses as well. But since Dracot's body was never found, there's just the off chance—"

"That he's alive," Diana whispered.

A small silence fell on the study. In it, they could hear Lord Radley's voice in the hallway exhorting his lady not to tax her feeble strength.

Molhouse looked at Diana and then at his employer. "Shall I go to Belgium, me lord?" he inquired.

"I must think about it." Then, as Molhouse exited, he turned to Diana. "It's a very slim hope," he said.

She had clasped her hands tightly together. In a low voice she agreed. "I know. It's most likely that Dracot perished and that some chance passerby took the horse and later sold it. I know that things like that happen during wartime."

She bowed her head. Abruptly Blaize asked, "If Dracot were alive, would you still marry him?"

Something in his voice caused her heart to thump painfully. "Yes," Diana whispered. "I would marry him. We were engaged when he went away and nothing has changed."

Everything has changed, Blaize thought. He loathed himself because he realized that he was actually hoping that Dracot would never be found.

"I am giving you so much trouble, my lord. Perhaps the best thing for me to do is to leave. None of these problems are really your concern," Diana said unhappily.

She was right, Blaize thought. If he had any sense, he would encourage Diana Gardiner to leave—and take her toad-eating relatives with her.

But seemingly he had no sense left, at least not where she was concerned. Blaize heard himself say, "Running away never solved anything. And you're wrong when you say that none of this is my concern. Dracot was my friend. Molhouse will go to Belgium to see what he can learn. And if that trail, too, ends in nothing, then—"

He broke off. "What then?" Diana whispered.

She looked so woebegone, so worried that he could not help taking her hand in his. "We'll cross that bridge when we come to it."

8

With a heart as cheerless as the gray sky, Diana readied herself for Colonel Pratt's hunt. She would rather not have gone at all, but Archie was nervous about Midnight's maiden hunt and had asked her to come along.

Archie's respect for the earl and his liking for the colonel had been put to a severe test. He hated the thought of Midnight's riding to hounds, worried about the effect of unfamiliar sights and sounds on his favorite black stallion, and yet at the same time he wanted to please Lord Lion.

There was a knock on Diana's door and Miss Flor stepped in, neat as wax in a well-fitting high-waisted dark blue walking-out dress with a matching, fur-trimmed pelisse and a bonnet lined with dark blue silk—all creations of a local seamstress.

"Is my bonnet on straight?" she asked anxiously. "It is too provoking, Diana. I seem to have mislaid my spectacles."

She tripped over a hassock, grasped at an occasional table for support, and knocked a figurine to the floor. "My reticule is missing as well," she sighed. "I cannot think where it has got to. Inside was the little ivory mirror Mama gave me long ago and my best linen handkerchief worked with lace."

Diana murmured a reply, but her mind was not on Miss Flor's problems. She was thinking that it had been nearly two weeks since Molhouse had left on his mission to Belgium and that since then there had been no word from him.

Could something have befallen the earl's valet? As she

and the nearsighted Miss Flor went downstairs, Diana felt cold at the thought. Better to think that Molhouse was on the continent, somewhere, asking questions and following a promising trail.

"If indeed there is a trail to follow," she muttered out loud.

"What did you say, Diana?" Lady Radley, with Edward in tow, had come up behind them. "Speaking to yourself is *not* a good sign."

Lady Radley was dressed in a bright yellow round dress and a bonnet with a jockey front edged with honeycomb trimming. She looked bilious and unhappy. Going to the colonel's boring hunt was not her idea. She had told Lord Radley so, but Simon had all but torn Lady Caroline Lamb's delicious new novel from her hands and commanded her not to be a crackbrained fool.

"This is your chance to butter up Lady Kerwinkle and Lady St. Aubrey," he had snapped. "Don't you know what their friendship can mean, madam? Invitations for the season—entrée into their circles. Kerwinkle's well-known in the House. By my head, who knows where this'll lead to?"

Lady Radley had obeyed her lord, but she felt resentful. And that resentment increased a thousandfold when she followed Miss Flor and Diana out of doors and saw Archie. Why, the wretched boy was leading Midnight as if he owned the horse *and* riding next to Blaize himself.

"Look at Archie on Midnight," Edward exclaimed.

His discontented voice fueled Lady Radley's wrath. *Why* should the earl insist on treating that want-wit with such respect and affection while her darling Edward was hardly noticed? She glared at Lord Radley, who had ridden up to the earl's other side, smiling and saying, "It will be a fine day for the hunt, my lord—very fine."

"It's going to rain," was the dampening reply.

The earl was tired of his uninvited guests. He did not credit for a moment that Lady Radley was prey to a recurring weakness that kept her from leaving Blaize Manor, and he loathed her husband.

Blaize would have gladly thrown the lot out of doors long before now, but the thought of any disgrace to Diana stopped him. No doubt the Radleys' poisonous tongues could harm their niece, and she had been hurt enough.

"A word if I may, my lord," Lord Radley was saying now in his unctuous tones. "It is about Edward, alas. It seems there has been a misunderstanding in the stables. My son says—I can't credit it, but there it is—that your groom will not allow him to see the horses."

Lord Radley's tones quivered with indignation. Blaize cast a fulminating look at the youngest Radley, who was standing just behind his mother and watching Archie with a jealous eye. Though Master Edward had been on his best behavior since his arrival, there had been small incidents. Salt had been found in the sugar bowl, spiders had found their way to Miss Flor's room, and small items—gold cuff links, a snuffbox, Miss Flor's ivory cameo—were missing. No one could connect Edward to these events, but Blaize did not trust the brat any more than he trusted the parents.

He spoke curtly. "Urse caught your son teasing the horses, and he's not to set foot in the stables again."

Lord Radley opened his mouth to remonstrate but shut it again quickly as the earl added, "It is by *my* order. Make no mistake, Radley, you are not here by my invitation and I don't consider you my guests. You are here on sufferance only."

Lord Radley gulped hard. He had never before noticed how fierce and lionlike the earl's green eyes could appear. "Y-yes, my lord," he faltered. "Of course, my lord earl. I am grateful that you—"

"I will be obeyed on my land and in my own house. If your son—or any of your household—oversteps the mark, you'll be shown the door immediately," Blaize continued. Then, without waiting for Lord Radley's reaction, he spurred away.

Diana saw the earl's grim expression and felt sick at heart. Since Molhouse had left, she and Lord Lion had seldom been alone together, and on the rare occasions that they had an uninterrupted moment, they spoke only of Molhouse and his search for Dracot.

Daily Diana watched the earl grow more silent, saw the hard lines reappear around his mouth. The laughter and pleasure that had lit his eyes had given way to a cold civility, and he now resembled the Lord Lion she had encountered when she first came to Blaize Manor.

And how could she blame him? As she seated herself in the carriage next to Miss Flor, Diana vowed that as soon as there was word about Dracot, she and Archie must leave Blaize Manor. It was the only way to give the earl peace.

These cheerless thoughts accompanied her on the short drive to Pratt House, where preparations for the hunt were already under way. The colonel, resplendent in the scarlet coat of the Master of the Hunt, was anxiously awaiting them.

"Horse looks to be in high croak," Pratt hailed the earl. "Dashed generous of you, lendin' me Midnight. Yes. Is he ready for the hunt, young Gardiner?"

"Midnight will do well, sir," Archie said. He could not help adding, "But he doesn't *like* hunting for the poor fox."

"Well, each to his own, young Gardiner, yes. I'm in your debt."

Lady Radley's eyes narrowed to slits as the colonel solemnly shook hands with Archie. Beside her, Edward hissed, "Archie's getting above himself."

The jealousy in his tone gave Diana a twinge of disquiet. She did not want anything to add to Archie's present nervousness. "He has worked hard to train Midnight," she pointed out. "Naturally, he is worried about the horse."

Lady Radley sniffed.

"Dear Archie has done wonders with that horse. Midnight used to be so unmanageable, and look at him now . . ." Miss Flor said loyally.

Her words trailed off as the colonel came striding up to the carriage. "Ladies, your most obedient," he boomed. "Good day for the hunt. Glad you could come, ma'am, very glad."

Miss Flor, to whom this last was addressed, blushed and stammered that she hoped it would not rain.

"Rain? never!" the colonel exclaimed. "Sun's goin' to come out."

He opened his mouth to say more but seemed to have run out of steam. He harrumphed several times and tugged his mustaches while Miss Flor looked down at her feet.

"Egad, yes," the colonel finally went on. "Sun's goin' to come out, and—hoy, there's my sister. Come on, Blaize, young

Gardiner. Want to give Midnight time to get used to things."

Looking relieved, he retreated as Lady Kerwinkle, a martial figure in a jade green riding habit and matching shako, advanced upon them. "Hello, hello," she boomed. "There you all are."

She caught her guests' hands in a crushing grip then added, "I'll be huntin', but Marion and the others will be at the viewin' pavilion. Horatio's had the place heated, so you'll be comfortable there and have a good view. You goin' that way, too, Lord Radley? Just follow James, here. Take you m'self, but the hunt's startin'."

Edward pulled loose from his mother's hand and darted off to get a better view. Diana could hear the colonel bawling commands for the hounds to move off to draw, and the noise of yelping accompanied Lord Radley and the ladies up a grassy knoll. Here a large and elaborate pavilion had been erected.

As Lady Kerwinkle had intimated, the pavilion was quite comfortably enclosed on three sides and warmed by charcoal braziers. Several gentlemen and ladies were seated in comfortable chairs or standing about a long table laden with platters of chicken, ham, duck, and roast beef. No one paid any attention to the newcomers.

Lord Radley, who had been considerably chapfallen after the earl's set-down, now rallied. He had sighted Sir Rupert Grue and Lady St. Aubrey standing to one side. As he steered his lady toward them he muttered, "Mind you compliment Lady St. Aubrey on her bonnet. Turn them up sweet, madam. Turn them up sweet."

Meanwhile, Miss Flor was peering about. "How I wish I had not lost my spectacles," she sighed. "I cannot see much of anything. Are Lionel and the colonel on the field?"

"Lady Kerwinkle is riding next to the colonel, who looks very well on Midnight," Diana reported. "I don't see the earl anywhere."

"Perhaps he has stayed back to talk to Archie." Miss Flor added in a mournful tone, "Oh, Diana, I am a bird-wit. I *promised* myself that I would be as bright and witty as Lady St. Aubrey is, but the moment I saw him, I didn't have two words to rub together. What a ninny he must think me."

"I do not believe so," Diana said. "Actually, I am persuaded that the colonel is also shy. He shouts so that people will not guess."

Miss Flor looked astonished at this, but before she could comment, a horn sounded on the field and Colonel Pratt shouted, "Tally-ho! Here we go!"

As if in response to this announcement, a shaft of sunlight burst through the clouds. It shone down on the master's scarlet coat, and on Sir Ogden, who spurred forward to take lead of the field. He was followed immediately by his wife. Blaize was nowhere to be seen.

"Look at Colonel Pratt," Lady St. Aubrey exclaimed. "I vow that he resembles a lobster in his hunt clothes."

Miss Flor stiffened as Lady Radley joined in the lady's laughter. Sir Rupert Grue tittered and said, "He reminds me more of a dancing bear than a lobster."

"The colonel is a fine figure of a man."

There was a startled silence and everyone stared at Miss Flor, who continued firmly, "I see nothing to laugh about."

Sir Rupert raised his quizzing-glass. Lady St. Aubrey tossed her curls. "Fol rol," she exclaimed satirically, "Horatio has found a champion."

"Pay no attention," Diana whispered to a blushing Miss Flor. She herself concentrated on Midnight, who was truly a magnificent sight to behold. As a shaft of sunlight beamed down on him, the stallion gleamed like black satin.

"Give you my word," Sir Rupert Grue was saying, "that black horse is a fine specimen."

When a ripple of admiration was heard through the pavilion, Miss Flor caught Diana's arm. "How I wish I could see. What is happening?"

"The colonel leads the field," Diana reported. "No horse can outrun Midnight."

Then, suddenly, Midnight seemed to go wild. Bucking and rearing, the black gelding slashed at the air with its hooves. In that second it had become the wild, mad horse that it had been when first it came to Blaize Manor.

"What is it?" cried Miss Flor as the ladies under the pavilion began to scream. "What is amiss? Diana, has something happened to—to the colonel?"

There was another, collective scream, and Lord Radley exclaimed, "By my head—that black devil's thrown Pratt."

"*Thrown* him!" Miss Flor repeated. In the next moment the little lady was stumbling out of the pavilion and running blindly down the hill toward the field below.

"Where is he?" she gasped, as Diana caught up to her. "I cannot see. *Tell* me he is not hurt, Diana."

"I hope not," was all Diana could say. The colonel was lying motionless on the ground. Lady Kerwinkle and Sir Ogden had both dismounted, and Lady Kerwinkle was kneeling beside her brother. Archie had run onto the field in pursuit of Midnight, who was stamping and snorting some distance away.

Sir Ogden scowled after Archie. "I told you you ain't ought to have ridden that horse. Beast's dangerous, by Jove."

"But Archie said the horse was tame."

Diana looked up sharply and saw that Edward and Lord Radley had joined them. "That's what Archie said, wasn't it, Papa?" the child repeated. "He *said* Midnight was as gentle as a lamb and now the colonel's dead."

"Dead!" wailed Miss Flor. She let go of Diana's arm and blundering forward, nearly tripped over the prostrate colonel. As she sank down on her knees beside him, the colonel spoke faintly.

"Not dead, egad." He tried to sit up then sank back again.

"Better lie still," Sir Ogden advised. With patently false sympathy he added, "Took another rattling fall, didn't you? Paltry thing to happen, by Jove."

"It's Archie's fault," Edward reiterated.

Diana stared at her cousin. She did not like the thought that was beginning to build in her brain.

The colonel made another attempt to sit up and this time succeeded. "Nobody's dashed fault," he croaked. "Not the dashed horse's fault, neither. There was a flash of light—drove him wild. Thought I had him under control till that dashed light got in *my* eyes. Blinded me, too."

Sir Ogden curled his lip. "So you say."

Turning a brilliant shade of crimson, the colonel demanded to know what his dashed brother in law was hinting at. "There *was* a flash of light," he roared. Then, noting the smirk on

Sir Ogden's face he added ominously, "You callin' me a liar, Kerwinkle?"

He got no further as Miss Flor cried indignantly, "No one with any sense could believe such a thing."

Sir Ogden sneered, "Hiding behind a woman, now? Too loud, Horatio, too loud."

The colonel uttered an outraged bellow and struggled to get to his feet. He was held back by several members of the hunt whilst Lady Kerwinkle loudly entreated her husband to stop being an ass. "M'brother's never told a lie, and you know it. If Horatio says there was a blindin' flash of light, then there was."

Both she and the colonel glared at Sir Ogden, who said grudgingly, "It was the horse's fault, I said. Beast's dangerous. If it was mine, I'd shoot him."

"No!" The shout came from Archie who was returning with Midnight in tow. "Midnight was frightened, that's all."

"A likely story," Sir Odgen snapped. He was in a bad temper for having been taken publicly to task by his wife and glad for a chance to vent his spleen. "The brute's savage. Heard what it did to one of Blaize's grooms. Heard it nearly killed the man."

Everyone began to speak at once. Sir Ogden, supported by Sir Rupert Grue, railed against Midnight. The colonel reiterated that Sir Ogden would suffer for questioning his veracity. Looking frightened, Archie protested that none of what had happened was Midnight's fault.

"The fault is not with the *horse*." Lady Radley's spiteful voice cut through the babble. "*You* trained the animal, Archie. It is because of your incompetence that the colonel has been hurt."

"Lady Radley's right." Sir Ogden pointed an accusatory finger at Archie. "This chitty-faced brat led you on, Horatio. Made you believe the brute was tame."

"That is not true," Diana cried, but her protest was cut short as Miss Flor turned on Sir Ogden like an indignant wren.

"You must not speak of Archie so, Sir Ogden, and Midnight is Lionel's horse, not yours." Her usually timid blue eyes snapped as she added, "Besides, the colonel has no need for a gentle animal. He is an excellent rider."

There was a dead silence broken by Lady St. Aubrey's trill of laughter. "La, who'd have thought it? The little lady has formed a tendre for our colonel."

Lady St. Aubrey began to laugh. For a moment, Miss Flor stood stock-still. Then, with a bleat of dismay, she plucked up her skirts and began hurrying away from the group on the field.

Diana started to follow, then stopped as she saw Edward's satisfied grin. All her suspicions rekindled, she followed her cousin as he skipped away from the others and caught him by the arm. "Edward, you must return Miss Flor's reticule immediately," she ordered.

Blue eyes radiating angelic innocence swam up to meet hers. "What do you mean, Cousin Diana? What reticule?"

"You know very well what I mean." Diana watched her cousin's face closely as she added, "Let me see what is in your pockets, Edward."

It was a stab in the dark, but she had not been mistaken. Diana felt sickened as she saw the spurt of fear in Edward's eyes. "You're telling whiskers," he protested. "I never stole anything from the old lady."

"Then empty your pockets."

Edward turned to escape, but she held him fast. As he struggled, a small, ivory-backed mirror fell from the boy's pocket.

Diana pounced on it. "You used Miss Flor's little mirror to reflect the sun in Midnight's eyes. What you did was not only wicked but dangerous. Supposing the colonel had been hurt?"

Edward stuck out his bottom lip and pretended to be close to tears. It was a ploy that worked with Mama, but his odious cousin only stared sternly down at him. "Well, he wasn't hurt," Edward sulked. "I didn't mean any harm. I was just playing."

"You mean you were jealous of Archie and wanted to play a wicked trick to make Midnight look bad."

She got no further before Edward kicked at her, squirmed out of her grip, and ran toward his mother. Feeling weak with disgust and outrage, Diana watched him go. She had always distrusted Edward, but she had never believed he was capable of such wickedness.

The Radleys had to leave, and the sooner the better. She would talk to Blaize and tell him about Edward . . .

Her thoughts trailed away as she saw Archie walking Midnight toward her. "I'm taking him back to the stables and rubbing him down," he said. "He's had enough for one day. And, Di, Midnight says the colonel's right. There *was* a bright flash of light, and it scared him into rearing up. He didn't mean to hurt anyone."

"You must tell that to the earl," she interrupted. "And I have something to tell him, too. We must find him—"

She broke off as a familiar figure came riding toward them. "There he is, there's Lord Lion," Archie cried, joyfully. "He seems to be in a hurry."

With relief, Diana awaited the earl's arrival. But there was something about the set of his mouth that made her catch an apprehensive breath. Something had happened.

She queried the earl with her eyes as he reined in his horse beside them, but he turned to Archie first. "I've heard about the hunt," he said. "There's no need to fear for Midnight, so rest easy. No one will lay blame to the horse again. Take him to Urse, lad." Then, as Archie joyfully took his horse away, Blaize turned to Diana. "There has been word from Belgium."

Diana's heart had begun to pound, but she spoke steadily. "Then Molhouse has returned?"

"No, but I've had word from him. That's why I didn't join the hunt." Blaize swung down from his horse and faced Diana directly. "A courier from Molhouse arrived here just as the hunt was riding out. There's a possibility that Dracot's alive and living in the village of Lesec, in Belgium."

Diana felt suddenly dizzy. Earth and sky seemed to cartwheel around her, and she might have fallen if the earl had not put his arm around her waist to steady her.

"Alive?" she said in a dry voice.

"I said, there's a *possibility*."

Diana became aware that the earl was holding her tightly and that something deep within her was responding to that clasp.

"I am sorry to have broken the news clumsily, but there's little time. I must travel to Dover at once."

He was going in search of Dracot. Dimly she registered this, realizing also that together with her excitement and apprehension, there was something else within her that ached unbearably. "You mean, Dracot may return with you."

Her eyes met the earl's, and in that heartbeat's time Diana knew what caused the throbbing pain in her heart. She wanted Dracot to return, prayed for his return, and yet there was a flip side to that coin. If her fiancé were indeed alive, this would be the last time she and the earl could be alone together like this. Hastily she tried to repress the forbidden longing within her by stepping away from Blaize's protective arm, but another wave of dizziness kept her where she was.

"I wanted to tell you first and to send word to Guenevere," Blaize said, but in his eyes she saw an echo of her own tumultuous thoughts.

"Thank you," she whispered.

"No need to thank me. Dracot was—is—my friend." Blaize spoke sternly as if reminding himself of honor and duty. "I will do my best to return him to you, if he lives."

"Return—to me." The words burst out of her without her own volition, and as if in response to all that had not been said, almost as if he were compelled to do so, Blaize bent to touch his lips to hers.

The kiss lasted a second—maybe less. Then he drew away from her and without a word remounted his horse. She took a step toward him, stopped, drew a deep breath to still the hammer of her heart.

"A safe journey, my lord," she told him. "And—and Godspeed."

Green hills, rolling plains, far-off castles and scrubbed-clean, pastel-hued villages, a whitewashed church shaded by fruit trees—it was, Blaize reflected, almost as if he were riding down an English country road.

Only, he was far from home. "How far to Lesec?" he asked.

"Not far now, Major—I mean, me lord." Glancing down at the tough little man beside him, Blaize noted how easily Molhouse had slipped back into his old role of batman. The valet seemed to have hardened and become leaner over the past few days, and there was a reminiscent sparkle in his shrewd eyes.

"There 'tis, me lord," Molhouse announced. "This 'ere is Lesec, and hif I'm not mistook, that there's the Rochards' farm."

Some distance west of the village, dappled in late afternoon sunshine, lay a good-sized farmstead.

"You're sure," Blaize asked, but there was no need for confirmation. The tightening in his belly had already conveyed that this was his journey's end.

Journeys end in lovers meetings—impatiently the earl slammed his mind shut to such foolishness. "So this is where the trail led you," he said aloud.

When young Mathews had brought Molhouse's courier to Pratt House, Blaize had felt the same sinking feeling he had often experienced before riding into battle, but he had not stopped to analyze his feelings. Pausing only to speak to Diana and send a message to Miss Flor, he had ridden to Blaize Manor, called for his carriage, and set off to meet Molhouse.

It had been a long journey. He and the courier had traveled by carriage to Dover and from thence to Oostende in Belgium, where Molhouse was waiting. Here the courier left them and Blaize and his valet had hired horses. They had ridden through Ghent, where they lay over the night, and then on toward Nivelles. Now it was near sunset of the second day, and they were within sight of the Rochards' farm.

With Molhouse riding close behind, Blaize urged his hired horse up the slope of a rutted road toward the farmhouse. It was a large, sprawling property crowned by a thatch-roofed farmhouse and surrounded by a barn, a henhouse, and a well-kept kitchen garden.

At their approach, a young woman came out of the henhouse and stood blinking uncertainly against the light. Molhouse called a greeting in execrable French, to which the girl answered and then ran into the house.

Blaize halted his horse, and both men waited until the door opened again. An older woman came out finally and stood in the doorway. She said something to the girl, who came shyly forward and dropped a curtsy.

"Messieurs, Maman asks, what is it that you want?" she asked, timidly.

Blaize introduced himself adding, "I have heard that you may know something about a friend of mine who was lost at Waterloo. His name is Dracot Gardiner."

A frightened look had come into the girl's eyes, and Blaize wondered if she had understood him. "We don't mean to intrude on you in any way," he reassured her. "I just want news of my friend."

The girl began to speak in French to the older woman. Blaize wished that he could understand what she said. She was buxom and fair and had a small, upturned nose sprinkled with freckles and a soft mouth. Wide, cornflower blue eyes regarded the earl anxiously as she said, "If you please, monsieur, Maman says to come inside."

She gestured to the house. The older woman dropped a knee and murmured in French. "Maman does not speak Eenglish," the girl explained, her words inflected with a French accent. "She says, the men are in the fields for the 'arvest. I will go now and tell them you are 'ere."

Both women looked nervous. Blaize smiled reassuringly at them and said, "Please thank your mother, Mademoiselle Rochard. *Do* you know anything about my friend?"

The girl translated. Her mother spoke rapidly and gestured. "*Eh bien.* Maman says to please come into the 'ouse," the girl repeated.

She then caught up her skirts and ran down the road, her wooden clogs making clopping sounds as she hurried toward the fields. Blaize stifled his impatience as he dismounted. He was certain these women were hiding information from him. Handing the reins to Molhouse, he followed the older woman into the farmhouse.

Inside there was a large and spotlessly clean room. Near the large, shallow fireplace there was a large table surrounded by benches and chairs. The table was set with wooden plates and pewter pitchers, and the mouth-watering fragrance of fresh-baked bread was everywhere. Fresh wildlflowers stood in a vase by the door and reminded Blaize of Diana. But then, everything seemed to remind him of her.

Restlessly, he walked to the room's one window and looked

out at the fields, where the girl, Annette, as he had heard the older woman call her, was talking and gesturing to a group of men.

"Monsieur?"

Madame Rochard was offering him something in a mug. He tasted, and found it was beer, strong and pleasant. When he thanked her, she smiled, but the worried look he had seen earlier remained in her eyes.

There were footsteps hurrying up the road, and a man burst into the farmhouse. He wore plain homespun and rough wooden clogs, and his head was covered by a round, Flemish hat. For a moment Blaize thought it was Farmer Rochard until the man gasped out in a choked voice, "*Lion*? it can't be you, Lion?"

Blaize started as though stung. Though he had accepted the possibility of finding Dracot, the moment caught him unprepared. For a moment the shock of it held him immobile, and then he strode across the room, caught the other man by the shoulders, and stared searchingly into his face.

"Thunder and hell," he said in awe. "Man, you *are* alive."

There were tears in the other man's eyes. He nodded, wordlessly, and the gesture seemed to roll back the years so that Blaize suddenly saw himself and Dracot young, unsure of the world but certain in their friendship. A hard lump wedged itself into his throat so that he could scarcely repeat, "You're alive, after all."

Then speech failed. Mutely, Blaize reached out a hand—and found it gripped by Dracot Gardiner's left hand. When he looked down involuntarily, he saw that his friend's right arm ended in an empty sleeve.

Blaize cursed again, and a small, dry smile curled Dracot's lip. "I left my arm at Waterloo," he explained.

Blaize felt so dazed that he could hardly speak. "Molhouse told me that he'd learned that an Englishman had been seen at the Rochards' farm near Lesec," he said. "I hoped against hope it could be you."

He stepped back to look at his old friend. Only this was no longer a lanky, brown-eyed schoolboy but a lean, sun-darkened man with lines scored deep about his mouth and eyes. Those dark eyes held an expression that had never been there before.

"*Why*?" Blaize demanded. "Why didn't you let someone know?"

"It's a long story. And you have a story to tell, too, no doubt. How did you find me, Lion?"

Before Blaize could reply, there were footsteps and voices outside, and Dracot added, "The others are coming in from the field. Usually we work until last light but tonight Monsieur Rochard has made an exception because of your arrival."

He broke off as a big, barrel-chested man entered the farmhouse followed by four young men who closely resembled him. "Farmer Rochard and his sons," Dracot introduced them. "Gustave, Etienne, Jean, and Raoul." He paused and added, "And this is Mademoiselle Annette."

The girl dropped a curtsy. She then turned to help her mother but not before Blaize saw her anxious expression. What was the girl so afraid of? he wondered. But then, he reasoned, his arrival had probably been as great a shock to the Rochards as finding Dracot alive had been to him.

Still somewhat dazed, he followed his friend, who conducted him to the back of the house so that he could wash. "We haven't got many comforts here," Dracot apologized as he used his left hand to work the pump. "You'll have to share my room tonight, and tomorrow morning I'll make sure there's water to wash with." He paused. "You must be tired. You're a long way from home, Lion."

"So are you." Blaize had recovered enough to add, "I want to know how you got here and why you've kept yourself hidden all these years."

"Later. Now the family is waiting for us." Dracot motioned Blaize into the farmhouse and guided him to what must have been the seat of honor beside Farmer Rochard. Other men, apparently hired workers, were now coming in to seat themselves at the board, and Blaize saw Molhouse situated amongst them. Mademoiselle Annette and her mother then placed huge plates heaped with stew and large, round loaves of dark bread on the table so that the men could eat.

Before they began eating, the farmer extended his sinewy arms and pronounced grace. Blaize gathered that Rochard was calling upon the Almighty to bless the harvest until he saw all eyes turn to him. "He's giving thanks that my English friends have come safely to this table," Dracot whispered.

Blaize didn't realize how hungry he was until he began eating. The hearty fare was simple but well prepared. He ate and watched the Rochard women serving the men and remembered Diana's tortured imaginings about her cousin starving and alone. And all this time he had been well fed and well cared for. He felt a sudden stir of anger. Dracot's explanation had better be a good one.

The meal took a long time. When it was over, the farmer gestured toward the fire. Two of his sons set chairs by the hearth and then withdrew to the other end of the room, where they lit their pipes.

"It seems," Blaize said, "that the time has come for me to hear your story."

Still wordless, Dracot sat down in one of the chairs and picked up a long pipe such as the other men were smoking. Annette Rochard hurried up to light it with a spill, then returned to the table where the women of the house were eating.

Dracot took a long pull on his pipe. "I'll begin with Waterloo," he said. "During the first engagement, the pater's and my company sustained terrible losses. Our commanding officer asked for volunteers to try and hold off the French attack until our company could fall back with our dead and wounded."

Blaize nodded, somberly. "I was at Waterloo, too." he interrupted. "I lost many friends there."

"Then you know—" Dracot absently rubbed the stump of his arm. "We gave our comrades a chance to fall back, but the French overran our position after an hour. My father was killed, Lion, in front of my eyes, as were most of the others. Somehow, I managed to crawl away from the killing. I crawled on my hands and knees until I collapsed in a kind of ditch and lost consciousness."

He drew a long breath of smoke and slowly let it out. "The ditch was overgrown with weeds, and no one was really looking for me, so I was left to lie where I fell. The next day, Raoul Rochard found me. He's always taken care of animals, and he couldn't stand the thought of horses suffering because of the war. He saw Gallant standing over me, and he came to see what he could do. And then he saw me move."

Raoul Rochard had called his father and brothers. Realizing that Dracot would die unless he was given immediate attention, they carried the wounded man home to the farmhouse nearby. There, the women had nursed him.

At first Dracot remembered very little. He did not know where he was or that Gallant had been sold to pay for needed medicine.

"I was as helpless as a baby for three months," he explained. "I was out of my head most of that time, but I remember seeing Annette—I thought that I was dead and that she was an angel." He smiled ruefully. "I must have talked a lot of nonsense. Thankfully, nobody understood me since nobody spoke English."

"But since then you've taught Mademoiselle Rochard to do so," Blaize pointed out. He wanted to change the subject momentarily away from the horrors that Dracot was recounting. "But then you were always a good teacher."

As Diana is. The unbidden thought was so painful that the earl's voice turned harsh. "Why didn't you communicate with your family after you came to your senses?"

"Would *you* have?" Dracot's eyes asked no quarter, and his next words were as harsh as the earl's. "I went to war with two arms and prospects of advancement. My father was convinced that by covering ourselves with glory, we would recoup some of the family fortune. Now here I am a cripple with no fortune. All our assets, even our house, was sold long ago to pay off my father's debts. I have nothing."

He got to his feet and looked searchingly down into his friend's face. "If it had been you, would you have returned home?"

Blaize also got to his feet. "Your cousin has been grieving for you all this time. Can you imagine how she's felt?"

"My *cousin*?" Astonishment filled Dracot's brown eyes. "How did you come to know Diana, Lion?"

"I think we need to take the air," Blaize replied. "Let's go for a turn outside."

Outside, the shadows of twilight were stretching into night

and a white sliver of moon stood out against the dark sky. For a moment the two men were silent. Then—"I think you have a story to tell, too, Lion," Dracot said.

In silence he listened to Blaize's explanation of the library. "Ironic, isn't it?" Dracot asked at last. "Here you are, with the one thing you abominate being foisted on you. And here I was, a man who liked reading and books above all things, marooned on a farm surrounded by fields and cows and chickens. Odd, what life dishes up."

Blaize was tired of philosophy; he wanted this situation settled. "We'll travel back to England in the morning," he said. "I know you'd like to make adequate compensation to the Rochard family, and that can be arranged before we go, but we must leave at first light."

"No," Dracot said. "I have no money, Lion. Not for travel or for anything else."

"Damn your pride," Blaize exploded. Then, forcing a more reasonable tone he added, "Call it a loan if you like."

"I meant, no, I am not going to England with you," Dracot explained. "You haven't listened to what I've been saying, Lion. How can I go back—like this?"

He held up the remains of his right arm. "If I go back, Diana will want to honor our engagement. I'd hoped she'd have forgotten about me and married someone else."

"You should know her better than that."

Dracot looked sharply at the earl, but all he said was, "A fine suitor I would be for Diana—or for any other woman. No right arm, no money, nothing to offer. Diana deserves much, much more than that. Tell her that I'm dead, Lion. Tell her that."

He turned away to look over the darkening fields, and Blaize felt a sudden strong emotion that shook him to the bones. He realized that what he wanted more than anything else in the world was to agree with Dracot Gardiner.

And wasn't what the man said true? Dracot had nothing to offer a wife, but there was no doubt in Blaize's mind that Diana would insist on marrying him anyway. She would yoke herself to a life of poverty in the name of love and devotion.

It would be so easy to leave Dracot here on his farm and go back with news of his death. It was what the man himself wanted. It would be best for everyone.

But Blaize remembered the way Diana had looked up at him the night she had said she would teach him how to read and write. She had dared him to trust her, and he had done so. Now she would trust him, too, and take whatever he told her as truth. She would never question him.

"Thunder and hell," Blaize gritted. Then he added, "Will you stop playing the coward?"

"Was that to *my* address, Lion?"

He wasn't sure whether he'd been talking to himself or his school friend. All Blaize knew was that it hurt to say, "You can't leave it this way. Come back with me to England and tell your cousin the truth."

"But I just got through telling you—"

"You explained that you want to take the coward's way out. I understand how you feel. If I were in your place, I'd probably want the same thing. But Diana"—he caught himself and stiffly amended—"but Miss Gardiner deserves honesty. She should have the chance to choose for herself what to do with her life."

"The chance to burden herself with a penniless cripple, you mean?" Dracot's laugh was bitter. "I think not."

But by now Blaize had had the time to think. "Not penniless, you idiot. Far from it, in fact. Before I came out to find you, I had my man of business make inquiries. You've come into a small windfall by way of your—your cousin Sir Theodore Lampery."

Blaize thanked whatever powers that were for a good memory. He remembered Dracot's telling him about this ancient cousin, four times removed, and also of hearing, through Colonel Pratt who always read the obituaries in the *Times*, that the man had died some months back without leaving any heirs.

"Cousin Theodore," Dracot repeated in amazement. "Not that old rumstick who lived in Dorset? You're diddling me, Lion. Why should he leave me anything? I only met him once."

"You must have made an impression on him, because he left you a living of four hundred pounds a year." Blaize briefly wondered if he had set the sum too low, but he had not wanted to arouse any suspicions in Dracot. Four hundred pounds was plausible. More would be open to question.

"Four hundred!" Dracot looked stunned. "Are you sure?"

"Certain," Blaize vowed. He was thinking that Diana could manage on four hundred pounds a year and that he would make sure that Archie, as his protégé, was well cared for.

"It's not your happiness you care about," the earl said aloud. "It's hers."

And the truth of this had never been so apparent, or so bitter, as when Dracot nodded slow agreement. "You're right, Lion," he said. "Diana's happiness is what's important. I've been a selfish cad to think otherwise, to stay hidden all this time."

He drew in a deep breath that was almost but not quite a sigh. "All right. We'll leave in the morning."

9

After the colonel's accident at the hunt, Miss Flor had returned to Blaize Manor, where she immediately took to her room and stayed hidden until the next morning, when she emerged, wan and distrait, to preside over the breakfast table.

She sighed and said to Diana, "Lionel wishes me to act as head of the household while he is away on some most urgent business. I must respect his wishes."

Miss Flor did not know where or for how long Blaize would be gone and simply accepted his explanation that he was away on business. Diana, who did know the earl's destination, prayed desperately that he would return soon. But as more than a week passed without word from his lordship, her hopes dimmed. If Dracot were indeed alive, Diana reasoned, the earl would surely have sent word by now.

The only bright spot was that the Radleys seemed to be uncharacteristically cooperative. Lady Radley did not put herself forward as was her wont, and Diana's uncle seemed anxious to please—even cowed. Even Edward was not as odious as he had been.

Diana wondered if the earl had had any hand in the change in her relatives' behavior and remarked upon it to Miss Flor. But the little lady was oblivious to all but her own problems.

"*How* could I have made such a fool of myself?" she mourned once again as she and Diana walked in the garden one afternoon. "I do not know what possessed me to act like such a—I shall never be able to face the colonel again. I will not dare to face *anyone*! What Lady Kerwinkle must think—and, oh, Diana, I shudder to think of how Lady St. Aubrey is laughing about me."

"I would not give tuppence for anything that woman says or does if I were you," Diana replied with heat. "She is a—a commoner. The colonel will surely see that."

Miss Flor seemed to droop even further until she looked like a wilted flower. "If he thought that, he would surely have come to call. It has been eleven days, and he has not come anywhere near Blaize Manor." She heaved a deep sigh. "No, it is my fault that I acted like a fool."

Diana could not bear such distress. She hugged Miss Flor and said warmly, "No, indeed. You were magnificent, and if the earl were here, he would tell you the same thing."

She broke off as Lady Radley, hand in hand with Edward, came walking across the garden toward them. "You are taking the air, I see," Lady Radley said. "It is such a beautiful day, is it not?"

Miss Flor sighed deeply while Diana nodded in agreement. Lady Radley went on, "We have been wondering where the dear earl has gone. He has been absent so long."

"I'm sure he'd have told Diana where he was going," Edward piped up, suddenly. "The earl kissed her hand while they were riding on the lake path the day of the hunt. I saw him."

Diana directed a quelling look at Edward, who looked as though butter would not melt in his mouth. "I wish you would not talk such arrant nonsense."

"It's not nonsense. I *saw* him. And he called you 'Diana.' "

"That is not your affair," Miss Flor said, suddenly. More firmly than she had ever spoken, she added, "It is wicked to poke one's nose in other people's business, Edward. You should try to be more like your cousin. Dear Archie would never, never do such a thing."

Edward frowned. He was used to having his own way, yet since he had arrived at Blaize the tables had been turned. Here everyone, even this old trout, thought the world of Archie. Even Archie's disgusting little dog got better treatment than Edward, who was considered a pest and an interloper.

And now Papa was being so beastly about his behaving himself and Mama, who could always be relied upon, had apparently also turned against him for she said quickly. "Now, dearest, it is not polite to tell tales about people." With emphasis she added, "You *know* what your papa said. The earl would *not* approve of eavesdropping. Make your apology to Diana at once."

Before Edward could speak, the sound of wheels was heard in the distance. Shading her eyes, Diana looked down the road. A carriage, driven rapidly, was coming toward the manor house.

"Is that not the earl's carriage?" Diana cried.

She was interrupted by a shout from Archie, who had emerged from the stables. "Lord Lion's come back," he whooped.

He tossed his cap high in the air and commenced running down the road, waving his arms and shouting greetings. Claude bounced after him, yapping joyously. Diana stood where she was, trying to still the tumult in her heart. In a moment, she would *know* if her life would change forever.

She could see Molhouse sitting next to the driver as the carriage came sweeping into the courtyard. Diana picked up her skirts and hurried forward. Consciously she was thinking only of Dracot, but at the sight of Blaize's broad-shouldered form stepping down from the carriage, she involuntarily caught her breath.

As if hearing that small inrush of air, Blaize looked across the courtyard toward the garden. For an instant, their gazes locked, and she saw that he looked weary and grim. Then he smiled at her, and something joyous and wonderful stirred in her heart. *How I've missed him*, she thought.

"Lionel—my dear boy!"

Miss Flor started forward, but before she could reach the earl, another man emerged from the carriage.

"Dracot!" Diana gasped.

It could not be. Could *not*. For a second she stood transfixed. Then, catching up her skirts, she raced forward shouting, "Dracot!"

He looked up, saw her, and began to hurry toward her. The next moment, they were hugging each other. Laughing and crying, Diana whispered, "Drake, oh, dear Drake, you are *alive*."

When he didn't reply, she pulled back and looked at him. He was thinner, and his hair was cut differently. And his arm—

"Waterloo," he said. It was his first word.

"How terrible for you—but it doesn't matter," she cried. "Oh, Dracot, you are alive. I didn't dare hope, even after Archie found Gallant, but the earl said he would find you, and he has done so."

She knew she was babbling, and she didn't care. A miracle had happened, and she felt giddy with thanksgiving. Now Archie came up, beaming. He, too, hugged Dracot, who said in an astonished voice, "You've grown, brat! I wouldn't have known you."

"You've changed, too," Archie replied.

A third man had descended from the carriage. He was a few years older than Archie and was dressed in a countryman's simple clothes. He had a round, fair, gentle face and was looking around him with surprised pleasure.

"This is Raoul Rochard," Dracot explained. "His family took me in and nursed me after I was left for dead." He smiled at Archie. "Raoul likes animals, too, and he speaks a little English. He wanted to see what England was like, so he came along with us for a few days' visit."

"My boy—my dead brother's dear son!" Lady Radley had trotted up and now cast herself, weeping, into Dracot's embrace. She was instantly followed by Lord Radley, who called heaven and earth to witness that he was the happiest man on earth. Not to be undone, Edward threw his arms around Dracot's waist and burst into tears.

Dracot looked helplessly at Blaize, who said, "Time to go inside. There's a story to tell, and it should be told over something strong and warming."

Diana found herself dislodged from Dracot's side. A tearful Lady Radley now hung on his arm, while her spouse on the other side demanded to know how his favorite nephew had escaped the Frog assault. Archie, already deep in talk with Raoul Rochard, followed. Diana looked about for the earl and saw him walking a little apart.

She wanted to go to him, thank him, try to express all that was in her heart, but something in his expression stopped her.

But of course, she told herself. She must not do anything or say anything with Lord and Lady Radley within earshot. *Later*, Diana promised herself happily. Now that Dracot was alive and safe, all would be right in the world.

But even in her joy, as the evening progressed Diana was aware that this world was not as it had been before. Archie was correct: Dracot had changed. The change lay not just in his thinness or in the cut of his hair or even in his maimed arm. He appeared tense, and though he laughed and joked over dinner, laughter never touched his eyes.

Diana told herself that such changes were to be expected. Though he made light of his suffering and instead heaped praise on the Rochards for their generosity, she knew that Dracot had endured great pain. He had come back from the brink of death. Later, when they had time to talk together, Diana reassured herself, he would tell her everything.

She listened carefully as her cousin relayed the story of his convalescence. Dracot had always been a good speaker, and he soon had his dinner companions enthralled.

"When they were sure I wouldn't cock up my toes," he was saying, "Raoul carried me outside each morning. I rested in the shade of a grape arbor at my leisure while the rest of the family waited on me hand and foot."

"*Ma soeur*, Annette," Raoul Rochard begged to explain. In his labored English he told them that Annette had taught Dracot how to eat, and write with his left hand.

Diana watched a spasm of pain shadow cross Dracot's features. "Mademoiselle Annette was patience itself," he agreed. "And a good teacher to boot. She soon had me feeding the chickens and the ducks and even milking cows."

Lord Radley looked scandalized. "But, by my head, you ain't a farmer. Hey? Not something a gentleman's son would do."

"Since my kind hosts were tolerant enough to overtake my mistakes, I was only too happy to be doing something useful."

There was an edge to Dracot's voice, Blaize noticed, and he interposed, "Sometimes work is the best medicine for a wounded man. I wasn't grievously wounded as Dracot was, but after Waterloo I enjoyed riding my land. More than once I helped my tenants in their fields."

"But why?" Lady Radley looked sincerely puzzled. "Surely, my lord, you have more than enough servants to take care of such tasks."

"It felt good to be alive," the earl replied quietly.

Seeing that he had made a tactical blunder, Lord Radley agreed heartily. "Of course. You put it so well, my lord. And now, what, hey?" he asked Dracot. "What will you do now?"

"I have some thinking to do. The world has changed since I went to war." Dracot got to his feet and bowed slightly to the company. "I hope you'll forgive me, but I'm tired from the journey. I'm used to a farmer's hours and now go to bed with the chickens."

Taking her cue, Miss Flor rose and signaled that it was time for the ladies to leave the gentlemen to their port. Diana once again tried to catch the earl's eye, but he was talking to Archie and Raoul again.

Once outside the dining room, Lady Radley approached her niece. "It is incredible that Dracot is alive. And how good, how *noble* of the earl to go himself to Belgium to find your cousin. It was the act of a true gentleman." She paused. "Of course, dear Dracot is not *himself.*"

Diana halted in midstep and turned back to level a long, cool look at her aunt. "What do you mean, ma'am?"

"He is, alas, not *whole,*" Lady Radley pointed out. "It would not matter —if it were not for the fact that the poor boy has not a feather to fly with. Not to peel eggs with you, I recall that my brother Thomas sold everything he owned and borrowed from *your* papa. I can only hope that Blaize is generous with him and allows him some small allowance, poor boy."

Diana had been speechless during all of this. Now she exclaimed, "I beg you will not mention such nonsense in his hearing, Aunt Hortensia. Dracot won't take any man's charity."

"Well, but what else *can* he do?" Lady Radley asked, reasonably. "Work? With that arm? His right arm, too—so unfortunate. Otherwise he could have gone for a clerk in some establishment or other."

She started to walk away and then paused to add, "Of course, if you were to make an advantageous match, *you* would be in a position to help your cousin, would you not? It's a woman's duty to help her *family.*"

Fairness compelled Diana to admit that Lady Radley had touched the painful heart of the matter. Diana could now see why Dracot had seemed so restless through dinner. What, he must have been asking himself, had he come back to?

Sick at heart, Diana climbed the stairs to her room, where worrisome thoughts kept her company till dawn. Then, giving up all pretense of sleep, she dressed with the first light, took up her shawl, and went into the dew-wet garden.

Usually, walking helped her put her thoughts together, but this morning no order would come to her tangled mind. Instead, images came back to nudge her memory. Here at the paddock, Archie had tamed Midnight. Here Miss Flor had picked her chrysanthemums the day the colonel came to call. There on the path to the lake, the earl had kissed her hand.

"Diana!"

She turned quickly, her heart in her mouth, but it was not Blaize who was coming down the pathway toward her. It was Dracot.

"I don't remember your being a particularly early riser," he said.

Diana's spirits lifted. This morning Dracot sounded cheerful, even happy. He was smiling. The shadows on his face had been erased by a good night's sleep. *He was only tired last night*, Diana told herself. *He really hasn't changed.*

"I always got up early," she retorted. "It was you who was a slugabed. Don't you remember the time when Uncle Thomas particularly wished you to get up at the crack of dawn so that you two could ride to hounds?"

"And I woke up at half past twelve," Dracot grinned. "I'll never forget the jaw-me-dead father gave me."

He fell in step with her and they walked together. They had often walked in companionable silence, but today there was no comfort in Dracot's stillness and Diana's earlier uneasiness came back.

"So many things have happened," she said at last. "There is so much to talk about."

Dracot said nothing.

"I'm sorry about Uncle Thomas, Drake. I miss him very much."

"And I was sorry to hear about the loss of your parents." Somberly, Dracot added, "So many people we loved are gone."

The garden seemed to grow darker. Diana put her hand on Dracot's arm and felt not muscle and bone but sleeve.

Quelling the ache in her heart she whispered, "Don't think of yesterday, Drake. There is no use."

For a long moment he did not speak. Then he drew a deep breath that was not quite a sigh. "You're right, Dina. We have to take our fences. *You* are living proof of that, though. I don't know how you survived Uncle and Aunt Radley. Why in God's name did you go to live with them?"

"There wasn't anywhere else to go." It was such a comfort to talk to Dracot again—dear, familiar Dracot. "They were trying to marry me to such *toads*, but, then, luckily the earl sent you a letter."

Dracot listened as Diana told her side of the story. She told it well and with humor, but Dracot was not fooled.

"What a hard time you've had," he exclaimed.

"Not a bit—not compared to you," she said stoutly. "Now, we are well settled—all champion, as Archie would say. *He* is happy, and I have my work to do."

Dracot gritted his teeth. "I can't bear to think of you living on another man's charity," he muttered.

"I don't call it charity. Archie and I have worked for our bread. And there's nothing wrong with work, Drake. In any case, we plan to leave Blaize Manor soon."

"Yes, I know." Dracot agreed. He seemed to hesitate before he added, "Dina, we must be honest, you and I. Before I went away to Waterloo, we made a pledge."

Something sharp and hurtful seemed to have lodged in Diana's throat. Unable to speak, she nodded silently. Dracot said, "As you said yourself, a great deal has changed since then. So have we. Before I went to war I had something not much, I grant, but *something*—to offer you."

Each word that her cousin spoke seemed to filter down to her through a wall of fog. "None of that matters," Diana managed to say.

"I'm a cripple, Dina."

She rounded on him indignantly. "Don't you dare say such a thing, Dracot Gardiner! You know that nothing you have said makes a bit of difference. Don't dare tell me you don't know that!"

He caught both her hands in his one hand and looked down into her eyes. "I want the truth," he said sternly.

"If you love a man, it doesn't matter if he's poor, if he's maimed, even if he's a beggar by the road—" Diana stopped short.

"I don't want pity from my wife."

The word echoed dully in Diana's mind. *Wife*. And all the time she had been talking about love, she had not been thinking of Dracot but of a man with tawny hair and untamed green eyes.

She willed herself to meet his searching eyes squarely. "You'd never have pity from me."

"And this"—he moved his ruined arm, "doesn't matter? Truly, Diana?"

He must not see her hesitate. Dracot had come back from the edge of hell. He had returned poor, maimed, and without prospects. He was her oldest, dearest friend, and she could not abandon him.

"Never," Diana vowed.

Still, his eyes held hers. His mouth was a white line in his sunburned face. "You must be sure."

"Sure," she repeated stoutly. "We'll work together. I'm not afraid of working, Drake."

He drew a deep breath that was almost a sigh. "It may not be necessary," he told her, then. "I'm told that my cousin Theodore died and left me a decent living." He smiled down at Diana's astonished face. "We can buy a small property and a little house and fill it with books. We can take long tramps along the countryside, keep a couple of horses for Archie to enjoy. We'll have a good life."

Somehow he had turned the sentence into a question. Fleetingly, Diana wondered what would happen if her cousin could look into her heart and see the madness that reigned there. Because that was all that it *was*, of course. Madness and moonshine to think that she and the earl of Blaize—

Diana checked the errant thought and smiled back at Dracot who needed her. She had just promised to be his wife, and she would never go back on that promise.

"Yes, my dear, it will be a very good life," she said, and gently kissed his cheek.

They made their announcement together at lunch, and their listeners reacted characteristically. Lady Radley let out a little shriek of astonishment. Archie cheered. Miss Flor clasped her hands and, with tears in her eyes, wished dear Diana very happy. "It is not," she added, "often that love triumphs over disaster."

"Disaster," Lord Radley repeated. His small eyes were almost popping out of their sockets. "Oh, by my head. Disaster!"

"I cannot see why it is a surprise to anyone," Diana said. "Dracot and I were engaged to be married before he went to Waterloo."

"Oh, before Waterloo!" Lord Radley contemptuously waved ancient history aside. "You have to think of the future," he went on urgently. "Neither of you has a feather to fly with. How will you live?"

Dracot explained that he had inherited a living. He glanced at Raoul Rochard, who was listening intently. "I didn't know this when I was with the Rochards, but I've discovered that a distant cousin left me four hundred pounds a year. Neither Diana nor I are extravagant people. She and Archie and I will manage well on that."

It was as he knew it would be from the outset. Blaize had steeled himself for the inevitable, and yet as he looked across the long table at Diana, he felt a desolation so savage and terrible that he could not bear it.

He took refuge in anger, instead. Why had Diana not told him that she was going to announce her engagement today? Surely she owed him this much, at least.

"Will we be living in Somerset?" Archie asked in a subdued tone. "I'll be sorry to leave Midnight and Mr. Urse and everyone," Archie went on, "and both Claude and I will miss Miss Flor and of course, Lord Lion."

Abruptly, the earl rose from his seat. "I wish you happy, Dracot," he said, "and you also, Miss Gardiner. I'm sorry to leave you, but I have some pressing business with my land agent that can't wait."

He bowed to the company and walked out of the room,

which was now abuzz with talk about the reunited lovers' plans. He did not see Diana half rise as if to follow him, and then sink back into her seat. Aware only of his own sense of loss, Blaize did not notice the sorrow in Diana's eyes.

But Lord Radley noticed. Later, when he was alone with his wife, he exclaimed that all was not yet lost. "Blaize isn't happy with the engagement because he's in love with the chit," he said. "I have to think, by my head."

"About what, Simon?" Lady Radley asked timidly. "Since Diana and Dracot are betrothed—"

Lord Radley snarled that he would not countenance such madness. When he thought of all his hopes and schemes of using his niece to gain entrée into Naunce's select circle, he could have gnashed his teeth. "I have to think," he repeated.

While Lord Radley plotted and schemed, Diana spent the afternoon with Miss Flor. That lady had shrugged aside her own troubles to enjoy the happy ending to Diana's romance. "It would be *so* wonderful if you could be married here," she added, wistfully.

"Dracot wishes to return to Somerset, as do I," Diana said. Now that matters had been arranged, she wanted to leave Cumbria as quickly as she could. "The earl has been kindness itself, but we cannot continue to burden him."

"Lionel does not think you a burden," Miss Flor exclaimed. She nodded toward the window, adding, "He has just ridden up. Will you not at least tell him what you plan to do?"

She had not even thanked him properly for bringing Dracot home. He had been so aloof and silent lately, and this was no doubt due to her lack of courtesy. "I will go and talk to him now," Diana said.

The afternoon had turned to a heavy, dusty gold and shadows had begun to grow longer as she left the house and walked down the garden path toward the stable. But the earl was not there, and Archie, who was sitting on the paddock fence with his new friend, Raoul Rochard, told her that Lord Lion had gone walking toward the lake in order to stretch his legs.

As Diana followed the trail to the lake, it came to her mind that everything about this place held memories. Here she had met the earl that day of the ravens. Here they had ridden together when she was trying to teach him to read—Diana's thoughts trailed away as she saw the earl himself standing by the water's edge.

He looked around to see her coming. His somber expression reflected her own mood, and she blurted out the first thing that came to her mind. "You must think me unmannerly beyond all things."

His eyes narrowed, but he only asked, "How so?"

"You have done so much for us—for Dracot and me—and I have not even thanked you."

He turned back to look at the lake. "There's no need for thanks."

There was an edge to his words. He sounded almost like the old Lord Lion, but Diana knew him too well now not to understand. "We owe you everything," she said, firmly. "I wanted to tell you first that we were to marry, but we could not find you. And since we were all together, we thought it best—"

Her words trailed off, and her face was troubled. Blaize took a deep breath and with it let go the unreasoning anger he held against her. The dice had fallen as they should, he reminded himself.

Turning to face her, he smiled wistfully and said, "I'm glad you made your announcement, and I do wish you happy."

But even as she listened to him, all the tumultuous magic between them came surging back along with the feeling that nothing and no one mattered save this one moment together. *Madness*, Diana told herself.

"I'm glad I have the chance to talk to you," the earl was saying. "I needed to ask you something."

Diana's heart had begun to beat faster. "Yes, my lord," she said.

"Dracot's a proud man, I know. I want to do something to ease his way, but he'd refuse me. You, I know, are too sensible to deny a friend the pleasure of giving a wedding gift."

A wedding gift. *Idiot*, Diana named herself. Idiot to have hoped, even for a moment, that the earl was going to tell her that he loved her.

She said in a low voice, "It is kind of you, but there is no need. Dracot and I will do very well together." She managed a smile. "We will rattle along very happily, in fact. We have so much in common that we'll never be lonely."

Lonely, lonely sighed the autumn wind. Blaize felt the chill of it deep in his bones and clenched his teeth against words he knew he must not say.

"You have given us so much," Diana went on earnestly. "Thank you for finding my cousin. If it had not been for you, he might have been lost forever. You have been so kind—so good."

Blaize recalled his moment of temptation in the farmhouse back in Lesec. "I'm neither of those things. You make too much of nothing."

"Not nothing—though I know that Dracot is your friend, too," Diana said in a subdued voice.

I almost succeeded in forgetting, Blaize thought. Aloud he said, "When will you be leaving for Somerset?"

"In a few days. You do not need me any longer."

"But I do need you."

She looked up quickly, her eyes wide; and meeting that velvet darkness, Blaize felt a madness sweep through him. He wanted to pull Diana into his arms and kiss her senseless, kiss her until he had erased every thought of Dracot Gardiner from her mind. He wanted to tell her he loved her and would not let her leave.

He locked his hands behind his back and said in as dispassionate a tone as possible, "I meant that I *have* needed you to make order of that wretched library. You've done wonders and I owe you my gratitude. Now, of course, you and Dracot have made plans for your life together."

Diana was sure that she had only imagined the intense look in Blaize's eyes. The earl was sounding and acting kind, reasonable, and quite calm. If he had a regret, it was because he was losing a satisfactory employee.

"We plan to marry as soon as we return to Somerset," she said finally.

Blaize had steeled himself for these words, but the thought of Diana in another man's arms was almost too much to bear. He forced a smile and changed the subject. "Pratt's asked me to go off for a few days' shooting over the border. I'll be leaving early tomorrow, so I'll say good-bye now in case I don't see you before you leave."

Not to see him again—Hastily Diana shut her mind to the thought. "In that case, good-bye, my lord."

She held out her hand. It was a mistake. The moment he touched her, the old treachery in her blood reignited, and they seemed once more linked in heart and spirit.

With an almost-painful effort of will, Diana disengaged her hand, turned, and began walking hastily toward the house before he could see the tears gathering in her eyes.

"Diana."

She stopped at the sound of his voice. If he came after her now, if he put his arms around her—Instead, he stayed where he was. Only his voice reached out to her as he said, "Diana, thanks aren't enough for what you did for me. I hope you know that you can command me in anything. If I can ever be of service to you, you have only to ask."

She tried to thank him but no words would come. *Put your arms around me*, she wanted to tell him. *Hold me*.

There were footsteps behind her—running footsteps. The earl tore his eyes away from Diana and turned to frown up the path. When Diana looked over her shoulder, she saw Witton racing down. He nearly stumbled, caught himself, and practically careened against a tree in his eagerness to reach the earl.

"What is it?" Blaize demanded sharply. "Where are you going in such a hurry?"

The footman gulped at the fierce look on the lord's face. "A letter from their graces of Naunce, my lord," he quavered, uncertainly. "The man that brought it said it was urgent, like."

The earl snatched the envelope from Witton's hand. The envelope was of heavy cream-colored vellum and bore the ducal crest. Diana watched as he slit the envelope open and scanned the contents.

"Thunder and hell," he exclaimed.

Diana did not need to ask whether the news was bad. She could see that in his face.

"Inform the staff that I want them to assemble immediately," the earl rapped out. "Their graces of Naunce are coming to Blaize Manor for a visit. They arrive tomorrow."

10

Archie whistled under his breath as he made his way toward the stable. It was an hour before dawn, and though the servants were already up and stirring in Blaize Manor, none of the guests were awake.

In spite of his whistling, Archie wore an uncharacteristic frown. He was perplexed about his sister and did not know what to do about it. Though she was outwardly cheerful about leaving for Somerset in a day or two, Archie was sure that Diana was not happy at all.

"I wish I was cleverer in the brainbox," Archie sighed to Claude, who was pattering along at his heels. "I wish I knew what to do."

The dog whined, and Archie bent down to scratch behind Claude's ear. "I don't like the thought of leaving any more than you do."

He sighed and bounced the carrots he had brought for Sultan and Gallant and the lump of sugar that was for Midnight. He himself had mixed feelings about leaving Blaize Manor. And it was not only because of Midnight.

"I like the idea of living in Somerset, but I'll really miss Miss Flor and Mr. Urse and the others," he told Claude. "And I'm really, *really* going to miss Lord Lion."

Claude barked and looked up at his master's face. "I know you want to help," Archie said. "I do, too, but it's all a muddle. I *am* happy that Dracot came back. But Dracot isn't happy, even though he pretends to be." His brows creased in a frown. "And Di and Lord Lion are miserable."

But perhaps this misery was caused by the impending visit of their graces of Naunce. Last night when Lord Lion had ordered his domestic staff to make preparations for his parents' arrival he had looked almost as grim as when the Gardiners first arrived at Blaize Manor. Since then there had been an incredible amount of polishing and washing in the grand house, with the servants rushing about and colliding with each other. Even Molhouse, who always had a ready smile and a joke to share, wore a harassed look.

Archie was silent a moment, musing on the comings and goings at Blaize Manor. The duke and duchess and their entourage were coming while Raoul Rochard had decided that it was time to return to his family in Belgium. It was harvesttime, after all, and he was needed in Lesec.

Raoul was to leave later today. The earl had offered him the use of his carriage all the way to Dover, where Raoul was to take ship to Belgium. "I'll miss Raoul," Archie told his dog. "He's a champion lad who understands animals. And Claude, do you know what? From the way Dracot looked when Raoul said he was leaving, he'll miss Raoul, too."

He paused to scratch his own head. "Tell you the truth, Claude, there's a lot that I don't understand. You can never tell with people. Animals are easier—they don't tell whiskers or hide things from themselves—"

He broke off as he realized that he was not the only one awake at this early hour. On the other side of the paddock, Dracot was walking with Raoul Rochard. Archie waved to them, but they did not see him. They were talking earnestly, their heads bent close, hands jammed into their pockets.

Understanding that they were saying their good-byes, Archie went silently into the stables. Midnight whickered a greeting, as did the other horses, and Archie stroked the animals and dispensed his store of treats. "I wish I could be in two places at once," he told Midnight. "I want to go back to Somerset, but I want to be here, too. Maybe that's how Dracot feels."

He glanced out of the open stable door toward his cousin and Raoul. They were standing by an old stone wall, still deep in conversation. Archie was about to turn away tactfully when he realized that a small figure was hiding in the shadow of the wall.

"What's Edward up to now?" he wondered.

The boy was obviously eavesdropping on the conversation between Dracot and his friend. Archie's eyes narrowed as he watched how Edward flattened himself behind a stone fence as Dracot and Raoul embraced in apparent farewell. Then, Raoul went one way and Dracot the other. Edward remained crouched where he was, and Archie had the feeling that he was vastly pleased with himself.

Edward was smiling. He had had a satisfying morning, and he was bursting with news which his father was sure to find interesting.

Edward thought, he might be able to demand the new pony he had been wanting for a long time. Or, perhaps he would go to Diana first. It depended on who was willing to give him more for the information.

Humming, Edward left the safety of the fence and almost collided with his cousin Archie. For a moment, Edward was too surprised to do anything but stare. Then he managed to call forth an engaging smile.

"Good morning, coz," he said cheerfully. "It's a fine morning. Are you taking the little dog for a walk?" He then attempted to pat Claude, who drew back his upper lip and growled.

"Why were you sneaking up on Dracot and Raoul?" Archie demanded.

"I wasn't sneaking!"

Edward's air of wounded innocence was convincing, but Archie was not fooled. "You were, though. And you'll tell me what you heard," he insisted.

Knowing he had been caught red-handed, Edward pondered his alternatives. His cousin looked as if he meant business, but what he had overheard was too juicy a morsel to let go easily. He eyed the stretch of land between the fence and the house. If he got to the house, there would be mama.

Edward let his shoulders fall helplessly. "I'll tell you," he sighed. "I'll whisper it."

As Archie bent closer, the smaller boy kicked him hard in the shins. Archie howled and fell back, and Edward sprinted for safety. He eeled under the fence, leapt a brook, and was racing toward the garden when he felt something catch at his trousers. Turning, he saw that the small, growling, black-and-white animal had attached itself to his leg. He tried to shake Claude free, but the dog held on tightly.

"Good, Claude," Archie called. He came running up and dropped a strong hand on Edward's shoulder. "*Now*, you gormless young mawworm," he added sternly, "now you can tell us what you overheard."

The residents of Blaize were all so tense that it seemed the manor itself held its breath as the ornate carriage, followed by no less than two conveyances containing baggage and servants, swept through the gates. Molhouse nervously eyed the assembled staff, who stood at attention at the bottom of the front steps of the manor house. He knew from sad experience that he was not his grace of Naunce's choice of valet for his son and that the duke would find fault wherever he could.

Some distance from Molhouse, Urse was admonishing his underlings not to make great gowps of themselves. Meanwhile, the head groom wondered whether his grace and the master would have another grand set-to as they had the last time the duke had come to visit. *That* time, the master had been savage for days after.

Urse glanced worriedly at the earl who was walking down the stairs to meet the approaching carriage. He *looked* calm, but then that was only his training. The master had the cool blood necessary to a soldier, but *this* was different. "Nay, I'd rather face Boney a hundred times afore breakfast than meet up with that duke," Urse muttered under his breath.

Diana was thinking much the same thing. At Dracot's side, she apprehensively watched the ducal carriage's progress. She had been tempted to leave for Somerset the moment she had heard of their graces' impending visit, but she had stifled this cowardly impulse. After all he had done for her, she could not let Blaize face his father alone.

She listened as Dracot recalled, "The first and only time I met the duke was when he came to school and looked down his nose at everything his son did or said. He never raised his voice, but it was as if every word were meant to wound Lion."

The earl passed them on his way down the steps. He was dressed impeccably in a coat and breeches of dove gray superfine, and his white linen gleamed in the sun. He appeared quite calm, but Diana misliked the look in his eyes.

The ducal carriage had come to a stop at the front steps. Urse snapped fingers at the undergrooms, who leapt to hold the horses' heads. Witton moved forward to place steps underneath the carriage door, and the senior footman opened the door with a flourish.

"Where the *hell* is that woman?"

Diana fairly jumped as her uncle's voice resounded almost in her ear. "I'll strangle her, by my head," Lord Radley snarled. "The most important day of m'life, and she's not here."

"Oh, heavens," gasped Miss Flor. Since the news of their graces' impending arrival, she had been in a state of constant agitation. "Has something happened to Lady Radley? Where is she?"

"I don't know!" Lord Radley was almost in tears. "She *knew* she had to be here when the carriage arrived. "By my head, this is the end of everything. We will never have such a chance again. To greet their graces on the steps of an earl's house—*how* could she do this to me?"

As he spoke, Lady Radley came panting down the stairs. "I cannot find Edward anywhere," she exclaimed. "I have *searched*, but he has vanished."

"I'll strangle the brat, too," vowed Lord Radley. He gave his wife a furious glare. "Pull yourself up and straighten your skirt," he snapped, "and then get over here and stand still, madam! The duke's coming out of the coach now."

Diana tried to shut out her uncle's angry voice. Since she had voluntarily removed herself from the duchess's favorite room and was now ensconced near her uncle and aunt, she was unfortunately privy to her relatives' constant brangling.

"His grace of Naunce," Dracot muttered.

A tall, middle-aged gentleman had emerged from the carriage. He descended and looked about him. "Well, Blaize," the gentleman said.

Diana felt as if her heart was being squeezed in a vise. In those two words, his grace had managed to compress an ocean of disapproval and contempt. She held her breath until Blaize replied calmly.

"Welcome to my house, sir."

The duke and his son eyed each other. They were, Diana noted, almost of a height and the family resemblance was keen. But the duke's hair was darker, his features heavier and harder.

Now Blaize was handing down the duchess. Her grace was tall, fashionably slender, and dressed in emerald green, with a pelisse trimmed in ermine. Her modish bonnet trimmed with flowers and leaves bobbed as she raised her cheek to be kissed.

"Lionel," she said in a soft voice. "My dear boy, I did not know that you were already entertaining guests. Have we come at an inopportune time?"

"Not at all, ma'am." The earl offered his mother his arm and strolled with her up the stairs. "My old school friend has come to visit with his family. May I present you?"

The duchess smiled while the duke looked pained. He raised his quizzing-glass as the earl said, "This lady is Miss Diana Gardiner. Miss Gardiner has been kind enough to put my library in order."

Diana felt the duke's cold and intolerant eye settle briefly on her as she curtsied to the ground. Meanwhile the duchess exclaimed, "The library—yes, indeed. How clever you must be, Miss Gardiner. It is good news that the library is in order, is it not, Naunce?"

But the duke was now examining Dracot through his glass. "Dracot Gardiner was my friend at school," Blaize explained.

"I don't recall the name." The duke dropped his glass, gave it a little spin. "Where do you hail from?"

"Somerset, sir." Under Naunce's piercing green gaze, poor Dracot looked vastly uncomfortable. "Lion—I mean, Blaize and I became friends in our last year at school."

"I hope you did better at Harrow than my son," the duke remarked.

Diana held her breath, but Blaize simply introduced her aunt and uncle, who immediately burst into a prepared speech.

"Permit me to say, your graces," Lord Radley began, "that it is an inexpressible honor to meet your graces—"

He was cut short by a freezing stare from the duke. For a full minute, Naunce examined Lord Radley as if he were some interesting species of worm. Then, murmuring a dismissive, "Quite so," the duke walked up the stairs toward the house.

As the earl passed her, Diana saw the tension in his eyes.

"It will be all right," Dracot reassured her. "Lion will know how to deal with Naunce. Besides, they'll all be gone soon."

But watching the seemingly never ending stream of servants carrying trunks and bandboxes into the house, Diana was not so sanguine. "I have never seen Uncle Simon speechless before," she told Dracot. "No doubt their graces will terrorize everyone, especially Archie. He is probably hiding in the stables until the fearsome duke goes away."

She would have liked to have gone in search of her brother, but Miss Flor now professed herself faint. "Give me your arm, Diana," she whispered. "I feel ill and must go and lie down."

Leaning heavily on Diana's shoulder, she tottered up the stairs. "I was afraid of this," she moaned. "It is always this way when Naunce comes to visit. He glares at everyone and disapproves of everything and criticizes all the time. And he picks at Lionel until there is an explosion, after which Lionel is beside himself for a week."

"And the duchess says nothing?"

"The poor lady is too downtrodden by her husband to speak up." Miss Flor put a hand to her head. "My head aches and I cannot think. Perhaps—no, I am *sure*—I will be too ill to come down to dinner. It is no loss. Mrs. Pruitt will do very well."

But the harassed housekeeper soon sought out Diana for advice. "For the cook had planned to serve prawns at dinner," Mrs. Pruitt said. "But his grace's valet says that the duke can't abide them. The cook's in a stamping temper, and his grace's servants are so toplofty that Mr. Molhouse is ready to have spasms—"

She broke off to look mournfully at Diana, who asked, "Is there anything I can do to help?"

The housekeeper was so pathetically grateful that Diana descended to the kitchen, where she discovered Molhouse glaring up at a tall, slender, balding individual.

"Ay *believe*," this disdainful personage was drawling, "that the question of precedence cannot be disputed. The manservant in service to a duke cannot be *compared* to the valet of a mere earl."

He flipped his handkerchief from his pocket and waved it in the air as if to dismiss such a foolish notion, and a cloud of cloying perfume wafted through the air.

Molhouse bristled. "I'll 'ave you know that this is the 'ouse'old of the earl of Blaize," he said with a growl, "and 'is lordship is no 'mere' anything."

Diana looked about the kitchen in dismay. Everything and everyone here was at sixes and sevens. The cook had folded his arms across his chest and was brooding in a corner. The chambermaid, ladies' maids, and housemaids appeared cowed and scared. The footmen were glaring at the duke's servants, who were looking down their noses at everything.

"That pompous turnip," Molhouse grated as the duke's valet minced out of the kitchen with his entourage of underlings in tow. "I'll show *'im* a thing or two if 'e don't take care."

Diana drew him aside. "It's you who must take care," she warned. "You are much more sensible than they are, Molhouse—surely you can see that—and the earl's honor depends on your good sense."

She continued to speak calmly and reasonably until Molhouse stopped fuming to allow, "You may be right. But—"

"The servants of his grace are all puffballs," Diana said. "They like to bully people because that makes them feel important."

The earl's domestic staff then gathered close to listen.

"I know that the earl trusts all of you and has confidence that you can rise above irritating snubs," Diana went on. "Miss Flor is unwell, and the atmosphere is full of tension. If we do not all pull together, we will all be in the soup."

There was silence until Molhouse roused himself. "Miss Gardiner's right." The light of battle shone in his shoe-button eyes as he added, "They're below hour notice, see? Let them twiddlepoops puff and blow. We won't care. We'll be terribly, terribly polite to them. Make them madder than 'ornets, that will."

The staff laughed somewhat nervously. Mrs. Pruitt began to issue directions. Leaving her and Molhouse to restore harmony, Diana went back up the steps to the main floor.

The house seemed at rest, but there was a brooding silence to it that made her think of the quiet before a storm. As she walked up the stairs toward her room, Witton came running up to her and said that her presence was requested in the library.

"Requested by whom?" Diana asked, whereupon Witton abandoned his footman's gravity and whispered that the earl and duke had gone into the library half an hour since.

"And I 'eard them talking back and forth, ma'am, but neither of 'em 'as come out," he concluded.

No doubt his grace disapproved of the work she had done. Steeling herself to meet this ducal censure, Diana walked slowly across the hall toward the library. The door was closed, but as she approached, she could hear the rise and fall of male voices. She paused, took a deep breath, and knocked.

A familiar, deep voice bade her enter, and as Diana stepped into the room, she saw Blaize standing by the oriel windows. He was watching his father walk about the room.

"Thank you for coming," Blaize said. "My father wanted to meet the lady who accomplished all this."

His tone and smile were reassuring. Not so the appraising look the duke leveled on her.

"So you're responsible for all of this?" he demanded. When she curtsied silently by way of acknowledgment, he said roughly, "Don't gammon me. Do you tell me that a chit like you put all this to rights?"

The patent disbelief in his voice was galling, but Diana replied evenly, "Yes, your grace. Of course his lordship the earl helped me on occasion."

"Ha!"

The bark of laughter was followed by yet another unnerving stare. "My son has never bothered to touch a book much less frequent a library," the duke said. "He is not *interested* in matters of the mind. His brothers, on the other hand, are of a different breed. Nicholas will go far in the House, and Theodore is a likely lad. Ah, well, there is always one in a litter who disappoints."

Blaize's face did not change, but Diana knew that this barb went deep. "Perhaps," she dared to say, "you do not know your son as well as you think you do."

The duke's eyes narrowed at this impertinence. But before he could speak, Blaize said drily, "I doubt you asked Miss Gardiner to come here so that you could discuss me." He turned to Diana. "My father was impressed with the way you organized the books. I doubt if his library at Naunce is better."

"How would you know? You were never in it."

"It was not my library, sir. This one is since my cousin willed it to me." Blaize held his father's eyes as he added, "I must thank you for suggesting it to him. His bequest has given me a great deal of pleasure."

The duke started to speak, stopped, and gave his son an odd look. "Knew about that, did you?"

"As you've always said, a man must know his enemies. The same can be said about a man's family."

It seemed to Diana that the earl and his father locked eyes across drawn swords. The duke attempted to stare his son down, but Blaize's gaze did not waver, and after a while the duke turned back to Diana.

"You've done satisfactory work here," he grunted. "Are you staying on at Blaize?"

"No, your grace. I am leaving for Somerset in a few days' time."

"Then the library will go to dust and damnation again—unless Blaize can find a replacement."

"I can never replace her," Blaize said without looking at Diana. "I plan to take over where she left off."

I can never replace her. Diana spoke through a suddenly tight throat. "If that is all, your grace, I must be on my way. Miss Flor is not feeling well, and I must look in on her."

The duke waved a dismissive hand. Once Diana left the room, he added, "A bit above herself for an employee. But then she's got a fine head of hair and those black gypsy eyes, so I don't blame you. If I were young, I'd probably think I couldn't replace her, either."

Anger flashed deep in Blaize's eyes. "Miss Gardiner is a lady. I have every respect for her. I'm sure you knew that, or you wouldn't be trying to goad me into losing my temper."

The duke frowned. He was not used to his son's even tone. By now, Lionel should have been baring his teeth. Instead he was regarding his father with a calm detachment that was somehow unsettling.

He tried again. "So she's a lady, is she? But down on her luck. 'Fallen on hard times,' as the saying goes. Otherwise she wouldn't have been forced to earn her bread by working in some damnable library, and those mushrooms, her aunt and uncle, wouldn't be toad-eating you." Still, Blaize remained unruffled. "Did they think they could arrange a marriage between you and their niece?" the duke sneered.

As was his wont, Naunce had managed to get to the heart of the matter. Silently cursing his father, Blaize turned away and walked to the window. "Miss Gardiner is engaged to my friend, Dracot."

"But that would be changed in an instant, if that rapacious Radley could have his say. Young Gardiner's lost an arm and he doesn't have a title—or well-connected parents." He paused. What's the matter, boy? Cat got your tongue?"

"What does your grace want me to say?" Blaize asked coldly.

Something in the younger man's voice made the duke frown. His son had changed, and this kept him off balance. "You usually say too much," he prodded. "The last time I was here, you raised your voice like a stevedore."

Blaize smiled.

"You find that amusing?"

"If I said too much then, I'm taking care to balance the scales by saying nothing now." Blaize leaned back against the window, folded his arms across his chest and met his father's eyes. "You see, sir, I intend to please you for once."

Before the duke could respond, there was a scream from the other side of the door. It was followed by something heavy falling, then running footsteps and finally Witton's voice shouting for Miss Gardiner. "What the devil is that?" Naunce demanded.

Blaize strode across to the library door and pulled it open in time to hear Lady Radley wailing, "Oh, my child, my child.

Oh, I *knew* something terrible would happen if I brought my innocent to the ends of the earth."

"Damn that woman," Blaize muttered. "What is the matter with her now?"

He strode down the hallway and found Lady Radley collapsed on the daybed in the morning room. Diana was on her knees beside her aunt, chafing her limp wrists while Lord Radley alternately ordered and pleaded with his wife to stubble it.

"I tell you, the brat's just gone off somewhere," he snapped. "Probably taken a walk with Dracot or that half-wi—I mean, with young Archie. Nothing to carry on about, by my head."

Like a rearing cobra, Lady Radley sat up and fixed her husband with a penetrating stare. "How *can* you, my lord! How can you speak of your only son in such a cavalier and unfeeling way! You have no proper family feeling. You are debased!"

"What," snapped the duke, "is the meaning of this farce?"

Lord Radley literally jumped. He turned as if stung, saw who was addressing him, and his countenance, which had been quivering with aggravation, suddenly attempted to transform itself into an ingratiating expression. "Nothing, your grace, nothing," he stammered. "My dear wife—susceptible to emotion as all females are, your grace. You know how the fairer sex is disposed to enacting Cheltenham tragedies—"

"No," said the duke coldly. "I do not." Then he turned to Lady Radley. "Madam," he snapped, "cease howling at once and tell us what the matter is."

Lady Radley stopped in midshriek and stared at the duke. She then began to cry noisily. Above her sobs, Diana explained, "Edward seems to be missing."

"Missing? For how long?" Blaize demanded.

"Since breakfast, I think Aunt Hortensia said." Diana bent over her wailing relative and spoke firmly, "I know you are distressed, but you must tell the earl what is the matter. He can't help you unless he knows what has happened."

Lady Radley lifted her tear-stained face and whispered, "Edward has been gone since this morning. I did—did not see him at breakfast, but that is not unusual. My darling often likes to get up early and walk about enjoying the fine morning air and the dew on the leaves and buds—"

"I think we can dispense with the buds and flowers," Blaize interrupted. "If he's only gone since morning, I agree with your husband. The boy's up and gone for a long walk. Still, it won't hurt to look about. I'll have Urse take one of the other grooms and ride over the estate."

"What can *servants* do?" moaned Lady Radley. She fixed a fulminating eye on Lord Radley. "If you had any feeling at all, *you* would go, my lord. It was *your* idea, after all, to come here to the ends of the—"

"All right," Lord Radley said with a snarl. "All *right,* madam, I'll go. Better to go riding than sit here and listen to your plaint, by my head. But," he added savagely, "that brat will be home for his supper, see if he ain't. And he's not going to be able to sit for a week, neither."

11

Having prevailed upon her lord to search for their missing child, Lady Radley tottered off to bed. Blaize, along with the duke, repaired to the stables to give Urse instructions. Diana gave the frightened housemaids last minute directions for the dinner and then went wearily in search of Dracot, whom she found reading in the library.

He looked up smiling when she entered the room and asked, "Has all the hullabaloo died down yet?" he asked.

"More or less. The duke expressed a desire to see the estate, so Blaize and he went for a canter." Diana sank down beside Dracot with a sigh. "Urse is looking for Edward, but so far he hasn't been found. Where can that tiresome child have gone?"

"If I were Urse, I wouldn't look too hard," Dracot remarked. "The little bleeter followed me this morning when I went to say good-bye to Raoul, and I had to threaten him with a thrashing before he let us alone. He's a sneak and a liar, and I don't trust him."

"You sound like Archie." Diana knitted her brows and added, "I wonder where Archie has got to?"

"Perhaps he has gone for a ride on Midnight," Dracot said. "I know how sorry he is to leave that horse. Sorry to leave this place, come to that."

"It's only that this is the first place where he has felt happy since Papa and Mama died."

"And *you*? Will you be sorry to leave, too?"

She was unprepared for the rush of emotions that welled through her. For a moment the memory of Blaize's strong arms and passionate kisses was so vivid that she could not speak. She shook her head, instead.

"Are you sure?" Dracot asked. His direct eyes held hers as he added, "I want you to be very sure, Dina," he said. "I want you to be happy."

Rallying, she forced a smile. "What moonshine is this? Of course I will be happy, you sapskull." He grinned at that and she added heartily, "Do you think I am going to let you out of my sight again?"

He took her hand in his and held it tightly. "I'll make you happy," he promised. "No more broken hearts, Dina."

I can never replace her.

Ignoring the ache Blaize's words made her feel, Diana said, "I think I should look in on Miss Flor."

She was sure that this latest development at Blaize Manor must have thrown the little lady into spasms, but when she stopped by her chamber, Miss Flor was not only up, but preparing to confront the Naunces.

"I must deal with the matter at hand," she said in a determined little voice. "If Blaize is looking for Edward, the duke and duchess must be entertained." She paused to add hopefully, "Doubtless Edward will return before supper."

But come supper the boy was still missing. Lord Radley and several attendant grooms rode in later that afternoon, and Diana was astonished at the change in her uncle's face. From petulant it had become highly anxious. Lady Radley took one look at her spouse and shrieked, "You have not found him! I *knew* that he would come to harm. It was your idea to bring him to the ends of the world—"

"Oh, be quiet!" snapped Lord Radley. "Don't pull a Friday face with me just because the brat's playing one of his pranks. Hey? Urse will bring him home."

But when Urse rode in half an hour later, he was alone. Her hand on her heart, Lady Radley faltered, "Oh, my child, my poor boy! Cutthroats and footpads may have harmed him. Gypsies may have stolen him."

Diana noticed how unhappy Urse looked and remarked,

"There is something more. What is it, pray?"

"Master Edward was sighted," the head groom said reluctantly.

Lady Radley sat bolt upright, clutched her heart, and begged Urse to enlighten a Grieving Mother.

Lord Radley snarled, "I knew it. I'll have his hide, by my head. Where's he got to, hey?"

"Nay, he was seen leaving t'town," Urse said even more reluctantly. "He were riding pillion on one of t'earl's horses along wi' that young Belgian fellow. They were making for Grassmere."

"Haven't I always said, never trust a Frog?" Lord Radley reached forward and clutched Urse's arm. "Where was that foreigner taking my son?"

"I dunnot know." Urse swallowed hard. "I do know that—that Master Archie were with them. He were riding Midnight."

Lady Radley let out a banshee scream. "Those monsters have stolen my child!"

Everyone started talking at once. Lady Radley seized her husband by the lapels of his jacket and insisted that he go immediately and bring her baby back to her. Miss Flor protested that Archie would not be involved in anything shameful. Urse protested that Master Archie and Mr. Rochard had probably only taken the boy for a ride. Lord Radley announced his intention to ride immediately and apprehend Archie and hale him back by the scruff of the neck.

"The fellow's a horse thief and now he's kidnapped my son along with that poxy Frog," he fumed. He rounded on Diana. "This is how you repay our kindness, hey? By my head, when I catch up to your brother, he'll be sorry he was born."

"I don't know what this is all about, but I am sure that there is some explanation," Diana cried. "Archie would not hurt anyone."

"Hah!" was all Lord Radley said before leaving the room. Diana turned to Dracot.

"Please," she begged, "ride with Uncle Simon. If he should find Archie, he will do him harm."

As a grim-faced Dracot followed hard after his uncle, Lady

Radley turned on Diana. "If your brother hurts my son," she cried, "I will see him hanged!"

She then proceeded to go into hysterics. While Miss Flor and the servants attempted to minister to her, Diana backed slowly out of the room. She was shocked and horrified to her deepest soul. "It can't be," she whispered. "Archie would never steal Midnight. And—and he would *never* hurt anyone."

But, some part of her mind reminded her that Archie had been terribly distressed about leaving the black stallion behind. Archie seldom saw things as others did—he followed a logic of his own. He might have reasoned that if he took Midnight and went away, they could be happy together.

But why, then, would he take Edward—and why was Raoul Rochard involved as well? "Oh, what a mare's nest," Diana moaned.

At least Dracot had gone after Lord Radley to prevent him from hurting Archie—but even this reassurance failed when Diana recalled that Lord Radley had two good arms. In his fury he might harm Dracot, too.

"I should have gone after Uncle Simon myself," Diana exclaimed. Then she added, "I *will* go. Archie will listen to me."

Not waiting to change into a riding habit or even take her bonnet and shawl, Diana ran toward the stables. As she did so, Archie's little dog came pattering out. "Claude," Diana exclaimed.

The dog whined in a forlorn way. When she bent down to stroke his unruly fur, she could feel the little animal trembling.

"He has left you behind," she murmured distractedly. "That is not like Archie at all. Oh, Claude, now I *am* afraid for him. I must go after them at once."

The grooms were just bringing in the horses for the day and were astonished to find Miss Gardiner saddling Firefly with her own hands. And in the next minute, they were staring and scratching their heads at the way Miss was riding away from Blaize Manor as if the devil himself were nipping at her heels.

But the devil was the least of Diana's problems. As she rode, troubling images rose in her mind's eye. She thought of Edward's sly underhandedness, his small cruelties. Perhaps

Archie had found him trying to hurt the horses and had become so enraged that he had become violent. "Archie would never hurt anyone," Diana whispered to herself, but the terrible thought nagged at her.

She had ridden no more than a few miles when she saw a horseman cantering down the road toward her. It was Blaize.

"What's the matter?" he hailed her. "Has Edward been found?"

She shook her head and stammered, "Archie has taken Midnight and Edward and gone away. Raoul Rochard was with them. I must follow—"

"Follow them where? You're not making sense." Blaize caught Firefly's bridle, forcing her to stop. "Tell me," he ordered.

Almost incoherently, Diana told her story. By the time she had finished, dry sobs were racking her. The earl said nothing but swung down from his horse and came around to look up at her. "Get down, Diana," he directed. "No, I mean it. Walk with me and talk it out. It won't help your brother to come to pieces like this."

He held out his arms to help her down and mutely she leaned into his embrace. "I'm here and I'll help you," she heard him say.

Diana could not help herself. She clung to the arms that held her so strongly. "I'll find Archie," Blaize promised.

Wordless, she looked up at him, her eyes swimming with unshed tears. Blaize forced himself to ignore the need to kiss those tears away and with a superhuman effort, he let her go. He then locked his hands behind his back and asked, "Where's Dracot?"

"He rode after Uncle Simon. He will try and keep Archie from being hurt, but—but I was afraid that my uncle might be too strong for him. I told myself I needed to follow him, but I see now that that was untrue. . . . I needed to find you."

"Why, Diana?"

She could have said because Uncle Simon will listen to you. She could have said because you are much stronger than Dracot and besides Midnight is your horse. But instead of any of these reasonable answers Diana told the truth. "Because I love you."

"What about Dracot?" Blaize asked in a hushed voice.

"He is my friend, my dearest cousin, I love him—but not in that way. I never knew," Diana said, "what love even was until I met you."

Still he did not take her into his arms. He only looked down into her face with such an ache of longing that her tears dried and she whispered, "Don't you believe me, Lionel?"

"Yes," Blaize said. "God help me, I do."

He caught her hard against him then, holding her so tight she could hardly breathe, and she leaned against his hard chest and felt that she had come home after a long, hard, dark journey.

"I love you," Blaize said, passionately. "You don't know how damnably close I came to—I love you more than my honor, Diana."

He was going to kiss her. It was what she had thought about, dreamed about, wanted all these long days. Recklessly, Diana lifted her face to him, but he did not kiss her.

"I almost left Dracot in Belgium," he told her. "I almost convinced myself to lie to you and say that he was dead. But—he's not."

The bleakness in his voice brought sanity back. Diana felt as if she had been touched with ice, for Dracot was not dead. Dracot had suffered so much and lost so much and must never be hurt again.

They looked at each other with almost unbearable pain. Then, the earl dropped his hands so that they hung at his sides. In a bleak voice he said, "This was my fault."

She began to protest, but he cut her short. "We can't let it happen again. We mustn't be alone like this again. He mustn't know how we feel for each other. You loved him before. You'll grow to care for him again and be happy."

She nodded mutely. There was nothing she could possibly say. She could only watch as Blaize mounted his horse.

"Go back to the house," he directed, "and don't worry. I'll bring Archie back."

But as he rode away Diana knew that it was no longer Archie who was tearing her heart in two.

Even though there was hardly anyone to eat it, the grand dinner prepared for their graces proceeded as planned. Nervous footmen proceeded to serve up dish after dish at the long table attended by their graces, Diana, and Miss Flor, who attempted not to flinch every time the duke looked her way.

Actually, his grace seemed to be in a relatively benign mood. He ate with appetite, though no one else seemed to be very hungry.

"How is Lady Radley?" asked the duchess, waving away a platter of roasted capons.

"She is sleeping," Miss Flor replied. "I truly do not know how such a thing could have come about. What could have possessed Archie to run away and take Edward?"

Diana was too miserable to answer. The duchess looked down at her barely touched plate. "I am so sorry for Lady Radley," she sighed. "She looks so distrait."

"Good God, madam," the duke said irritably, "can we talk about nothing except those foolish brats?"

There was the sound of clattering hoofbeats outside, and a loud voice was heard to declaim, "Hoy! Where in hell is the groom *wallah* to hold my horse?"

Miss Flor gave a faint shriek. "It is the colonel," she stammered. "Oh, I cannot face him! Excuse me all, please. She jumped to her feet and fled from the room whilst the duke cast up his eyes and wondered why his son's domicile was populated by idiots. "First an exodus of Frogs and brats and now this," he exclaimed.

On the heels of his grace's words, Colonel Pratt came striding into the dining room. Both his riding clothes and boots were splashed with mud, but the precision of his salute to their graces of Naunce would have given credit to his former regiment.

"Servant, your grace," he roared at the duke. "Your most obedient, ma'am. Glad to see you back at Blaize Manor." Hardly waiting for a return of courtesies he swung toward Diana adding, "My groom brought news about your trouble, Miss Gardiner. Been out ridin' all day, unfortunately, and just came home. Mean to start tryin' to track down your brother at once. Yes. Got all my servants mobilized and ready."

He waved away Diana's thanks. "*Chut*, ma'am, *chut*. Neighbors, egad. Besides, this is dashed smoky business. Young Gardiner's not the sort to lope off with another man's horse."

As he spoke, the colonel kept looking about the table. Drily, his grace of Naunce asked, "Have you lost something, Pratt?"

The colonel looked embarrassed, and then said that he would be riding home. He refused the duchess's suggestion that he stay and dine but added, "If I might—a word with you, Miss Gardiner?"

Perhaps he knew something about Archie that he had not wanted to say in front of their graces. With a sinking heart, Diana followed the colonel into the hall, where he cleared his throat several times.

"I've been wonderin' how you were doin' with all of this. Naunce comin' and setting everythin' by the ears. Antagonizin' Blaize as he always does. And now all this about young Gardiner. A lot on your plate."

He lowered his voice to a solicitous rumble. "Worried that all this might be too much for Mi—for you ladies. Females don't have the stomach for trouble."

Diana did not know what to say, so she remained silent. The colonel cleared his throat again, and poked at the carpet with the muddy toe of his boot. "Miss Flor prostrated with worry, is she?"

"She is most distressed." Diana added cautiously, "She has been upset—for some time."

The colonel puffed so hard that his mustaches blew untidily about. "Can understand that," he said unhappily. "Horrible scene that day at the hunt. What with me thrown from Midnight and then that woman *laughin'* at her—Miss Flor's right to be hipped."

The colonel squinted balefully into the near distance. "Always thought myself a brave man," he declared. "Dealt with any amount of *budmarshes* in Inja—faced tigers and thuggees and never fought shy. But didn't dare ride out here to face Miss Flor again after I made such a dashed fool of myself."

As a deep magenta began to creep into the colonel's cheeks, Diana's sluggish brains finally commenced to work. "Is that why you have not come to call on us since the day of the hunt?" The colonel rumbled incoherently. "Miss Flor thought it was because she had disgraced herself forever in your eyes."

"Hey?" the colonel spluttered. He swung around to face Diana, his eyes bright with hope. "Mean to say she doesn't consider me an old duffer without any—any bottom?"

Diana shook her head.

"Such a shy lady, I always thought, but now I understand how bravc she can be. Stood up to them all like a *pukka sahib*. Took up the gauntlet for young Gardiner and the horse and—and for me. And then that St. Aubrey woman dared to *laugh* at her. Tell you the truth, Miss Gardiner—I wanted to strangle that woman."

"You must tell Miss Flor how you feel," Diana cried.

The colonel's mustaches seemed to bristle in agitation. "Couldn't do that," he muttered hoarsely.

"But she—"

"If I was Miss Flor," the colonel interrupted, "I'd shut the door in my face. Egad, yes, I would. Think of it, ma'am—there I was, lyin' like a dashed dead fish. Didn't even try to defend Guenevere—I mean Miss Flor. I let her be laughed at and scorned. No wonder she left the table tonight when she heard me comin'. Couldn't stomach lookin' at me, and I don't blame her."

In vain Diana tried to assure the colonel that he was wrong.

"Kind of you to try and soothe my feelin's, but I have to be a man and leave her be. Nothin' left for a gentleman to do." He tugged at his mustache for a long moment and then attempted to look cheerful. "Don't worry about young Gardiner, ma'am—he'll turn up all right."

Diana saw the colonel out and stood looking after him into the darkness. It had begun to rain, and a cold wind was blowing. "Where are you?" she whispered.

"Where, indeed." Diana started as she saw that the duchess had come to stand beside her. "I know you must be worried," she went on, "but do not give in to despair. My son will not rest until those boys are found. Lionel is the strongest one in the family, and he will never give up."

Surprised, Diana turned to look at the duchess and saw resignation and sadness in that lady's mild eyes. "I had thought," she said frankly, "that his grace would have that distinction."

"I said strong, Miss Gardiner, not strong willed."

The duchess smiled a little sadly. "We are all made as we are made," she said. "That is life. My dear papa used to say that I was a rabbit and that Naunce was a tiger. Our oldest son is like his father, Theodore is more subtle and cautious. And our daughters are like me."

Wind sighed against the ladies' skirts. Diana listened, astonished as to why the duchess was telling her such things.

"But we were speaking of Lionel," her grace continued. "Lionel is the only one who stood up to his father all these years."

"At what cost!" Diana checked herself. "I beg your pardon, ma'am," she added hastily. "I should not have said that."

The duchess shrugged the apology away. "Why not, when it is the truth? It is only what I have thought myself."

Without thinking, Diana replied, "And yet you said nothing? Even when your son was punished and humiliated?"

"I protested at first—but it was no use. In his household, Naunce's word is law. Lionel knew the consequences, but he rebelled. It was his choice."

The duchess looked hard at Diana and then smiled quite warmly. "Now, we must go in. It is growing colder and a wind is coming up from the lake, and it may be hours before Lionel returns."

It was considerably later and much colder when Dracot and Lord Radley rode in. Miss Flor and their graces had long since gone to bed, but Diana was up and waiting for news. Both men looked exhausted, and though Lord Radley attempted to bluster, his heart was not in it.

"Thought for sure they'd try to make a run across the border," he said with a low growl. "Nothing—not a trace of any of them on the northern road."

While Lord Radley climbed the circular staircase to his room, Diana caught Dracot's arm and held him back.

"Where are they, Drake? What could have happened to them?"

"God knows," Dracot replied. "We rode all the way up to Carlisle, but no one's seen or heard from them."

There were lines of pain around his mouth, but he waved off Diana's anxious queries. "I'm all right. Some sleep and I'll be ready to ride again. Don't despair, Dina—Lion may bring some news."

The earl did not return till morning. Diana, who had slept fully dressed in a chair by the window in her chamber, heard his voice and ran outside to meet him. One look at his face, and she knew that he had found out something.

"I found Midnight and the horse Raoul Rochard rode at an

inn in Grassmere," he reported grimly. "Apparently Archie asked the innkeeper to return the horses to me."

"But where *is* Archic?"

"He, Edward, and Raoul Rochard were seen taking the Yorkshire-bound mail coach. They got as far as Leeds, but there the trail went cold. I made inquiries all up and down Yorkshire, but they were nowhere to be found."

Diana fairly wrung her hands. "Then they must have come to some harm. Lady Radley spoke of footpads and cutpurses. Perhaps they are hurt—"

"Stop it." He caught her by the arms and held her for a moment, then abruptly let her go. "Don't look like that," he said fiercely. "They did get as far as Leeds, anyway. Raoul Rochard doesn't look like a fool to me, and I'd put money on Archie any day."

Diana wanted nothing more than for Blaize to put his arms around her and comfort her. It took effort to say, "You are looking exhausted. You need to rest, my lord."

It wasn't rest that he craved, Blaize thought. Looking down into her upraised face, he had to fight an almost irrepressible need to embrace her. Aloud he said, "I left Urse in Yorkshire. He'll continue to search. Molhouse has gone on to Dover, in case they think to go to Belgium with Rochard. Now, come to the house. You're shivering."

Word of the earl's return had awakened the household. When Blaize and Diana returned to the house, they found that even their graces had arisen and were waiting in the first floor morning room. When brought abreast of the situation, Dracot said that he would get ready to leave at once, and Lord Radley declared that he would ride as well. Lady Radley fell into a chair, her face the color of putty, and for once Diana truly felt sorry for her aunt.

"They are safe," she tried to say around the lump in her own throat. "Please try not to worry, Aunt Hortensia. Edward will be found."

Lady Radley began to sob. As the ladies attempted to comfort her, the duke walked up to his son. "This does not look well," he said. "They may all be dead by now."

Looking somber, Blaize took a cup of coffee from the tray that Witton had just brought in. "I've alerted the law to that possibility. But there's no use alarming the women."

The duke grunted. "You've done all you can, then. Let others do the rest."

"I promised Miss Gardiner I'd find her brother."

The earl glanced at Diana, who was kneeling beside her aunt, and then forced himself to look away. "I'll wash and eat and be on my way again."

"Headstrong as always." There was a grudging admiration in the duke's voice. "Once you have an idea in your head, you'll not let it go. You remind me of myself when I was your age."

The earl set down his cup and regarded his father. The hard green eyes of the young man met the identical set of his father's hard green eyes.

"Indeed," Blaize said.

The coldness of that one word made the duke wince. "We are of the same blood," he snapped. "What do you expect?"

"This is the first time you've ever suggested that," Blaize retorted. "At least without a cane in your hand."

He then walked out of the room. The iron control with which he had held himself was frayed from hours without sleep, hours of anxiety for Diana, for Archie. He needed an hour's rest before setting out again. But as he approached the stairs, he heard his father's voice behind him.

"Lionel," the duke said, "a word."

The hand that held the stair rail clenched momentarily, then eased. "Can it wait, sir?"

Foolish even to ask. The duke could never wait for anything that he wanted. He simply stood there waiting until his son walked down the hall and opened the door to the library. "After you, your grace," he said.

Frowning, the duke strode into the room. In contrast to the rest of the house, it seemed like an oasis of calm. Vases of Miss Flor's autumn asters had been arranged throughout the room. The curtains had been drawn back, and the pallid morning sun shone through the high oriel windows.

Blaize stood by the door waiting as the duke walked into the center of the library, looked around him and nodded. "Astonishing changes," he remarked.

His son said nothing, and after a moment the duke added, "I

don't mean just the library. You are not as you used to be."

"All life is change," Blaize replied.

"Don't try to diddle me with old saws." The duke took a turn around the room, stopped and added, "You said, a moment ago, that I always had a cane in my hand. I suppose it must have seemed that way to you. It was my intention to be cruel."

Again, Blaize remained warily silent.

"Life is cruel," the duke explained further. "It can defeat a weak man. Just because you were Naunce's son didn't mean that there were no dangers ahead of you. I've seen too many rich men's sons turn into pigeon fanciers and rackety care-for-nobodies who game and drink and throw their lives away. My own brother's sons are drunken sots. Your mother's brother gamed his estate away."

The duke clenched his fist, thumped it into the palm of his other hand. "I wanted my sons to be strong."

Something flashed deep in Blaize's eyes, but his voice was calm. "By your standards," he said. "By *your* measure. By *your* mark. It was always about you and what *you* wanted."

The duke snorted, looked ready to deliver a quelling set-down, changed his mind, and instead said, "Perhaps it seemed so."

"There's no 'perhaps' about it."

"It was the way I was raised myself. Your grandfather was a stern man." Naunce frowned as if at some unpleasant memory. "Your mother is a weak woman. Her brother was worse than weak. I did not want you to be like them."

"So you toughened me up with a cane. Effective, sir!" Bitterness hardened Blaize's voice as he added, "If I ever fill my nursery, I'll not use a cane. It degrades. It hurts the spirit. You wanted me to be strong, but you almost convinced me I was worthless. If it hadn't been for—"

If it had not been for Diana. Diana sitting on Peavey Hill with the book in her hands. Diana, patient and serious and absorbed. Diana with tears in her eyes crying, "I *knew* you could do it, I knew!"

The passion died from Blaize's voice. "If that's all, I need to be on my way."

"Wait," the duke commanded, as his son strode to the door. "Perhaps I was wrong."

The earl stopped short, his hand on the door. He turned and looked quizzically at his father.

"I *was* wrong," Naunce said.

"I can't believe it. *You* admitting a fault?"

"Well, believe it," snapped the duke. "I say to your head that I was wrong. Not in what I tried to do but in the method. I did not beat you because I despised you, Lionel. It was because you were my son."

For a second, the duke's harsh voice sank, almost shook. As silence fell heavy on the room, Blaize felt a sudden ache slice through the bitterness in him, touch a place in his heart that he believed had withered long ago.

"If you had said all this years ago," he began, but his father interrupted him.

"What Cheltenham tragedy is this?" he demanded, harshly. "Do we now fall on each other's necks and weep?"

He turned his facc away and added in his old, arrogant way, "At any rate, I succeeded in what I set out to do. You've grown strong after all. That's all I had to say to you, and now you can go to the devil."

And that, Blaize thought, was about all he could expect. He started to leave the library, then paused to look at his father. He could not believe it, but he had just seen the duke's shoulders sag. He had never seen that ramrod straight back ever droop before. It was almost as if the proud duke knew that he had been judged and found wanting in the eyes of his son.

Blaize watched his father's averted face and wondered at himself. Why he should feel any kind of sympathy for Naunce was beyond him. Such an emotion would be as unwanted as it was unwarranted, and yet—

And yet he could not hate the man any longer. When he searched his heart, Blaize found that instead of the usual roil of bitterness and impotent anger, he was feeling sadness and a vague sense of pity.

"What, still here?" Naunce turned to look hard at his son. "You look exhausted. Best rest—or at least ride carefully."

And then, lest Blaize see the anxiety in his eyes, he said, "All that's needed in this havey-cavey affair is for you to break a leg—or your damned, stiff neck."

12

Dracot Gardiner stood by the window and looked past the pellets of rain beading the glass. Long, long ago the first countess of Blaize had planted fruit trees in the south garden, and the faithful old trees still bore fruit. Glimmers of red apples showed even though most of the fruit had been picked.

"Why the sigh?" Diana asked from behind.

Dracot looked up, smiled, and shook his head.

"Are you thinking of Archie? I know he has been gone ten days, but the earl says there is still hope."

"Of course there is. I wasn't thinking about Archie, though, not just now. I was remembering Lesec, all green and gold in the spring rain. In many ways, it is like Somerset." His smile changed, turned pensive. "I miss being home."

Diana bit her lower lip to stop the tremble. "I know you want to go home," she said in a low voice.

"You do?" Dracot looked astonished for a moment before comprehension dawned in his eyes. "You mean home to Somerset."

"I realize that it will soon be winter and the roads will be hard to travel. But I cannot leave—not until Archie and Edward have been found."

If indeed they ever would be found. The local constabulary had been called in, and the possibilities they raised tormented Diana. Archie could have taken Edward for a ride, or the boys might have accompanied Raoul Rochard as far as Leeds and then fallen afoul of criminals. They could be lying dead in the woods or in a roadside ditch, or they might be in London, where handsome young boys were in demand for unspeakable perversions—

As Diana closed her eyes against that terrible thought, Dracot put his arm around her. "Bear up, Dina. Bear up, my girl. I don't believe that Archie's dead. Nor that brat Edward, either."

But the horror and fear of the first few days had given way to a leaden misery that lived with her day and night. Diana wished that she could weep and fall into hysterics as Lady Radley did daily because that would at least be an outlet for her feelings. As it was she found herself turning icy, numb.

"I keep listening for them at the door," she admitted. She wiped her eyes. "I didn't mean to snivel, but, oh, Drake, I wish we had never come here."

But if she had not come to Blaize, they would never have discovered Dracot alive. Good balanced against bad, Diana thought numbly. As the duchess would say, that was life. "And where there's life, there is hope," Diana said aloud.

"There's also dinner," Dracot said bracingly. "I just heard the bell. Shall we go?"

Diana tucked her hand in Dracot's arm as they walked down the stairs toward the dining room. Not for support, but for the comfort of having a warm, familiar presence near her. For a moment that warmth touched a memory, and she thought of strong arms and the feeling that nothing could touch or hurt her while those arms were around her. Then, she rejected the thought. It was forbidden ground.

She had not seen much of the earl during the last ten days. He was always on the move, searching for Archie and Edward and questioning would-be witnesses, but there were no clues anywhere. Molhouse had raised no trail either in Dover or in London. Still, Blaize refused to admit defeat. He searched, or caused others to search.

Sometimes, Naunce accompanied his son. Another good to weigh against bad, Diana thought. Blaize and his father seemed to be trying to mend their fences. Small consolation, indeed—but Diana held tightly to that thought as they entered the drawing room. Here Miss Flor announced that since their graces had not yet descended, they would wait to go in to dinner.

"And Lionel has just gone upstairs to change." She looked sad and anxious as she added, "Claude has not been eating well, again."

Half-hidden by Miss Flor's skirts, Claude whined, softly. Since Archie's disappearance, Claude had attached himself to Miss Flor, who had removed him from the stable and taken him to her room so that she could better care for him. The small dog pattered over to Diana now and licked her hand as she stroked him.

"Is there any news?" Diana asked.

Lord Radley raised his head at this. Otherwise, he did not move from his place near the fire, which had been lit against the November chill. He seemed to have shrunk in the past few days, and the pettiness and the spite had vanished from his face, leaving it heavy with fear. He had even stopped making threats about what he would do to Archie if he ever caught him.

Lady Radley was looking very pale and sickly. "I am not well," she said in a sigh to Diana's inquiries. "I did not want to come down to dinner, but your uncle insisted."

Lord Radley nodded. "Can't *not* come down when their graces are at table," he said quietly. "Insult, by my head. Not eating don't make things better."

As he spoke, Blaize walked into the room and nodded to the company. He did not look at Diana, but he was very much aware of her, and his heart ached because he knew how sad she was.

It had been difficult to avoid her this long time. Difficult not to put his arms around her and comfort her. But now, though every instinct warned him to keep his distance, he crossed the room to her.

"Don't give up," he told her.

She felt as if his deep voice was reaching into her heart, wringing it unbearably.

"I won't," she murmured.

"More people than we can count are combing the country-side for two boys and a black horse. They're looking in all the towns and villages and cities from Cumbria to Dover. Something is bound to happen, Diana."

She closed her eyes against the sweetness of her name on his lips.

"Thank you," she said.

"No need to thank me. You know that I'd do whatever I could for you—and Dracot."

The duke and duchess appeared in the drawing room at this moment. At the same moment a gust of rain-soaked wind was heard crashing outside, which prompted Lady Radley to moan, "Oh, such bitter weather. Can no one tell me where my precious innocent is tonight?"

As if in answer to this plaintive cry, there came a loud banging on the door.

"Who would call at this hour?" the duke demanded testily.

The outer door flew open with a loud thud that resounded through the manor. This noisc was followed by Witton's excited voice and a babble of men's voices speaking in a foreign tongue.

Miss Flor turned deathly pale and put a hand to her heart. "It is the French," she breathed. "We are being invaded!"

Blaize strode across the drawing room and looked out into the hallway. "Thunder and hell," he exclaimed.

Diana ran up behind the earl and saw that several men were massed at the foot of the stairs. They were wrapped in sodden cloaks and hoods, and looked most villainous. In their midst was one with hair so fair as to be almost white.

"Archie!" Diana shrieked.

She darted past the earl and down the stairs, throwing her arms around her brother so impetuously that she nearly knocked him down. There was a sharp bark, as Claude also bounced down the stairs and hurled himself into his waiting master's arms.

"There you are—I've missed you." Archie added in a muffled voice. "I'm sorry to have left you, Claude, really I am, but we had to travel fast, and you'd have slowed us down."

"Sorry you couldn't take the dog! What about us, you wretched boy?" Diana scolded and laughed and hugged and cried at the same time. "Oh, Archie, are you all right? I was so worried—so worried."

"Let me at that little bastard!"

Lord Radley came bounding down the hall landing toward them. "I'll tear him limb from limb," he vowed. "I'll wring his bloody little neck. Where is my son, you scoundrel?"

He would have rushed down the stairs, but Blaize grasped him by the arm and hauled him back. "Well, Archie," he said grimly. "Where is Edward?"

There was a stir amongst the wet group, and a small, shivering bundle of humanity was pushed forward.

"Here I am," Edward stuttered. "I'm cold, and I'm *wet*."

"Edward! Come to Mama!"

Lady Radley attempted to descend, but her legs gave way under her and she could only hold out her arms. Edward ran upstairs into his mother's clutching embrace. "Tell me you are here, my angel," the lady declaimed. "Tell me you have returned to your mother."

"Well, he has, ain't he?" demanded her husband irascibly. His old bullying manner had returned, and he glared at his wife and his heir. "Don't be a bigger fool than you are, madam. Hey? Now, Edward, what I want to know is, where was you?"

"*He* took me," Edward accused with a pointing finger. "Archie made me go. He said if I didn't go, he'd do something horrible to me. I'm cold *and* wet, and I'm hungry." He began to sniffle.

"We will be avenged," Lady Radley announced. "Simon, deal with that—that *serpent* which we have nourished in our bosom."

Once again, Lord Radley attempted to descend. Once more, Blaize prevented him. "First things first," he commanded. "I recognize these gentlemen as the Rochards. What are they doing here?"

Before Archie could answer, Dracot gave a gasping cry. "Annette!"

"Oh, Monsieur Dracot!"

Everyone stared as one of the cloaked figures started forward. Her hood fell off revealing blond hair, a plump, pretty face.

"Who is this Annette?" the duke was demanding. "What Cheltenham tragedy is this?"

Dracot surged forward, then stopped where he was with a great effort. "This lady is Miss Annette Rochard," he said in a strangled voice.

Annette looked yearningly up at Dracot, and he looked down at her with despair. "Why did you bring her, Archie?" he grated.

"Because," Archie said patiently, "you were going to marry the wrong lady. Di doesn't love you, and you don't love her. You love Mam'selle Annette."

There was a deathly silence. When he finally found his voice, Dracot stuttered, "Wh-what did you say?"

"You and Mam'selle Annette love each other." As if reciting a lesson to a particularly dull child, Archie added, "You admitted it to Raoul the day he went back to Lesec. Edward overheard you."

Enlightenment filled Diana. "You mean that the wretched child was eavesdropping again!"

"Yes, and I caught him, and he confessed. He was going to tell Uncle Simon," Archie went on in accusatory tones, "because he was sure Uncle Simon would have given him a pony for the news."

"Nonsense! By my head, the brat is as mad as a March hare," spluttered Lord Radley. "Why would I want to set my son to eavesdrop?"

"Because," Archie said patiently, "you want Di to marry Lord Lion."

Pandemonium ensued. Lord Radley denied such perfidy at the top of his lungs, while Lady Radley bewailed the slurs to her angel's good name and accused Archie of foul lies.

Meanwhile Diana turned to Dracot and asked, "Is this true?

"Unhappily, he nodded.

"Oh, Drake, *why* didn't you tell me?"

With tears in her eyes, Diana put her arms around her cousin and hugged him gently. "I wish you very happy, Drake, indeed I do."

"Truly, Dina? but I thought—You had waited for me all this time." Dracot faltered into silence.

Diana smiled at him through her tears. "With all my heart," she said. "I will always love you as my dearest brother, Drake. But—that is all."

She turned to embrace Annette, who was staring about her with scared eyes. "You are the lady who nursed my cousin back to life," she said, warmly. "I already loved you for that, Annette. And now that we will be as close as sisters, I love you even more."

Annette began to cry with relief. Dracot would have taken her from Diana's arms into his own, but one of the Rochard brothers stepped forward to shoulder him aside. "My brothers want to know if there will be a marriage," Raoul explained. "We do not understand what is going on."

"That makes two of us," Naunce declared. "Blaize, must we be standing here like fools?" He glared at Molhouse, who was beaming at everyone from the top of the stairs, then at the earl's staff, avidly listening near the ground floor stairs. "This *interview* should be conducted out of hearing of underlings."

No one paid his grace the slightest attention. They were all spellbound as Archie described how he had forced Edward to tell him what he had overheard.

"I couldn't let him go and report to Uncle Simon," Archie added. "I had to take him with Raoul and me."

"Why not simply tell me what you'd learned?" Diana wanted to know.

"I didn't think you'd believe me. And even if you did, I didn't think you could *do* anything. I mean, you were marrying Dracot and he was marrying you because you felt sorry for each other and because it was the honorable thing to do." Archie said. "I had to go and get Mam'selle Annette."

"*Mon ami* Archie follows me and asks me to tak 'im back to Lesec with me," Raoul added. "When I discover the *raison*, I agree."

Archie turned to Blaize. "I'm sorry about borrowing Midnight and that other horse from your stables," he apologized. "We needed to reach Grassmere quickly, and we didn't dare take the carriage for fear your coachman would report to you." Anxiously he added, "*Did* that innkeeper give the horses safely back to you?"

Reassured by the earl's nod, Archie resumed his narrative and said that he and his companions had taken the mail coach to Yorkshire. "There we went to an inn and met a man who was going to London. He offered to take us. His horses told me that he was a champion good person, so we went with him. Then, someone else took us to Dover."

At Dover they had narrowly missed being discovered by Molhouse and boarded a ship bound for Belgium. It had been a long journey, but at the end they had reached Lesec and explained matters to the Rochards.

"Monsieur Rochard didn't want Mam'selle Annette to come with us, but *she* wanted it." Archie looked pleasedly at Dracot and Annette, who, oblivious to the world, stood hand in hand. "That's when the brothers said they'd come along to make sure nothing happened to their sister."

At this point, the oldest Rochard son interrupted Archie. "Marriage," he said in English. He looked very hard at Dracot and demanded, "Yes, or no?"

"Yes," Dracot said.

"Very much, yes," Diana agreed. She smiled at Dracot, who was happily kissing the blushing Annette's hand. "I am persuaded that Dracot has been pining for Lesec all this time."

"So all's well that ends well." The duchess glanced timidly at her lord and master's fulminating countenance and added, "Though it was extremely naughty of Edward to eavesdrop, it all came well in the end."

"Reprehensible," the duke said, glaring at Edward. "Not the act of a gentleman."

Lord Radley blanched at the scorn in the duke's voice. He was horrified to realize that his grace was holding his son in contempt—and probably blaming *him* in the bargain. He turned on Edward like a fury.

"I can't believe that a son of mine would stoop to listening in keyholes. Hey? It's, er—it's reprehensible."

"But, Simon," Lady Radley pleaded, "he's only a child."

"Your fault, madam, that he's turned out as he has. You've cossetted him. But, by my head, things will change. As soon as we return to Sussex, he's going straight to school. Meanwhile, it's bread and water for him."

Lady Radley wailed protest while Edward sobbed aloud.

"For God's sake," the duke exclaimed impatiently, "is there no end to this damnable farce?"

The outer door swung open with a crash that nearly splintered the wood, and into the house strode Colonel Pratt. His face was almost magenta, and his mustaches bristled ferociously. In his hand he wielded an enormous saber.

"Come on, you *budmarshes*," he bellowed at the Rochards. "Come and deal with an officer of the king!"

The colonel advanced farther into the ground floor anteroom and looked about until he discovered Miss Flor standing on the staircase landing.

"Guenevere! Are you all right, my girl?" He roared. "Have these villains dared lay a finger on you?"

Miss Flor could only shake her head.

"For God's sake, Pratt, put down that damned sword before you kill someone. What're you doing here?" Blaize exclaimed sharply.

"Just spoke to my dashed groom. He said that a group of Frogs were headed for Blaize Manor. Knew they were up to no good, so I came to save Guenevere—mean to say, I wanted to make sure Miss Flor didn't come to harm."

"Oh, how gallant of you. How noble!"

At Miss Flor's heartfelt cry, the colonel grasped his saber with even more ferocity.

"After my poor showin' at the hunt, you don't think I'm beyond the pale?" He asked her. "Mean to say—I'd go to the ends of the earth to keep you from harm. Dash it—I esteem you. What's a few Frogs?"

The colonel swung about to face the Rochards, who seized hold of pieces of furniture with which to defend themselves. Annette screamed and got behind Dracot. Diana cried, "Colonel, it's all right. The Rochards have just brought Archie and Edward home."

The colonel paused. He tore his eyes away from the Rochards and blinked hard at Archie. "Well, I'm blessed," he trumpeted. "If it ain't young Gardiner. Thought you were dead, my lad."

"Nobody's dead," Blaize said. He added significantly, "At least not yet. Put up your sword, Colonel, and stay to have a drink. I know *I* need one."

It had been a night to remember, Diana thought.

As she climbed the stairs to her room, she stopped to look out of the hall window. The rain had stopped, and a halo of mist obscured the garden.

By rights she should feel weary to tears, but the excitement that had bubbled through the long evening buoyed her even now. She could not yet believe that Archie was home, that Dracot had been united with his lost love, and that the world, so hopeless this morning, suddenly looked new and bright again.

The house had finally settled down after a late and hilarious dinner. Wine flowed freely, and soon the duke unbent so far as to tell a joke about stuffy members of Parliament, while the Rochards vied with each other at singing Gallic songs. Miss Flor and the colonel sat on opposite sides of the table and beamed in tongue-tied bliss at each other. Dracot and Annette remained in a celestial realm of their own. The duchess and even Lady Radley, who had been dipping quite heavily into the wine, laughed at the jokes, applauded the songs, and sighed over the toast that Blaize proposed for the lovers. Even Lord Radley appeared to cheer up.

Diana had not touched the wine. She was drunk on life, exhilarated and happy beyond her wildest dreams. It was all she could do to stop herself from singing, too. Whenever she looked at Archie, or at Dracot, who looked well and so happy, she felt a thanksgiving that welled up from her soul.

The dinner took a long time, but not even the servants seemed to mind. By the time the colonel took his reluctant leave and the Rochards went to their readied chambers, it was nearly two in the morning. Diana, who had stayed behind to make sure that the arrangements for Annette's room were made, slowly climbed the stairs.

"I tell you, it's for the best."

Diana stopped dead in her tracks as Lord Radley's hissing whisper came from the darkness overhead. Now she could make out that her uncle was in the staircase hall, talking to his wife.

"Now that Dracot's out of the running, it will turn out right," he was saying. "By my head, Blaize couldn't take his eyes off her all evening. There's a *good* chance he means to offer for her."

Lady Radley did not sound pleased. The thought that her darling Edward had been so badly used *and* disgraced by Diana's brother made her angry and resentful enough to snap,

"He may not do so. He is an earl and she is as poor as a church mouse. More likely he will make her a dishonest proposal."

"Y'mean a slip on the shoulder?" Lord Radley scoffed. "Not Blaize. Too honorable. Besides, if he does, we've got him. Don't you see, woman? I'll act angered and outraged, and so on. As the chit's protector, I'll demand—"

"Satisfaction? No, Simon, it cannot be. He would kill you."

"Not satisfaction, you ninny. I'll demand money," Lord Radley said bluntly. "I can button up this scheme as quick as a flea's leap, so I can."

Feeling soiled and degraded, Diana backtracked down the stairs and went into the drawing room where the ghost of the fire kept time with the ticking clock. All her earlier happiness had dissolved into dismay at the thought of what her unscrupulous relatives were planning.

"I must leave," she murmured. "I must leave at once."

"You really should stop talking to yourself."

Blaize had come into the room. His coat was damp, and there were raindrops in his thick tawny hair. "I thought I saw you go upstairs," he said. "What are you doing here?"

"What were you doing outside?" she parried.

"Seeing Pratt off." Blaize grinned, looking suddenly young and happy. "He was on the mop and as happy as a king. I sent him home in the carriage and he swore that he would return it tomorrow when he came to declare himself to Guenevere. 'The fair Guenevere' as he called her."

"I am so glad."

"So am I. Guenevere is happy, Archie is triumphant, Edward is in disgrace. Good conquers evil—or at least, this time it beat out spite and malice. All's well that ends well, as my mother pointed out."

"It would seem so."

He looked at her in sudden concern. "You're unhappy," he said. "Why, Diana?"

"I am only tired. Really, my lord, I must go—"

He stayed her. "You don't mind about Dracot loving Annette Rochard?"

Her eyes widened in surprise. "Of course not! I like it above all things. Dracot tells me that he was happier in Lesec than anywhere else on earth, and he will be so content with that dear girl. They love each other."

"As I love you," Blaize said.

The words were said. Once, they would have made her sing with happiness. Now, Diana felt only the leaden weight of her uncle's perfidy.

"I love you," Blaize went on. "And I thought you cared for me. Have you changed your mind?"

She could not lie to him. "Your father the duke—"

"Is not the issue here. What bothers you, Diana?"

In a low voice she said, "I would bring nothing to a marriage. You know that. Neither birth nor fortune. And then, there are my relatives."

"Ah, the *Honorable* Radleys," Blaize said. He began to laugh as he added, "Now we get to the heart of it. Has rapacious Radley been scheming again?"

"It is no joking matter," she reproved. "He means to haunt you."

"If I have survived Naunce all these years, don't you think I can handle a little toad like your uncle? Tomorrow I shall send the lot of them packing." He came over to her, caught her hands, and swung her into the circle of his arms. "Now, let's talk of important matters. Do you love me?"

"Even if you send him away, he means to blackmail you."

"Only one cure for that, then. Miss Gardiner, will you do me the honor of becoming my wife?"

"It is not at all that easy," Diana tried to say, but when she looked up into Blaize's eyes, her heart began to quiver and dance like a flower in the wind.

"There is nothing easier. You are the lady of my heart. Diana, if Miss Rochard hadn't come all the way from Lesec to claim her lover, we would have been condemned to misery all our lives. Now, miraculously, the sun is shining."

"That," Diana said shakily, "is patently untrue. It is the middle of the night. There is not even a moon."

"Oh, yes, there is." Blaize turned her toward the window and there amongst the tatters of rain clouds shone a silver new moon.

Diana could not help smiling. She looked so beautiful that the earl could not help kissing her. Once having done so he kissed her with even more concentrated passion until dark spots and streaks of light danced before their eyes.

"A new moon for a new beginning," Blaize declared. "Well, Diana, shall we live here at the foot of the mountains and let Archie revel in Midnight's progeny and watch our own children grow? As Rochard put it: marriage, yes, or no?"

Diana laughed and lifted her lips once more to his. "Marriage, yes," she whispered. "Oh, my love, *yes*!"

Avon Romantic Treasures

Unforgettable, enthralling love stories, sparkling with passion and adventure from Romance's bestselling authors

CAPTIVES OF THE NIGHT ***by Loretta Chase***
76648-5/$4.99 US/$5.99 Can

CHEYENNE'S SHADOW ***by Deborah Camp***
76739-2/$4.99 US/$5.99 Can

FORTUNE'S BRIDE ***by Judith E. French***
76866-6/$4.99 US/$5.99 Can

GABRIEL'S BRIDE ***by Samantha James***
77547-6/$4.99 US/$5.99 Can

COMANCHE FLAME ***by Genell Dellin***
77524-7/ $4.99 US/ $5.99 Can

WITH ONE LOOK ***by Jennifer Horsman***
77596-4/ $4.99 US/ $5.99 Can

LORD OF THUNDER ***by Emma Merritt***
77290-6/ $4.99 US/ $5.99 Can

RUNAWAY BRIDE ***by Deborah Gordon***
77758-4/$4.99 US/$5.99 Can

Buy these books at your local bookstore or use this coupon for ordering:

Mail to: Avon Books, Dept BP, Box 767, Rte 2, Dresden, TN 38225 C
Please send me the book(s) I have checked above.
❑ My check or money order— no cash or CODs please— for $________ is enclosed (please add $1.50 to cover postage and handling for each book ordered— Canadian residents add 7% GST).
❑ Charge my VISA/MC Acct#________ Exp Date________
Minimum credit card order is two books or $6.00 (please add postage and handling charge of $1.50 per book — Canadian residents add 7% GST). For faster service, call 1-800-762-0779. Residents of Tennessee, please call 1-800-633-1607. Prices and numbers are subject to change without notice. Please allow six to eight weeks for delivery.
Name________
Address________
City________ State/Zip________
Telephone No.________ RT 0894

Avon Regency Romance

SWEET FANCY
by Sally Martin 77398-8/$3.99 US/$4.99 Can

LUCKY IN LOVE
by Rebecca Robbins 77485-2/$3.99 US/$4.99 Can

A SCANDALOUS COURTSHIP
by Barbara Reeves 72151-1/$3.99 US/$4.99 Can

THE DUTIFUL DUKE
by Joan Overfield 77400-3/$3.99 US/$4.99 Can

TOURNAMENT OF HEARTS
by Cathleen Clare 77432-1/$3.99 US/$4.99 Can

DEIRDRE AND DON JUAN
by Jo Beverley 77281-7/$3.99 US/$4.99 Can

THE UNMATCHABLE MISS MIRABELLA
by Gillian Grey 77399-6/$3.99 US/$4.99 Can

FAIR SCHEMER
by Sally Martin 77397-X/$3.99 US/$4.99 Can

THE MUCH MALIGNED LORD
by Barbara Reeves 77332-5/$3.99 US/$4.99 Can

THE MISCHIEVOUS MAID
by Rebecca Robbins 77336-8/$3.99 US/$4.99Can

Buy these books at your local bookstore or use this coupon for ordering:

Mail to: Avon Books, Dept BP, Box 767, Rte 2, Dresden, TN 38225 C
Please send me the book(s) I have checked above.
❑ My check or money order— no cash or CODs please— for $______________is enclosed (please add $1.50 to cover postage and handling for each book ordered— Canadian residents add 7% GST).
❑ Charge my VISA/MC Acct#________________________Exp Date________________
Minimum credit card order is two books or $6.00 (please add postage and handling charge of $1.50 per book — Canadian residents add 7% GST). For faster service, call 1-800-762-0779. Residents of Tennessee, please call 1-800-633-1607. Prices and numbers are subject to change without notice. Please allow six to eight weeks for delivery.

Name____
Address____
City________________________State/Zip_______________
Telephone No.____________________

REG 0494